My Three Dogs

My Three Dogs

W. Bruce Cameron

TOR PUBLISHING GROUP
New York

MY THREE DOGS

Copyright © 2024 by W. Bruce Cameron

A Forge Book
Published by Tom Doherty Associates / Tor Publishing Group
120 Broadway
New York, NY 10271

www.torpublishinggroup.com

Forge® is a registered trademark of Macmillan Publishing Group, LLC.

The Library of Congress Cataloging-in-Publication Data
is available upon request.

ISBN 978-1-250-90020-3 (hardcover)
ISBN 978-1-250-90021-0 (ebook)

Our books may be purchased in bulk for promotional, educational,
or business use. Please contact your local bookseller or the
Macmillan Corporate and Premium Sales Department
at 1-800-221-7945, extension 5442, or by email at
MacmillanSpecialMarkets@macmillan.com.

First Edition: 2024

Printed in the United States of America

0 9 8 7 6 5 4 3 2 1

For my big sister Amy:
thank you for teaching your students to love all books,
especially mine.

My Three Dogs

Prologue

"Here's the thing," Liam Young blurted one evening a couple of years ago, agitation pushing just those words and no others to his lips. He shot his brother, Brad, a helpless look.

How do you get a woman to do more than glance in your direction? is what he was struggling to ask.

Because apparently it took more for a woman to fall in love than just a glance, though for Liam, that was all that was needed—out of the corner of his eye, he saw her sweeping her thick blond hair back from her face, and before he even turned to gawk, his brain was filled with a shrieking incoherence, too many signals coming in to separate into distinct threads.

Brad waited encouragingly. He was doing that thing Liam found so irritating: wearing a paternal expression, his dark eyebrows lifted. Their entire relationship in one facial expression. Brad, the older of the two, ready to head off some impulsive decision by Liam, and yes, of course it was impulsive; you can't really fall in love with a woman without even having at least a conversation with her. But that's how it felt.

"So," Liam foundered as if he were making sense, "I'm not usually about blondes, but this woman . . ."

"Jennifer Burr was a blonde," Brad reminded him brightly. "Jan Cowan was a blonde. Patty Pasternack was a blonde."

"Shut up," Liam corrected gently.

The brothers grinned at each other, sharing a comfortable moment. They were sitting in Brad's downtown Denver "bachelor pad," as Liam called it, takeout Mexican on the table, a few empty Pacifico bottles abandoned with practiced negligence next to the remains of the frijoles refritos.

"Just watching out for you," Brad finally explained.

"As you always do. I'm taller, younger, much handsomer—"

"Ha!" Brad snorted.

"Yet you," Liam persisted, "think you always have to watch out for *me*." Liam's grin gradually faded.

"You're thinking about me going to Germany," Brad concluded from Liam's expression. "But that's a process that could take another couple of years to pull off. Heck, it's already taken half a decade. So you're not getting rid of me just yet, brother."

Truthfully, that wasn't at all what Liam was thinking about.

His mind was back on the woman.

This was how it began for Liam. She walked past his jobsite nearly every day, so he had plenty of time to gaze at her. He didn't know she lived a few blocks down from the school where she taught English. He just knew that reliably, first thing in the morning and then again in late afternoon, this woman would stride by and leave him with a feeling of having fallen from a great height. Every time she walked past, he caught his breath and didn't release it for what seemed like hours.

Normally pretty confident around females—he'd certainly, as Brad tried to imply, had plenty of girlfriends in his nearly thirty years of existence—he was utterly flummoxed by this one. What *do* you say when it feels as if blowing this opportunity would wreck your life? She'd seen him staring enough, so she must know he wanted to speak to her. But the stakes were so high he was always strangled by them.

Finally, he approached her on the sidewalk and asked if she had any interest in seeing the kitchen he was remodeling.

She seemed baffled by the question. He didn't know that she had been listening to *The Talented Mr. Ripley* in her earbuds and hadn't really registered his approach until he was standing in front of her, grinning like the fool that he felt.

She snapped off her AirPods and asked him to repeat the question, which made him feel even worse.

"I'm a builder. We're gutting the kitchen and adding a sunroom. I don't know if you're into that kind of thing . . . ?" He trailed off miserably. What did he think he was doing? Her expression was filled with suspicion. Of course, here's this man, he realized, inviting her into a vacant house where no one else was currently in attendance. It certainly seemed like a bad idea for her to follow him inside, so he shrugged, acknowledging her decision before she uttered it.

"I'll take pictures and show you next time," he promised her.

Well, that was ridiculous. Next time? What? What did he even *mean*? He almost rolled his eyes at himself, but restrained himself and tried another grin. Thankfully, she offered a small grin back. She possessed the sort of smile that lit up her whole face.

"Okay," she agreed cautiously.

He saw her the next morning and ran out and fell into step next to her, agitatedly showing her his photographs on his phone. He had taken forty, which was probably a little excessive. He walked with her and swiped photos and then realized she was reacting with very little enthusiasm. What if she didn't care? What if she hated kitchens?

Okay, who hated *kitchens*?

He ended the slideshow presentation and asked her about herself and gleaned important information. Her name was Sabrina. She was a schoolteacher. She was a few years younger than he was. She liked to walk to work and listen to audiobooks.

He asked her if she would like to meet him for a cup of coffee after school. She smiled and said that she didn't own her own house, it was a rental, thus she was a poor prospect for a remodeling job. So, okay, he was coming across as a salesman. That was bad. How could he do or be anything but totally, completely wrong with this particular woman in front of him? He was intoxicated to the point of absolute thought extinction. Then he surprised himself by suggesting that they go for a hike the next day up in Evergreen, around the lake.

He explained, "Just a walk. Unless, of course, you're tired of walking from going back and forth to work."

Well, as it turned out, she was the kind of woman who liked hiking. Liked it a lot. The next several times they met, it was to hike together. They hiked in the canyon. They walked along the paved path in Cherry Creek. They went farther into the mountains up into Summit County and strolled the streets of Frisco, and hiked the Mount Royal trail.

"The thing in Germany looks like it's not going to happen for a while," Brad mournfully reported to him one day on the phone.

"Sabrina likes hiking. I bought new boots," Liam replied.

Clearly, they were not having the same conversation.

Sabrina liked his new boots. Even better, she liked his *dogs*. Riggs, the miniature Australian shepherd, was a bit cool at first—that was just Riggs, being his alpha self. But Luna, Liam's Jack Russell, greeted Sabrina as if jetting on a caffeine overdose, dashing around and wagging and crying and licking every single time. Sabriana's laughter at Luna's antics left Liam a little speechless, awed by his own reaction to the way a simple chuckle from this woman could make him feel.

When he bought her lunch on these hiking excursions, it didn't seem like a date, it seemed like a natural extension of what they were doing, which was good—no pressure—but frustrating. He wanted to be more than just a hiking buddy!

When he finally asked her to dinner at her favorite restaurant, he wore a suit but didn't put on a tie, because he'd been unable to remember how to do one, and the video he'd watched made him realize his tie was more than a decade old.

His dogs seemed offended they weren't invited along. Hadn't it been established they were key to the enjoyment of any meal? Lying loyally at the human feet at outdoor tables, the pair of canines was satisfied they were the whole reason Sabrina and Liam kept laughing happily.

The first dinner was a remarkable success. The next day, Sabrina introduced him to a friend of hers. When the friend asked how long they had been dating, he was shocked to hear Sabrina say, "Four weeks." He thought they'd just had their first date, but apparently, all those hikes added up to something else.

"Good dog, Luna," he later told his bright-eyed little terrier. This caused Riggs to thrust his nose forward so he could be petted—obviously, if Luna was a good dog, Riggs must be as well.

It didn't really matter if it was the dogs or the forced marches in the mountains or the lunches at Bagalis in Frisco—Liam, almost despite his desperate efforts, had gotten into a romantic relationship with the most beautiful, amazing, intelligent, funny, kind woman he had ever met.

What Liam had been trying to tell his brother was that Sabrina was the *one*. His relationship with her was the best thing that had ever happened to him. He was determined that no matter what, nothing would go wrong, not this time.

And for a couple of years, nothing did.

1

The morning air brought Archie the scent of freshly cut wood, a peculiar odor with which he had become very familiar over the past several weeks. Barely out of the puppy stage, the six-month-old Labradoodle was too young to really remember the snow from earlier in the year. For him, the strong Colorado sun had always warmed his brown fur and of late had even become a little uncomfortable. A thin tree nearby was struggling to fully leaf out and provided scant shade. He contemplated scratching at the dirt to try to excavate down to cooler soils, but felt too lethargic in that moment to move.

Archie didn't like being alone and wished anyone or anything would come along to relieve the tedium, but today was much like the day before and the day before that. Sharp percussions punctured the stillness, but the dog was accustomed to the noise and didn't so much as flick an ear. The man with a name that sounded to Archie like "Face" was doing something inside a structure several yards away. Other men were there, too, and handed long pieces of wood to each other and carried heavy tools and would sit and eat at least once in the middle of the day. They spoke to each other continuously, but rarely to Archie.

Archie was connected to a short chain that drew furrows in the soil when he dragged it over to his water bowl. Sometimes he drank without thirst as a way to relieve his boredom.

Archie yawned and stood up, shaking his curly fur. A fragment of memory came back to him. He'd been dreaming. His dream concerned the first man he had lived with, a man named Norton.

Norton was very friendly and played with Archie every day.

Archie could still remember, though, the time when all the play ended. Norton had come and knelt and held Archie's head in his hands, staring into his eyes. Something about that occasion had stilled Archie, and he ceased his puppylike capering and gazed back at Norton.

"I am going to be leaving you now, Archie. I'm so sorry," Norton had intoned solemnly. "I may not be coming back for a long time. You'll be living with my brother, Damien. He'll take good care of you. Okay, Archie?"

Archie had heard a question associated with his name, but had understood nothing else other than the odd, vague sense that something weighty and grave was happening. He wagged when Norton stood and embraced the man people called Face. "Take care," Face said. And then Norton left, and Archie never saw him again. Instead, Archie went to live with Face.

Face was not much like Norton, though they carried similar odors. Human skin gave off a distinctive smell when frequently baked in the sun, and both men had darkly tanned faces and arms. But where Norton had laughed a lot and was very amused when Archie would pounce on tossed balls or thrown sticks, Face didn't seem to have time or inclination for any games like that. He rarely spoke to Archie, but he did bring him every day to this place of banging wood and buzzing machines. When it rained, Archie lay in the resulting mud, and it clung to his snarled fur. When it was hot, like today, he sprawled out in the sun and panted.

With Norton, Archie had slept inside on a bed. With Face, Archie went home and was led into the backyard where a chain very similar to the one he was wearing would be affixed to his collar, and then he would remain there overnight. This was the life of a dog, and Archie just accepted it.

Archie felt abandoned on the end of his chain. He could smell his own feces nearby. Norton always scooped up his leavings, but Face just left them lying there in the dirt. This was something else Archie had to accept.

He had gone back to lying down, yawning, not so much sleepy as just exhausted by the sheer inactivity, when his ears picked up the sound of a vehicle bumping its way up the short, rutted driveway to where all the other trucks were parked. Archie raised his head, curious. The vehicle stopped, and a cloud of dust pursued it and then overcame it, settling on the gleaming finish.

There was a creak, and a man stood up out of the truck, a man Archie had never smelled before. He took a couple of steps forward, his hands on his hips, watching Face and Face's friends working. Then the new man turned and looked at Archie.

Riggs watched in irritation as Luna attacked yet another dog toy, a stuffed lamb with a missing ear. Luna went after the thing as if in a fight for her life. A five-year-old, quick-moving Jack Russell, she more than outmatched Riggs's own energy. Australian shepherds are far from lazy dogs, but after six years of living with Liam, Riggs had become accustomed to a simple life of patiently waiting for their person to come home before going berserk. Luna, it seemed, simply couldn't suppress the need to move.

Most days, after lying in her dog bed for a little bit, Luna would suddenly go at her toys, growling, jumping on them, even throwing them across the room and then racing after them as if the animals had assumed actual life and run away from her predatory pursuit.

Riggs was not sure why it bothered him that Luna played like this. There was a disorder to the whole thing, something that offended Riggs's basic sensibilities. The toys were now scattered around on the rug as Luna gave up on the lamb and suddenly went after a small, brown, monkey-faced animal that had long ago lost its shape to dog teeth.

Luna kept glancing at Riggs as if trying to entice him into helping her with her assault. Riggs just watched, feeling his irritation grow. He knew that when Liam came home, he would patiently round up the scattered dog toys and put them all back in the basket. Why didn't Luna understand that the basket was where the stuffed animals belonged?

Just as abruptly as she had pounced, Luna decided to put an end to the mayhem. Abandoning the monkey, she ran and nimbly jumped on the sofa, ignoring Riggs's glare.

Dogs were not supposed to be on the couch. This had been made very clear by both Liam and Sabrina. Though Sabrina had only been around for a few winter-summer cycles, she was as in charge as Liam as far as Riggs was concerned. If she didn't want Luna on the couch, Luna should obey her. That was just good dog behavior.

From her raised position, Luna triumphantly surveyed the room. Her gaze managed to avoid meeting Riggs's eyes. Then her attention became riveted on a stuffed cow that was lying like a corpse on a throw rug. Riggs knew what she was going to do before she did, watching the excitement spread through her muscular little body like an electric current. She tensed, lowering herself, and then, with a quick burst of speed, Luna dove off the couch and charged at the cow, her nails scrambling across the hardwood floor as she built momentum. When she pounced, her forward motion pushed both the rug and the stuffed cow under an easy chair. She turned and stared at Riggs in disbelief. What had just happened?

Riggs wasn't sure why the stuffed cow was now under the chair, nor did he have much interest in what Luna proposed to do about it. It was her fault.

Riggs watched as Luna circled the chair, sniffing frantically at her prey. She tried lying down and shoving her face toward the stuffed animal. Her teeth fell just short of snagging one of the cow's limbs. She circled a few more times, clearly frustrated. Riggs watched with his usual disapproval. What did Luna propose to do? She kept snorting as she jammed her face as close to the cow as she could manage. Then she sat back, her eyes bright, cocking her head.

Was she now pondering how to tip over the chair? Riggs didn't know but thought that even if the two of them worked together, they would find such a task physically impossible, and anyway, there was no way the two of them were going to work together. Riggs simply refused to participate in her silly games. Sabrina would be especially aggrieved if she came home to find the furniture upended.

Luna eased forward, put her front paws on the throw rug, and began digging at it, pulling it with her forelimbs. She pulled and heaved, tugging with her teeth.

It seemed pretty pointless, but then Riggs watched in astonishment as the rug came out from underneath the chair, pulling the stuffed cow with it.

When Luna jumped on the toy, she turned and faced Riggs in absolute triumph.

Unwilling to give her any satisfaction at all, Riggs looked away, put down his head, sighed, and closed his eyes. His senses told him they were a long way from having either Sabrina or Liam come home. Luna's antics were just one of those things Riggs had to accept.

Archie saw exciting potential in everything, and the arrival of this new man was no exception. When their gazes locked, Archie wagged his tail vigorously, pawing a little bit at the air, indicating to this new person that he should know that the most fun dog anyone could ever imagine was straining right there at the end of this chain, ready to play, ready to chase balls, ready to go for car rides or do anything else any human could think of.

The man named Face walked out of the construction project,

smacked his hands on his pants, and came forward with one hand extended. The new man reached out and shook it.

"You're Liam?" Face asked.

The man nodded, glanced one more time at Archie, and then turned back to talk to Face. "I am. And you're Face?" he asked tentatively.

Face nodded. "Name's Damien Fascatti, but people just call me Face. Almost thought your call was a joke—who puts money down on a place sight unseen? But that's your business." He turned and gestured to the structure. "Well, there she is. Framing's just about done. Plumbing, electrical, everything's ahead of schedule, if you can believe it. Got a good crew this time. Come on in. I'll show you around."

The two men moved toward the half-built structure, but before stepping inside, the new man turned and locked eyes with Archie.

For some reason, Archie shivered.

2

When the new man broke off his gaze and turned back to speak to Face, Archie's excitement faded. The two men moved out of earshot, and the dog went back to lying in the dirt. Whatever had just happened was over. That was Archie's life: an occasional burst of elation, followed by the stillness of his existence, waiting for humans to decide what would occur next—which, since Norton vanished, amounted to almost nothing.

On the threshold of the framed-in house, Liam paused, nodding for Face to proceed him into the new structure. The men were of similar build, both lean and sinewy, with hands rough from shaping wood, carrying tools, and building things. Liam was taller and his dark brown hair neat and trimmed, while Face's hair, virtually the same color, hadn't seen a comb or a brush in some time.

"So you know they're getting divorced?" Liam asked. "I don't think it's a secret or anything."

Face nodded. "Yeah, we heard, but it's no surprise, if you get my meaning. All they ever do is fight. I think they decided building a new house would bring them together."

Both men laughed ruefully at this preposterous notion.

"Where does that leave you, then?" Liam asked after a moment.

Face shrugged. "Well, I'm paid through this week. Obviously, they're selling it or you wouldn't have called. You get the inside scoop on it or something?" Face raised his eyebrows at Liam with a speculative expression. "Made a bid, put money down before it even got listed?"

Liam shrugged. "Maybe."

"That what you do? Go around buying up distressed properties?"

Liam smiled. "Well, I don't know if I'd say *distressed*, exactly. I usually find a place in the right neighborhood at the right price that just needs some TLC, put in a new kitchen maybe, add a bedroom." Liam shrugged. "Then I sell it, or sometimes I rent them out."

"I hear being a landlord's no fun," Face observed.

Liam nodded. "Oh, you got that right. You got to do a really good job picking your tenants, or you could be in a real jam. That's why lately I'm mostly interested in selling. House I'm in now, though, I've got a buyer on the line. Sold their home in California, so the offer's all cash—they're not bothered by mortgage rates. I time it correctly, I could move right in, make it my home." Liam smiled, acknowledging Face's curiosity. "So yeah, I've got a few friends here and there, put me together with the wife's divorce attorney. Saw her photos online, made an offer, contingent on an inspection by a licensed builder—me. And . . ." Liam waved. "I'd say it passed inspection."

"Well, if you're taking this project over, what would happen to me, to my men?" Face asked bluntly.

Liam gave him a careful look. "I do have my own team."

"Right," Face replied. "I figured, but we're doing good work here. You can check it out. Maybe . . . maybe you'd keep me on. Put your new team on something else. That could happen."

Liam nodded noncommittally.

Archie's gaze tracked the two men anytime they were in view in the unfinished house. He still had the sense something important could be happening today. He wagged involuntarily at the thought that the new man might come over to say hello. This occurred sometimes—people would be affectionate and give him hugs. Other times, they were stiff and formal, and from them, the best a dog might expect was a hand extended, palm up, offering a sniff. Though there was never a treat associated with this gesture, Archie always went ahead and sniffed anyway.

Every so often as the two men strolled, the new man would glance over at Archie. Archie registered each one of these brief looks as if it were a physical gesture. Suddenly, Archie wanted nothing more than to have this man come over to talk to him. Archie wagged at the thought, but the man seemed intent on his conversation with Face.

Luna was back on the sofa. In her triumph, she had pulled the stuffed cow up with her, not to chew on but simply to have as a hard-won prize. Her challenging glances at Riggs indicated she thought he was probably lusting to grab the thing from her. Riggs ignored her and the cow. Luna growled, shaking the toy. Riggs ignored that, too. But he couldn't tolerate it when Luna began scratching and digging at the pillows on the sofa, knocking them askew. It upset the order of things. Riggs pictured Sabrina coming home and finding the pillows scattered and putting them back in place with a negative shake of her head. The thought was too much for Riggs to bear. He felt it was his responsibility to maintain order in the pack. Luna had her own agenda and was apparently intent on stirring things up.

Riggs rose and eased out of his dog bed, padding across the hardwood and leaping up on the couch with Luna, who greeted him joyously. Riggs gave a corrective growl.

Luna was not at all intimidated. In all their time together, they had never had a fight, and Riggs had never done so much as bare his teeth. His growl, though, communicated his stern disapproval, a disapproval that turned into action when Riggs pointedly pushed at Luna, steering her to the edge of the sofa. Luna willingly jumped down, and Riggs followed. Riggs determinedly guided her over to her bed.

Something about Luna suggested to Riggs that she enjoyed this daily ritual, that she wanted this. She needed the discipline. She craved the order that Riggs imposed on her. It was much the way Riggs craved to be told "sit" or "lie down." Often Liam followed up these glorious commands with a treat, and that was wonderful. But even when there was nothing offered by Liam but a smile, just pleasing their person was good enough for Riggs.

This felt much the same. Luna wasn't so much pleasing Riggs as ceasing to annoy him, but he could tell she felt like a good dog when she behaved the way he wanted her to.

Luna ceased her maniacal play and curled up on her dog bed, her mouth open, her tongue slightly out, her eyes glowing with satisfaction. Whatever had been the game, it had come to a conclusion. Riggs watched her for a few moments, because sometimes she bolted from her place and ran back to the sofa, but when she seemed content to remain still, he turned and padded back to his own bed.

It would not be long now before either Liam or Sabrina came home. Usually, the first person through the door was Sabrina, but something told Riggs it would be Liam today.

Archie was ecstatic as Liam and Face approached him. It wasn't so much that they were heading straight to the dog as they were meandering, pointing out things in the yard, wandering ever closer. Archie was nearly overwhelmed with impatience. Would a yip be inappropriate? That's how Archie felt, that he needed to give voice to his excitement.

As they neared, Archie could separate Liam's smell from Face's. It was clear that Liam had other dogs in his life. With a smile, Liam stepped forward and extended his hand, and Archie licked it, nearly swooning. It felt so good to be paid attention to by a human being.

"So who's this?" Liam wanted to know.

"That would be Archie," Face replied.

"Archie?"

At the sound of his name, Archie fell on his back and extended his legs in the air, willing Liam to give him a tummy rub.

Liam squatted and complied. "Got a lot of dirt and stuff in his fur."

"Yeah," Face agreed noncommittally.

"It's a Labradoodle. They take a lot of attention, I guess. His coat might be hypogenic, but it scoops up crap like a vacuum." Liam pulled a stick from Archie's fur and frowned at it.

Archie licked Liam's hand.

"Not my dog," Face explained. "It's my brother's."

Liam glanced up. "Oh, does he work here with you?"

Face shook his head. "Nope. So what happened was my brother Norton decided he wanted to go to Australia. Not sure why, exactly, but that's just how Norton rolls. He calls me one day and says that he's going to be gone for a while, would I mind watching this dog? And what am I going to do? He's always dumping things on me and blowing out of town." Face shrugged. "Good thing he never had a kid."

"So when's your brother coming back?"

Face shook his head. "Well, that's the thing. I don't hear from him very often, and when I do, he sounds pretty happy. I guess he's met a girl down there. Her name is either Sheila or something like Sheila. That's what he calls her anyway. Sometimes it sounds like he's talking about more than one girl, both of them named Sheila." Face shrugged again. "I don't know. He'll come back when he feels like it."

"You're just stuck on dog duty, then?" Liam asked.

"That's about it," Face agreed wearily.

Liam stood and looked down at Archie, thinking of something that brought a frown to his face. "Well," he finally remarked, "it's a beautiful dog inside of all that tangled fur. Puppy, too."

"I guess maybe six months," Face responded.

"Is it fun having a dog here?" Liam probed. "I never take mine to a jobsite. Always thought of it as being too dangerous."

Face thought about it. "You know, I'm pretty busy. I feed the dog, I give it water, but I don't really have time to do much else. Too much going on."

"I know how that is." Liam nodded agreeably. "Sometimes I'll be on a project twenty hours a day. I got a girlfriend, though. Her name's Sabrina, so she can take care of the dogs."

"Oh." Face gave Liam a blank look.

Archie sensed something, now, a tension coming off the new man. And something told him that tension had to do with him.

"So," Liam announced decisively. He put his hand out to Archie, and Archie licked it again, then closed his eyes and groaned when the man gently put a knuckle up by his ear and rubbed out an itch that had been plaguing Archie for days and days.

"You're a good dog, Archie," Liam praised. "Really good dog." Liam stood and turned to Face. "I wonder . . ." He trailed off, scratching his chin, internally struggling.

Face raised his eyebrows encouragingly.

Liam nodded decisively. "I wonder if you'd consider selling me this dog."

3

Archie was in a full swoon. He was riding in the front of the pickup truck and could not stop himself from barreling across the seat to jump excitedly at Liam, who pushed him away with a grin. Then Archie ran to the glass and stared out at the passing scenery, and then returned at full gallop back to Liam.

Whenever Face gave Archie a car ride, it was always in the back bed of the pickup. The smells there were marvelous, but Archie always felt almost abandoned by the man driving, walled off by steel, glass, and attitude. It was as if they were taking separate car rides, but now Archie could smell and even feel the presence of Liam behind the wheel. It was absolutely exhilarating.

Archie saw a dog on the street and barked with joy, wincing when Liam called to him, "Archie, stop that. All right. All right. Stop!"

Archie could remember a time when he was yelled at. It was back when he was living with Norton. Archie found a piece of furniture that was redolent with Norton's sweat. Near it were iron bars, stacked and dusty, and Archie could tell from the smell of the thing that Norton sometimes would lie on the bench with his head at one end. The supporting structure was made of metal, but on top was a spongy rubber padding that yielded under Archie's teeth. His mouth at that point was on fire, a sensation compelling him to gnaw on things, and this fragrant bench seemed the best outlet for his obsessive urgency.

Norton did not agree with Archie's judgment and was very displeased to find bench padding strewn all over his floor. He yelled the word *no* and even smacked Archie above the tail with an open palm. Archie wasn't quite sure what the precise lesson was other than that he had displeased his person, somehow. The thought made Archie quail inside.

But this felt like a new chance, away from Face, away from Norton. Archie decided he would be a good dog, the very best dog, so that Liam would always want to be with him, and they would take car rides and he would bark at other dogs. Life would be perfect.

Liam kept laughing. "Have you never been for a ride in a pickup truck before, Archie? Settle down. It's not as amazing as you think."

Archie couldn't help himself. He wanted to sit in Liam's lap. He wanted to lick the man's face. He wanted to climb all over him. Liam kept thrusting him away, but in a good-humored action, not one that communicated anger or displeasure. "You are such a silly dog, Archie." There was something, though, a creeping feeling that was coming off the man. Liam would grow pensive, and that's when Archie would decide another assault with his tongue and paws was called for.

"You just have no idea the kind of trouble I'm going to be in, Archie," Liam advised at one point. "This is a really bad idea."

Archie heard something in the voice and wasn't sure what to do about it. Liam seemed a little wistful and sad. Archie stretched out in his seat and looked up at Liam and beseeched him with his eyes to see how wonderful life had become, now that they had found each other.

It made Liam smile.

Riggs had evolved to the point with Luna that the two of them fed off each other's moods and reactions. When Luna suddenly came alert and trotted to the door, Riggs knew it meant that very shortly, one of their people would be walking through it, and from the way Luna was acting, Riggs knew that person would be Liam and not Sabrina. Then Riggs felt it, the change in the air, and went to join Luna. He yawned with excitement because soon they would be with people.

Both dogs were sitting at full attention when, with a rattle, the door swung open. Neither dog was prepared for what confronted them next. In charged a dirty, smelly puppy, less than a year old, streaking straight at them. Luna and Riggs froze, and this new dog crashed right into their bodies.

"Down, down," Liam called.

Riggs and Luna reacted instantly, lying down and being good dogs. This new interloper did not. He dashed into the kitchen, ran around in there, came racing back, and threw himself joyously on Luna, who looked to Riggs for an explanation. Riggs reacted stiffly when this dog leaped at him, unsure if Liam wanted Riggs to control the situation or not.

"Archie, Archie," Liam called. "Get down. Stop that." The new dog was apparently Archie, and he showed no signs of understanding anything that Liam had just said. He certainly was wild and unruly, an undisciplined dog if Riggs had ever met one.

Riggs didn't like undisciplined dogs.

Riggs wasn't sure what to make of this situation. This had never happened before. Luna's arrival, long ago, seemed to Riggs a perfect way of increasing the size of the pack, with the Jack Russell instantly acknowledging that the Aussie was in charge. Archie was so berserk Riggs wasn't sure the other dog even knew Riggs and Luna were *there*.

Then things became worse. Liam reached down, grabbed the twisting, licking, squirming puppy, and lifted him up off the floor, grunting a little. He carried the young dog down the hallway and dumped Archie into the bathtub. Moments later, water was thundering out of the faucet.

Riggs and Luna regarded each other in horror. This unexpected bath seemed like the worst news possible. They had not even had time to properly greet their person, and now he was running water in the bathtub? Was the new dog getting a bath?

Though they each felt in the other an impulse to flee, Riggs and Luna could not help themselves—they were compelled to watch, even as they were horrified to think that they might be next for the torture.

Archie's enthusiasm for life had dimmed considerably now that he was in the tub. Liam was grinning, but he was using his hands to cup water and splash it up on top of Archie's back. The water ran dark with dirt and debris from Archie's gnarled fur. It was a tangle that resisted straightening even under direct assault from the spray out of the faucet. "Good dog. Good dog," Liam praised.

Those words made no sense to any of the canines in this particular context. How was this a good dog? He was getting a bath.

When Liam pulled Archie out of the tub, the look Archie shot at Luna and Riggs was miserable. He perked up considerably when Liam fished out an old towel and vigorously rubbed it up and down his back. Archie shook and sprayed water everywhere and then, panting, tried to roll on the floor, and then took off running into the other room. Riggs and Luna, feeling doomed, stared at Liam. "Well, guys, long as I've got the tub going and Archie's splattered water everywhere, I might as well clean the two of you as well." Sure enough, Liam reached for Luna, scooped her up into his arms, and placed her into the bathtub. The expression she aimed at Riggs was full of resentment, and Riggs understood why. Whoever this new dog was, his coming here meant all three dogs were being punished. Punished in the worst way possible.

Riggs watched as Liam scooped up water and poured it over Luna's back, hoping to escape similar torment. His stub of a tail wasn't long enough to tuck between his legs, but it was bent down toward the floor anyway, and his ears were back and his eyes hooded. Archie was wild, so there was no wonder he'd been punished, and Luna's attack on the couch pillows was probably what earned Liam's ire, but Riggs, as far as he knew, had done nothing wrong.

So why did he feel sure he was about to be subjected to the same humiliation?

"There now, you're going to smell so sweet," Liam crooned as he massaged soap into Luna's fur. It smelled terrible. Riggs felt sorry for Luna. When Liam turned to reach for more liquid soap, Luna stood up on her rear legs and pushed with her paw on the lever that controlled the flow of water, shutting it off. Liam burst out laughing. "You are such a smart dog," he praised her. "Such a good dog." Riggs heard the words *good dog*, but then Liam turned the water back on, so Luna couldn't have been that good.

Riggs decided to abandon Luna to her plight. Perhaps, he reasoned, if he slunk into the other room, Liam would forget about him, and only two of the three dogs would be wet. He found Archie racing around, rolling on his back on the rugs, which had been kicked up so they were little mounds at each end of the room. Archie's nails made a sharp clicking noise as he launched himself at Riggs, and Riggs felt compelled to push out his chest and give Archie a stern warning look that did nothing to deter this wild animal from slamming into Riggs in a wet spray.

"Riggs! Come," Liam called from down the hall. Well, Riggs knew what that meant. His head low, he padded down the hallway. One did not ignore the word *come* when issued by Liam; that was an ironclad rule in this house. Yet Riggs did not want to go in there. Riggs did not want a bath.

Liam scooped up Riggs and put him into the tub next to Luna. Then he lifted Luna out and wrapped her in a towel while the water poured into the tub. Riggs was miserable, especially when the water was aimed directly onto his fur and the soap was rubbed in. Now all three dogs would smell terrible, and they would all be wet.

This was shaping up to be one of the worst days of his life.

It felt good, though, when the ordeal was over and Liam

wrapped Riggs in a towel and cuddled him. This was actually the best part of getting a bath. Riggs felt comforted and loved in Liam's arms.

"All right," Liam announced. "Sabrina is going to be so, so mad at me. I need you to be on your best behavior tonight. Okay? I'm going to make her favorite dinner, chicken stroganoff. All right?"

Riggs heard the question in Liam's voice. He wasn't sure what Liam was saying, but he had heard Sabrina mentioned and calculated that it had something to do with the entire pack. Riggs felt responsible for that pack and took it to heart that whatever it was, he needed to do something for Liam.

"Sabrina," Liam muttered, "is going to absolutely kill me."

4

In the kitchen, Liam mentioned Sabrina several more times as he chopped and sliced things. Each time her name passed his lips, Luna's ears perked up. Luna's love for Sabrina was unrestrained, while Riggs felt more strongly that it was Liam who was at the center of the pack's world.

Both dogs, though, seemed in complete agreement that the arrival of this new, young, crazy dog who was still running around, jumping on furniture, and behaving in an entirely insubordinate fashion, was an absolute violation of the usual order of things. Luna kept glaring at Riggs as if demanding he do something about the interloper and the chaos he'd brought to the house.

Finally, Riggs could take no more of it and ran straight at Archie, cowing the dog, who shrank to his belly at the sudden lunge. Riggs let Archie get up, satisfied that the younger dog now understood who was in charge. Archie meekly followed Riggs back into the kitchen.

Liam carefully cut the chicken into bite-size pieces, and the dogs adored him for this. His recipe was simple, but Sabrina loved it. A little sour cream, a little organic mushroom soup, mushrooms, onions. They would pour it all on cauliflower rice. Sabrina was on what she called a keto diet, though she still ate several small squares of chocolate fudge every night, and Liam had learned that to comment on this fact was considered treason.

Archie had calmed down, Liam noted. The puppy was attentive to the smells in the kitchen and kept glancing at Riggs as if for approval. "I just need her to meet you, Archie," Liam advised optimistically. "She meets you, she'll see how wonderful you are,

and when she hears that you were all alone on that chain, day
after day"—Liam shook his head—"she won't object. Much." He
shrugged. "I hope she won't object much. Oh, man. What was I
thinking? *Three dogs?* Riggs, you think you can keep a handle on
this?"

Riggs heard the question and straightened, ready for whatever
was going on. Luna also picked up on the name and regarded the
Aussie curiously.

Archie threw himself on the ground and rolled onto his back.

Liam's tension started to increase just as the smells from whatever he was doing at the stove achieved a level of wonderful the
dogs could not have imagined. The canines prowled the kitchen,
lifting their noses, keeping their eyes on one another to make
sure no one was favored with a tossed piece of chicken when the
other two weren't watching. People were generally evenhanded
when it came to doling out treats, but sometimes they made mis-
takes.

At some point, Liam picked up his phone, made an exclama-
tory sound, and called his dogs. Archie was unsure but followed
Riggs and Luna down the hall at Liam's beckoning. The older
members of Archie's new pack seemed to know what was going
on, and Riggs radiated something of a command presence to Archie. Liam steered all three dogs into one of the back rooms and
pulled a wooden accordion gate across the doorway. It was an
effective way of keeping the dogs locked in the back bedroom,
though Riggs wasn't sure why they were being banished from the
wonderful-smelling kitchen. He and Luna exchanged distressed
glances. What if some chicken fell on the floor and they weren't
there to clean it up?

"Okay, let me talk to her and get her used to the idea, and then
I'll come get you," Liam informed them.

Riggs wagged his tail stub but kept his eye on Archie, who
prowled this new room, examining the odors. Riggs didn't know
that the bench beneath the weight station in the corner was

pretty close to being identical to the one that Archie had destroyed at Norton's house. Archie seemed smugly self-satisfied when he sniffed it and then turned deliberately away from it. Riggs did not understand this behavior.

Luna was pacing. Liam was home, which meant Sabrina should be home. For Luna, that was the simple fact of it all. The Jack Russell remembered smelling and seeing Sabrina in bed that very morning, and the memory brought a concern it might never happen again. As the light began to change character with the setting sun, Luna's anxiousness grew. Then they heard it. The jangle of keys, the opening of the door.

"Hey, honey," Liam called. They heard him walk across the floor.

Sabrina answered, "Hi, Liam."

They heard the rustle that they all associated with the two humans coming together in an embrace. Luna's tension increased. The dogs were supposed to be out to greet Sabrina!

With an almost inaudible whimper, Luna eased over and sniffed at the gate latch. Riggs watched her curiously.

Sabrina stepped into the kitchen, smiling appreciatively.

"Whatever that is, it smells great. I thought it was my night to cook."

Liam shrugged. "When you said you were running late, I figured I should make my chicken stroganoff."

"Oh?" Sabrina arched an eyebrow.

With that one gesture, that lift of her thin eyebrow, Liam was completely enthralled. More than two years together, and she could still make his stomach flip. "How was work?"

Her face fell. "Not good. We were on lockdown—somebody called in another threat."

"I don't understand why people would do that."

She sighed. "For the attention? I don't know. I just know that once the kids have sheltered in place for an hour and a half, we've lost them. They're probably going to be impossible for the rest of the week."

"I hate that you had to go through that."

"Honestly? It's almost better to be sitting in silence than it is to try to get them to talk about *To Kill a Mockingbird*. Sometimes I think we're shepherding high school students into a bookless world. They just don't care." Sabrina's mouth twisted bitterly.

Liam stared in concern. This wasn't the Sabrina he knew. The light seemed to have gone out in her. "Beautiful day, though," he pointed out by way of diversion. "Only the first week of April and spring is already *here*."

"It's Colorado. Probably snow ten inches tomorrow."

Again. Not acting like Sabrina. Something was wrong. "What else?" Liam probed shrewdly.

Sabrina regarded him warily, then nodded in acknowledgment. "Yeah. He who shall never be named called me."

Liam stared. "He *called* you? How'd he get your number?"

"I honestly don't know. I'm sure he tracked down somebody who gave it to him."

Liam shook his head. "I don't believe that. None of your friends would even speak to Merrick, much less tell him how to get hold of you."

"Well, not a friend-friend. But a lot of people have my number. It's one of the problems with being an educator."

"Did you talk to him?"

"Of course not," Sabrina snapped. She caught herself. "Sorry. I'm just tired of this."

"What do you want to do, babe?"

"What *can* I do? I didn't answer, because I didn't recognize the number, but the second I heard his voice, I stopped listening to the message and blocked him. Now I'll get a new phone. Again.

That's really all he's got, I think, is the number. I'll get another Illinois area code so he doesn't know I'm in Denver."

Liam gazed at her sympathetically. For him, there was no sacrifice in giving up social media—he had a business website and a part-time helper to maintain it, and that was all he needed. But he understood how Sabrina's ex-boyfriend had distorted her life, cut her out of normal society because of the unwanted messages, calls, pictures.

Sabrina had advised Liam that Merrick was harmless in the physical sense: his harassment came in more subtle forms. Liam sometimes wished the guy would show up and *try* something physical—that would put an end to it.

She correctly read the grim set to his jaw. "He wouldn't ever show up in person, Liam. He's a lurker, an electronic stalker only. I showed you the police report. I just have to be unresponsive to his provocations. Eventually, he'll give up, move on to somebody else."

Liam nodded. Sabrina was all but invisible in the online world, but her ex-boyfriend had found her number once before, right when she and Liam were first dating; Sabrina told Liam she had a new phone number and explained why. Somehow, every few years, Merrick would find her and leave his messages.

Liam had never heard the messages.

"I shouldn't have said anything about it," Sabrina apologized.

"No, of course you should tell me."

"I just hate the hassle of it all, you know? We just get things settled, *normal*, and then he who shall not be named stirs everything up. It's like I don't have control of my own life."

"I'm really sorry."

"Thanks, honey. I know you're frustrated that there's nothing you can do, but it helps to just talk about it. And he's nothing. A nuisance, that's all. I shouldn't let him get to me. I *don't* let him get to me, not usually. It was just a tough day."

"I get it."

Sabrina cocked her head and smiled at him. "You do get it, don't you? I didn't feel under threat during the lockdown—it's just a part of being a schoolteacher in the modern world. And I don't feel under threat, not at all, by my ex-boyfriend. It's just the disruption to my life I can't stand. And you get that."

"I get that."

She stepped closer, and their kiss warmed Liam, so much so that he completely forgot about Archie—until he spotted the extra bowl he'd set out for the new dog's water. As their kiss ended, he subtly moved her so the three bowls weren't in her direct line of vision. "Want a glass of wine? I've got some pinot grigio."

"Yes, please."

Liam went to work with a corkscrew, and Sabrina frowned.

"Where did you get that?" she queried, gesturing to the bottle.

"Picked it up today," he replied lightly.

"You don't like pinot grigio," she observed suspiciously.

Liam shrugged. "You like it, though."

Now, Sabrina stood back and crossed her arms, watching him work with a suspicious expression on her face.

"Okay. What did you do?" she asked.

"What do you mean?" he replied defensively, barking out a quick, inauthentic laugh.

"You're cooking chicken stroganoff, the house is clean, you did the morning dishes—something's going on."

"I gave the dogs a bath," he replied irrelevantly.

As if on cue, the dogs in the back bedroom finally voiced their frustration. The racket was immediate, and it sure sounded to Liam's informed ears that there were three dogs.

Sabrina cocked her head. "What's going on back there?" she asked.

"Oh, I locked the dogs in the back room," Liam responded casually.

"Why?"

"How do you feel? Want a foot rub?"

"What do you mean, how do I feel?"

"I just mean," Liam fumbled, "are you feeling, um, open-minded?"

Sabrina just stared at him.

5

Once Archie began barking, he continued with mindless exuberance, even as Riggs fell silent to watch Luna work on the gate. Luna had observed how Liam reached his hand down to the latch to open it. Now she used her paws to dig at that latch. She wasn't able to grasp how the mechanism worked, but she knew that was the focal point, the key to opening the gate.

Her pawing had exactly the effect she intended. With a clicking sound, the gate eased away from the doorframe. She thrust her nose into the gap, and the gate slid sideways, admitting her and then Riggs and then Archie into the hallway. They were so excited to be released from temporary prison that their nails scrabbled for purchase on the floor, and Archie tripped over his own feet and literally crashed into the wall. Riggs followed Luna, who wasn't faster, per se, but had gotten a few steps ahead and was determined to make her way to Sabrina.

Riggs was frustrated at Archie, who didn't seem to understand what they were doing and was not pursuing Luna but rather darted curiously into a different doorway. Riggs doubled back and forced Archie to fall in line, steering the younger dog back into the hallway.

Luna dashed into the kitchen and leaped up, trying to lick Sabrina's face. Sabrina bent down, her long hair flowing onto the dog. "Oh, Luna. I love you," Sabrina crooned.

Riggs went straight to Liam, but Archie, spotting a new person, threw himself at Sabrina and nearly knocked her over when he collided with her legs. She staggered and crashed against the counter. Archie jumped up, trying to get to her face with his tongue, then fell to the floor and rolled on his back, cycling his paws in the air. Riggs and Luna both sensed the increase in tension between the two humans and paused their greetings, eyeing Sabrina warily. She watched Archie's antics with an open mouth, then turned, her expression somewhere between shock and dismay. "Who is this?" she demanded.

Liam cleared his throat. "That's Archie," he advised as if this were all the explanation required.

At his name, Archie flipped back over and ran to Liam and sprang up as if trying to land on the man's head. Riggs followed strongly behind him, pushing against Archie's rear quarters, trying to slow him down. Luna went to stand loyally by Sabrina, who put her hands on her hips.

"It's a long story," Liam explained inadequately. Sabrina raised her eyebrows. "Well, what happened was I went to this jobsite, and here's this poor dog lying in the sun on a short chain. I guess what happened was the owner left the country, and so his brother, who's running the construction project, was supposed to take care of the dog, but he wasn't doing a very good job. I could see that Archie was really unhappy, so . . ." Liam trailed off with a shrug.

"So wait. This is one of your jobs? Which one?" Sabrina probed.

Liam shook his head. "No, it's a . . . Okay. So there are these people, they're building this house, and all of a sudden, it turns out she wants a divorce, and so the project's being abandoned. I know somebody who knows somebody, and I was able to make an offer before anybody else. I went out to look at it. It's a pretty good deal." He began to feel some enthusiasm creeping into his voice, and he resisted the urge to start speaking more rapidly.

"So you go to look at a house, but you already own a house?" She gestured. "Then you've got the other house you're working on already? I thought you said you're overextended and wouldn't be able to take on another project until you sold one of them."

"Right. Yes. But that's what I do, Sabrina. I buy houses, fix them up, and sell them. This is a wonderful opportunity, and you know what?" His eyes grew brighter. "It actually would make a great house for *us*."

"For us," Sabrina repeated somewhat woodenly.

Liam nodded happily. "It's four bedrooms, four baths. The kitchen is going to be glorious. Like I said, it's not even on the market, but if we pay off the note and give a little equity to the owners, we can have it."

Sabrina was quiet, just watching Liam.

He seemed a little deflated by her silence. "Also," he continued finally, "I mean, it's got a great yard. All dirt right now, of course. Nobody has planted anything, but the plans call for a fence. You know, for the dogs."

"The dogs? You mean our three dogs?"

"Did I tell you we're having chicken stroganoff?"

"So this morning when I left, you owned two dogs plus two houses and you were having trouble making the payments, and now you own three dogs and three houses," Sabrina summarized.

"That's one way of looking at it," Liam admitted.

"And without even asking me, you bring home Archie. And you'll be at work, so it will be my job to walk him and feed him most of the time."

Liam felt like they had somehow lost the topic of the chicken stroganoff and wondered how to get Sabrina back on track.

The dogs settled down once it became apparent that the humans were going to sit on the couch, sip liquids, and talk in quiet tones.

"Archie's filthy," Sabrina noted finally.

"Well," Liam corrected, "not dirty filthy. More like matted-and-tangled filthy. I gave the dogs a bath."

At that word, Riggs, Luna, and Archie looked up quickly. Riggs was disappointed to hear the word uttered aloud.

"Do you ever think about how hard this is? I hate packing,"

Sabrina complained. "I never know when we move into a place how long we're going to be there before we move out."

"That's what I do for a living," Liam started to say again.

Sabrina waved off the interruption. "We've been together for two years now, and yet I don't know that I feel any more secure in our relationship than I did on the very first day we met."

Liam frowned at what felt like a radical and dangerous swerve of topic. "How could you say such a thing? You know I love you, Sabrina."

Sabrina bit her lip and nodded. Her eyes were moist now. Luna came over to her and sat, staring up in concern. "I know," Sabrina agreed quietly, "and I love you, too, Liam. But I feel my life is nothing but chaos."

With that, there was a sound outside somewhere in the front yard. The dogs reacted instantly and protectively, racing to the window, jumping up on the couch so that they could bark at the outside. Archie didn't know what was happening, but he pursued the rest of the pack with abandon. His leap was mistimed. He bumped into Riggs, fell sideways, and knocked over a floor lamp. They barked until Liam shouted, "Stop that noise!" At that command, Luna and Riggs went silent and dropped back down to the floor.

Archie didn't know why they had stopped barking, but then again, he hadn't really understood why they had started. He agreeably followed the other two dogs back to their people. Luna resumed her sentry position on the floor next to Sabrina's legs. Riggs sat and then sprawled down next to Liam, and Archie wisely decided not to try to chew on Riggs but rather satisfied himself by finding one of Luna's stuffed animal toys and grabbing it. With gusto, Archie tossed it up in the air, fumbled the catch, and then dove on it. Luna watched all this with an unreadable expression.

"I don't know how you could call this chaos," Liam protested, walking over to straighten the floor lamp. He turned and grinned at Sabrina, and she grinned back, but then her smile faded.

"I just have no control over *me*. I go to my classroom full of plans and don't get to do any of it. We keep relocating to new houses. I have to keep changing my phone number. Do you get how that feels? It's my life. When do I get to make my own decisions?"

"No, I mean, of course," Liam responded, trying to come up with the right answer.

"Do you know what your favorite expression is? 'Let's just play it by ear.'"

Liam frowned. "I wouldn't say that's my favorite," he corrected peevishly.

Sabrina shook her head. "Everything is that way. I suggest we make reservations for dinner, and you say, 'Well, let's just play it by ear.' I want to know where we're going to stay on a road trip, and you say, 'We'll figure it out when we get there. Let's just play it by ear.' I feel as if my life is subject to whatever whims of the moment strike you. Nothing's *set*."

"The table's set," Liam countered lamely.

Sabrina shook this off. "You're a commitment-phobe, Liam. You can't make up your mind about anything, and yet"—she gestured to Archie—"you brought home another dog. Like another dog doesn't represent one of the most important commitments in the world."

Liam's face went blank. "Well, sure, but if you could've seen how poor Archie was living . . ."

"You didn't think that maybe you should at least call me?"

"That does seem like it would have been wise."

"I don't know what made you this way, and I don't know what I can do about it," Sabrina observed simply. "But it's affecting me in ways I don't like."

Liam straightened himself. "Well, I'll try to—" He trailed off, not sure exactly what he could "try to" do that would be any different from the way he felt he essentially was. Sabrina nodded at him.

"I know you'll try," she agreed in a defeated voice. "You've been trying."

"Well, hey, this new house—" Liam began enthusiastically.

"Could we maybe not talk about the new house?"

"Sure." His expression was crestfallen, but he didn't pursue the topic.

Archie trotted over, took the now soggy toy, and thrust it into Sabrina's lap, knowing it would cheer her up. She brushed it away, and Luna snatched it instantly, giving Archie a very clear warning look. Archie sat down and then barked.

"Stop that noise," Liam and Sabrina chided together. That did not sound like they were enjoying the barking game, so Archie went quiet.

"I've never seen such matted fur," Sabrina remarked sadly, reaching out her hand.

"I'll take them tomorrow to the dog groomer's," Liam volunteered. "Riggs needs his nails done anyway."

Riggs glanced up. He'd just heard his name, but it didn't sound like anything fun was associated with it.

Sabrina gave Liam a small smile. "Did I hear something about chicken stroganoff?" she asked.

The three canines were enraptured by the dinner smells and sat loyally by the table, putting everything they had into deserving-dogs appearances. Archie followed the lead of the other two members of the pack. When he was tossed a delicious chicken morsel, he swallowed it so quickly he could barely taste the thing. It was divine.

Sabrina sighed.

"What's up, babe?" Liam asked.

She gave him a sad smile. "I just don't think I can manage three dogs, Liam. That's what I would have told you, if you'd bothered to call me. Can't you just take Archie back to his owner?"

6

The next day, the three dogs piled into Liam's truck. Luna was alert to the fact that Sabrina was not with them. Whenever Sabrina left in the morning, Luna always felt a gnawing anxiousness that the woman would not return. For Riggs, what was important was that unlike most days, they were all together in the truck. Riggs was hopeful they were going somewhere fun, and Archie assumed they were—after all, it was a car ride!

Riggs put his nose to Liam's hand, and Liam absently stroked Riggs's head. Liam seemed pensive and preoccupied.

The dogs were loyally facing forward. Well, Luna and Riggs were facing forward. Archie kept leaping up to look out the side window, and then would see something so exciting, he would turn and jump on Riggs, who at one point bared teeth in a silent snarl to make Archie behave. Archie, hurt, his ears back, sat down and stared at Riggs, feeling like a bad dog.

At their destination, Archie was as thrilled to arrive as he had been to leave the house, but Luna and Riggs seemed to know where they were and were not wagging. All three dogs received leashes securely clicked into their collars. They boiled out the side door when Liam opened it, and Riggs lifted his leg while Archie squatted. It was occurring to Archie more and more to lift his leg, but usually he was so excited he forgot and squatted instead. Luna and Riggs displayed great reluctance as Liam half led, half dragged them to a door through which wonderful dog smells came pouring out.

Once inside, canine odors were everywhere, and in a back room somewhere, they could all hear a dog's plaintive barking. It was a lost and lonely sound, and Archie felt a twinge of sadness but then focused on the matter at hand, which was that the three of them were together as a pack with Liam in a place where many dogs had gone before them. It was hard to imagine a better day.

Why were Riggs and Luna so apprehensive? Archie couldn't fathom what had them so stiff with concern. Whatever they were doing was bound to be fun!

Archie was led away first, taken to a small room where a very nice and gentle woman massaged him and then applied a buzzing machine against his fur. It felt wonderful. Archie was vaguely aware of his curls landing with soft impacts on the elevated table and the floor below. Each drift downward of dog fur carried with it some of Archie's scent. A part of him was ecstatic at the fact that he was leaving his smell everywhere in this small room.

"You are a good dog, a good dog," the woman told him as she busily worked her hands along his body. Archie glanced up when he smelled Riggs, Liam, and Luna—they came down the hallway, their canine nails clicking, passing by his open doorway. He saw them all proceeding into a room just across the hall and hoped he would soon be joining them.

After being shaved, Archie was shampooed. He didn't enjoy that at all, but at the end of the ordeal, his skin felt incredibly alive. He was allowed to jump down, and he raced around the room, thrusting his face along the floor, rolling on his back, and kicking his legs skyward.

The woman laughed delightedly. "You are such a silly dog, Archie!"

When Archie rejoined the two other dogs in the front room, Riggs was remarkably colder toward the younger dog.

Riggs did not know what Archie had done. He just knew that for the second day in a row, he and Luna had been subjected to the humiliation of a bath. This sort of thing had never happened before Archie arrived. Clearly, Archie had done something to bring this horrible fate upon them. As far as Riggs was concerned,

Archie was a bad dog, and Riggs looked forward to them going back to being just Riggs and Luna in the pack.

Face was waiting in the driveway, his arms folded, when Liam pulled up. All three dogs saw the man, but only Archie reacted. At the smells of this place, of the odd, naked wood frame, of the loud banging noises, of the men, of the sun on the dirt, Archie recoiled. No, he did not want to come back here. He had a new home now. He lived with Liam and two other dogs, and there was that nice woman, Sabrina. Why was he here? He did not want to live with Face anymore.

Liam came around and opened the door, and Luna and Riggs jumped down briskly. They were both well behaved enough to remain at Liam's feet and not run off, though clearly this was what Luna especially wanted to do, to lower her nose and sniff and hunt for prey. Riggs, on the other hand, was loyal to Liam, and until commanded otherwise, he was going to stay with his person.

Archie wouldn't get out of the cab.

"Here, Arch. Come on, Archie," Liam called.

Archie feebly wagged his tail but otherwise didn't move. His ears were down. His eyes seemed to be sunk in his head.

Liam gave him a kind smile. "Come on, Archie. You know where you are. You've been here before."

Liam reached forward with kind arms and gathered Archie up. Archie closed his eyes, luxuriating in the warm and comforting feeling of Liam's broad chest.

This felt like a parting. His time with the other dogs had only been temporary. He understood now that a dog like him did not deserve a new pack and a new family. He was meant to live in this yard on his chain with a bowl of fetid water and no shade. Dogs accepted the rules and determinations put forth by humans.

Archie, sad but resigned to his fate, did not move when his paws hit the ground, but he did glance up at Face's voice.

"Hey there, Liam."

"Face," Liam responded evenly.

The two men walked toward each other. Riggs followed. Luna broke away and went sniffing, and Archie pursued her a little bit. She made a beeline for the scooped-out area Riggs had called home for so many days. She sniffed it suspiciously, poking her nose in the dirty water dish. Then she touched her nose to Archie's as if understanding that this was Archie's home. Archie didn't put his nose to his own feces and urine, even though Luna thought the matter worth investigating. Instead, Archie turned and made his way back to Liam. He simply didn't know what else to do. Riggs watched Archie approach without enthusiasm.

"So I heard you're the new boss," Face announced to Liam.

Liam nodded.

"Same as the old boss?" Face suggested.

Liam shrugged. "Well, we have a deal. I told them everything looks good, so I'm buying the place. Obviously, the paperwork's not done. But even though that part will take a while, yes, effectively, this is my home now."

"What does that mean for me and my crew?" Face wanted to know.

Liam looked away from the question. He nodded toward Riggs, who was sitting at rigid attention, unsure of what was happening. "That's my dog, Riggs, and you know Archie, of course."

Face glanced at Riggs and then frowned at Archie. "Ah, Archie, you got shaved."

Riggs felt Archie shrink away when his name was spoken and snapped his attention to this new man. Archie knew the man and didn't like him, which was very unusual.

Luna came trotting over curiously. "And that's Luna," Liam introduced.

Face didn't so much as glance at Luna. Instead, he glanced

pointedly around, and Liam seemed to understand the significance of the gesture.

"I see you cleaned up the jobsite," Liam noted.

Face nodded. "I saw the back of your truck. I figured, yeah,
you're the kind of guy, likes everything nice and neat and orderly.
Me, honestly, I feel like it's more efficient to wait until the job's
done and clean everything up at once, but"—he gave a crooked
smile—"you're the new boss, like you say. So what do you think?
Am I fired or what?"

Liam's gaze was cool as he delivered the news. "Well, I'm going to pay you through the end of the month, and then my crew
will take over."

Face's lips twisted bitterly. "So it's like that?"

"I told you," Liam reminded him, "I have my own team. We
work pretty well together. This place"—he nodded to it—"this is
going to be my home, to live in, I mean, so that means I'm going
to pay particular attention. I'm going to revisit the plans, change
the finishes, the cabinets—I know what my girlfriend likes."

"I can do all that," Face objected.

"I know you can."

"We do damn good work here, Liam."

"I don't disagree."

"So then what's your problem?" Face asked angrily. "You can't
just show up here and get rid of us like we're nothing."

"I never said you were nothing," Liam responded patiently.
"That's why I'm willing to pay you through the end of the month.
I expect to get honest work out of you. By your reputation, that
shouldn't be a problem."

"But we're still fired," Face responded, returning to what was,
for him, the main issue.

"If you want to put it that way, then yes," Liam agreed. "I'm
hoping you see that giving you until April 30 is adequate notice."

"You want to tell me why?"

"Honestly, it's got to do with the dog. I didn't make up my

mind until just now, even though when I first met you, you had Archie on a short chain in the sun. You maybe didn't understand how a dog should be treated. But even though Archie probably thinks of himself as your dog, he wasn't happy to see you, and you didn't seem too overjoyed, either."

Face's expression turned darker. "I explained to you about my brother. I told you the dog just got dumped on me. I gave the dog a home. I could've taken it down to the pound and had it put to sleep, but I didn't."

"No, I agree," Liam said mildly.

Riggs still held his eyes on the man called Face. There was anger brewing inside him, and if that anger boiled up in any aggressive action, Riggs would defend Liam. That was what Riggs saw as his job in the world.

Face clenched his fists, and Riggs prepared himself to react.

7

Liam calmly assessed Face's red visage and balled fists. "You really want to do this?" Liam asked softly.

At the sound of his person's voice, Riggs let a low rumble settle in his throat.

Archie, on the other hand, was cowering. He had seen this anger from Face before, and it had never turned out well. Now Archie wanted to do whatever it took to be good. He would go back to his chain. He would not dig in the dirt. He would lie there patiently in the sun, but he did not want the full boil of Face's fury turned on him.

"You're going to sic the dogs on me?" Face demanded.

"No, of course not. Riggs! It's okay."

Riggs picked up Liam's meaning and stopped growling.

Liam nodded and turned back to Face. "And I'm sorry, I understand this will be a hardship for you. But I don't want to work with somebody who would treat a dog like that."

"You're firing me because of a dog?" Face repeated incredulously.

"Right. That's exactly right."

Face deflated. He glanced at the dirt as if to spit at it, and Archie quailed, but then the man turned and strode away in the dust.

Archie, Riggs, and Luna burst through the front door of their home, instantly aware that Sabrina was in the house.

Archie was ecstatic. Despite all expectations, he was not now lying in the dirt, waiting for Face to complete his day to take him home and feed him in the backyard. He was here with a pack, with loving people. He'd taken a car ride!

Even Sabrina, who had greeted him soberly the day before now, fell to her knees and stretched out her arms. "Oh, Archie, you look completely naked," she squealed. "What happened to all your fur?"

Archie threw himself into her arms. He kissed her face, he rolled against her. He loved her.

"They said there was no solution except just shave it off and take care of it from now on," Liam informed her. "How's your day off going?"

Sabrina smiled. "I'm enjoying just being home. Want to do takeout tonight?"

"Yes," Liam agreed. "I do want that."

The two of them smiled at each other. "I've been doing a lot of thinking, Liam, and I realize I haven't been fair."

"Okay," he agreed cautiously.

"I've been thinking about my sister a lot lately. Marcy has everything I want. She has a stable house, and her husband is still with the same corporation that he worked for when they first met. He gets promoted now and then. They're not rich, but they're comfortable. She's talking about getting pregnant. That means I'll be an aunt soon." Sabrina smiled at the thought. "It's sort of a perfect life."

"Well, a perfect life except for all of her cats," Liam objected mildly. "I think twelve cats means that you might look stable on the outside, but there's got to be a screw loose there somewhere."

Sabrina laughed. "Twelve! There are only five."

"'Only five cats' is like saying 'only five heads.' Nobody needs more than one," Liam insisted with a grin.

"Okay, you make a point about the cats. I mean, two cats, maybe, that would be okay."

"Or three dogs," Liam countered.

"Okay, three dogs." Then her smile developed a sadness. "I like it here, Liam. This is the nicest home we've ever lived in. I know you've got it on the market, but I'm not sure I want to move. I think we should stay here, even though I admit it's a little small now that we're raising an entire pack of wild animals. I also—" Her expression became even more serious. "I've been thinking about it, thinking a lot. Teaching isn't at all what I was expecting, and I don't think it's ever going to get any better. The ones who've been at the school the longest seem pretty burned out. I love my commute, of course, but I'm thinking maybe of making a change."

"Oh? I didn't know that," Liam replied guardedly.

She nodded. "So, I'm not my sister. You're right. Too many cats. Maybe three dogs will work out. I mean, how can I not love Archie the baldadoodle? But if we can just stabilize life a little bit, get it under control, give me an opportunity to find a different job, I think things will work out okay. I want them to. I love you, Liam."

"I love you, too, Sabrina." Liam sighed. "So this conversation is going to make it very difficult for me to tell you what I need to tell you, Sabrina."

She eyed Liam steadily. "What's that?"

"I sort of sold this house."

"Sort of," Sabrina repeated.

"I told you about the new place. The one where I found Archie. It's perfect. You know how you showed me the kitchen cabinets you said were your dream? They'll look great. It's roomy, and the two of us can cook together, and nobody needs to get stabbed." He smiled at his own joke.

"Let's go back to the part where you sold this place where we live," Sabrina suggested coolly.

"Right. That. So, for everything to work with the financing, I needed to let go of this one. But let's face it, we never thought this was a forever home or anything. I'm making good money on the flip—the buyers are all cash."

Sabrina absorbed this. "When do you think we would move?"

Liam shrugged. "Honestly, the best for the buyers would be first of July. I can negotiate around that, of course, but why not just get a temporary place until the new home is ready?"

"So," Sabrina summarized, "two moves. One in less than three months, and the new one just as school's starting."

"Okay, yes, that's terrible timing, I get that, but maybe you won't be teaching by then. Maybe this is a new life in a new house."

"A forever house?"

Liam seemed to pick up some deeper significance in this question than appeared on the surface, and he hesitated, unsure of himself.

"What do you mean it's a new life?" Sabrina continued. "What are you proposing, Liam?"

Liam blinked at the word *proposing*. Now, even Archie was focused on the two humans, sensing that something was going on between them that was far over his head but that might involve dogs somehow.

"Well, I just mean, you know, it's a new house," Liam responded lamely.

Sabrina waited a beat for more, but nothing else came. "All right," she finally summarized simply, "a new house, which I haven't even seen, another move, which I will manage again because you'll be busy working, a new dog, but other than that, no real change. Because everyone is in charge of my own life except me."

Liam looked uncomfortable with this, started to say something else, and then stopped himself.

Riggs was coming to grips with Archie, even though the newcomer had brought nothing but chaos into their lives. If there was one thing Riggs could not stand, it was chaos. Archie competed with Luna to see who could do the most violence to the stuffed animals she kept in her basket. It was upsetting to Riggs to watch the mayhem, but he tried to tolerate it as long as he could.

Much worse was any behavior from Archie that Sabrina and Liam disapproved of. Almost from the moment Archie came to live with them, the new dog would signal his readiness to pee by going to the sliding door to the backyard and squatting there.

Liam would yell, "No!" Sabrina would yell, "No, Archie!" But the outcome was the same. They would run to the door, slam it open, and all three dogs would barrel out into the fenced-in yard. Often, ironically, Archie would be too excited to complete his mission, and then they would have to remain in the yard until finally the dumb dog remembered why they were there in the first place and would wet the grass.

Archie spent a lot of time eyeing Riggs and following his examples, which is why it didn't take long for Archie to run to wherever Riggs had marked and lift his own leg over the spot. This was something else that irritated Riggs, to the point that he would often circle around and readdress the same spot to make the point that his mark needed to be dominant. Luna might occasionally lower her nose to the mix of odors but otherwise was disinterested in the pissing contest.

Archie found wonder and joy in everything they did, but this wasn't without a downside. Riggs was irritated that breakfast in the morning was no longer an orderly affair. Archie would wolf down his food so quickly that, despite the fact his meal appeared to Riggs to be a little more generous than what was fed either Luna or Riggs, he would finish first, and then the younger dog would approach Luna, who would glare, and then Riggs, who would growl.

There was no learning for this Archie dog. The next morning, the exact same thing would happen. When they all bounded into Liam's vehicle, Archie was so irritatingly enthusiastic, it was all Riggs could do to restrain himself from snapping at the younger dog.

It was worse in Sabrina's car because the three dogs were crowded together in the back seat. Liam would drive, and Sabrina sat next to him, but Riggs always thought of the vehicle as being Sabrina's. It did not have a long, open area in the back like Liam's truck. And the back seat, redolent with his and Luna's odors, was the only place where the dogs were allowed to roam, though Riggs often pushed his face between the front seats to see if anyone would invite the rest of him to squeeze through. Otherwise, he and Luna were obediently quiet, and Archie would climb on them and bite their faces.

One morning, Liam drove them in his truck, and Archie was as exuberant as ever, but then he sobered when the familiar odors came to him. They were back to the place where Face brought Archie every day, and though it had gone well the last time they'd visited, Archie was still wary.

The dogs jumped out and stretched. Archie noticed there was nothing but the faintest hint of Face's smell now. Further, to Archie's delight, when they were allowed out of the truck, there was no movement to put him back on the short chain. Instead, Liam led them around to the open ground behind the odd-smelling dwelling. From within the structure, sharp percussions landed on all three dogs' ears.

"You guys stay," Liam instructed.

Luna sat, and Riggs immediately trotted over and sniffed at Archie. There was a real sense that the word *stay* meant something to these dogs, but Archie couldn't at all fathom what that might be. He sniffed around the yard, conscious of the fact that Riggs was right there beside him. And after only a short distance, it seemed as if Riggs was moving to deliberately block his way, prevent him from straying too far from Luna.

Then Archie caught sight of a squirrel.

8

Luna saw it, too—the squirrel enthusiastically bounded at the base of a tree, oblivious to the carnivores watching it. To beat the Jack Russell to the prey, Archie instantly launched himself into a full-on sprint and was shocked when Riggs crashed into him, literally knocking him off his feet.

Archie jumped up and gazed in disbelief at Riggs's cold stare. This was crazy! Riggs would not let Archie leave this small area that apparently defined their new yard, not even to chase a squirrel. Archie looked to his presumed ally, Luna, but the little dog, while rigidly focused on the insouciant trespasser hopping around within easy hunting range, didn't break from the sitting position.

Riggs and Luna seemed to understand something he didn't, which was that the dogs were suddenly supposed to behave as if they were on leashes. Archie wanted to bark his frustration but was cowed by Riggs's stern focus on him.

This set the pattern for their lives, though thankfully not with any more squirrels, which would have been more than Archie could have taken. They traveled together daily to the noisy house where Face once chained Archie near his bowl, hung around, and then returned home.

Archie had humans who loved him and a pack that mostly tolerated him. As long as he did what Riggs seemed to want, every day was wonderful.

One evening, Liam walked in and found Sabrina sitting in the living room. Her manner suggested something serious was happening, and the dogs reacted to Liam's abrupt change in mood.

"You okay, babe?" Liam asked her.

Luna trotted over to nose Sabrina's hand, and Riggs sat and watched Liam's face. Archie darted to the basket and retrieved a stuffed rabbit.

"I have to tell you, I didn't get the summer school job. I won't be teaching summer school this year."

Liam brightened. "That's great. You'll have the summer off."

Sabrina frowned. "It's not great. I didn't become a teacher for summer breaks. I did it because I want to help educate children. And I wouldn't feel good sitting around all summer while you're going off to work every day." She gestured around the house.

"Okay, well—" Liam stopped talking, fumbling for his response.

"Maybe this is something I have to solve on my own, Liam," Sabrina suggested softly. "I do appreciate your help, it's not that, but I'm a grown-up now and I need to act like it. Maybe this is a sign that I should make a change."

"Okay." He regarded her warily, feeling as if they were talking about something else, but he wasn't allowed to know what. "Like, a career change?"

Her gaze was unreadable. "Maybe."

"Great," he responded with cautious enthusiasm.

"I mean, *career,*" Sabrina mused. "That probably would take some time. But I'll find something for the summer. Something flexible so that when your schedule changes without warning, I can adapt, still take care of the dogs."

There was an edge to her voice, but Liam elected not to ask what was behind it.

Because they were humans, Liam and Sabrina eventually decided to change everything. Now, Liam was on a schedule where he worked very late, coming home after dark and getting up before dawn. Sabrina, who normally would be up and out even earlier, slept in and only joined Liam as he was standing up from the breakfast table.

The dogs were happy. They could manage spending much of the day by themselves, but this was much, much better. Sabrina was good company, and she, rather delightfully, didn't seem to be going anywhere.

"This is driving me crazy," she informed Luna after a few days.

Luna wagged. Sabrina made delicious-smelling food and sat and ate it silently, looking at her phone and sighing. This happened the next day and also the next. Every morning, it seemed that Sabrina's muttering increased in frequency.

"I'm stuck here," she told the dogs. "I don't do anything."

Sabrina's life seemed wonderfully active. She took them for walks several times each day, sticking them all on leashes so that they could pull out ahead of her, sniffing everything. Archie, of course, could not master walking in a straight line, and the leashes often became tangled, but Sabrina's patience charmed them all. Riggs licked her hands when she unsnarled the leashes and set Archie back on a straight path, only to have him mess it all up again in a short distance. Luna, ever loyal, always remained right by Sabrina until Sabrina indicated, "Go on, Luna." Then Luna would trot to the end of the leash to catch up with Archie and Riggs.

It was the very best of times.

"I've made a decision," Sabrina told the dogs on one such walk. "God, I'm going to hate having the conversation, but honestly, I think I'm going insane."

Things were slightly different that particular afternoon. Sabrina's mood was dark. She walked into her room and brought out boxes and put clothing in them. She did the same thing in the bathroom. Luna, anxious, tracked her every move, following closely behind and gazing up at Sabrina expectantly whenever there was a pause in the activity. Archie, of course, had no clue and eventually wound up diving into the pile of animals in the basket, attempting to lure Luna into participating in a game of Let's Rip the Cow to Shreds.

But Luna knew something was amiss with Sabrina, and almost nothing mattered more than that. When Sabrina carried her boxes into the living room and then out and put them in her car, Luna's agitation increased. Luna would climb the couch and stare out through the big window at Sabrina and then run to the door when Sabrina returned. Riggs watched this silently from his dog bed, and Archie did what he often did, which was to collapse suddenly into a deathlike nap.

Luna did not take any comfort when Sabrina stopped moving things and sat down on the couch with some tea. She sipped it slowly, her inner dialogue occasionally slipping out in a few whispered words, and checked her phone every few minutes, impatience and apprehension settling over her in equal measure.

Sabrina's tea had turned cold when Liam rattled his keys and opened the door. Archie barked.

"No barks. Stop that noise," Liam greeted Archie automatically. Riggs and Luna ran to greet their person, trying to communicate that some subtle change had come over Sabrina. Liam knelt, obliviously giving them love, laughing when Archie joined the pile and nearly knocked everyone over. Liam stood up, grinned at Sabrina, and then the grin faded from his face. "What's wrong?"

"We need to talk," Sabrina advised somberly.

Looking frightened, Liam eased into the room and sat down in a chair. "Okay," he agreed. He took a breath. "What's going on?"

All three dogs reacted to his fear. Riggs went to Liam's side, Luna sat in the middle of the room, and even Archie paid attention, dropping to his stomach and watching Liam's face.

Sabrina cleared her throat and nodded. "I've packed up my things."

He took a minute. "It's a little soon to be doing that, don't you think?"

Sabrina impatiently shook her head. "You know what I mean,

Liam. I've packed to leave. I need some time. I'm—I feel like
I'm trapped. I'm going to go spend time with my sister and give
myself room to think."

"How is there room to think in that little house with all those
cats?" Liam demanded lightly.

"Come on, Liam."

His eyes narrowed. "Wait. You're leaving. Leaving me? Are we
breaking up?"

"I'm not saying that," she responded dismally.

"Okay, but you're leaving and you won't come back. People
never come back," Liam pronounced bitterly.

Riggs went to Liam and nosed his hand and sat staring at him.
Luna was distraught when Sabrina stood.

"Please, can we just—Don't. Can't we talk?" Liam protested
in a pitiful voice.

"We'll talk, of course. I promise. But I need to go. I told Marcy
I'd be there by now, but then you got delayed. See?"

"See?" he repeated, baffled.

"See how I have no control over my own schedule? I need to go
now, Liam. I need the space."

"Take the space here."

"That isn't how it works."

"Leaving is never how it works," Liam retorted.

Sabrina knelt and gave Luna kisses. Then she went to Riggs,
who lifted a paw in a gesture that he knew charmed her. She gave
him a sad smile and shook that paw. Then she went and knelt by
Archie, who gazed at her cluelessly. "Okay. Goodbye, dogs. I will
see you soon, I promise."

"Don't go, Sabrina," Liam urged, springing agitatedly to his
feet.

"This isn't forever, Liam. I just feel as if I've been too close to
everything. I need to take a step back. We've both been so busy,
life is just flashing past, unplanned, no structure."

Liam was distraught as he watched her walk out the door.

Luna followed her to the door and then sat, anxious, when it shut behind her.

The next day was unusual. Sabrina's odors were everywhere, but with that odd stale character that human smells take on when they're all that remain of a person who had departed.

None of the dogs were happy that Liam left them by themselves—they thought they had come to an understanding on that topic. He was gone all day, and Riggs watched sourly as their abandonment played out in a stuffed animal massacre. By the time Liam's keys rattled in the lock, there were dog toys scattered in several rooms, and the giraffe had become separated from its head. "No barks, Archie," Liam commanded tiredly.

That was nearly the only thing he said. Liam showered, scraped some food out of the refrigerator onto his plate, and then wandered back to bed by himself. The dogs expected Sabrina to walk in through the door but one by one abandoned their post. Riggs was first, loyally trotting back to the bedroom and jumping up next to Liam, who needed his dogs. Riggs put his head on Liam's chest and tried to let Liam know with that touch that whatever he was facing, he wasn't doing it alone.

Archie eventually came wandering in, unsure, smelled the dog beds, and then decided to start the evening up with Liam. He would jump down eventually. Riggs watched in something approaching resentment as Archie went to Sabrina's side of the bed, dug at the pillows, and then collapsed on them as if celebrating that he had claimed as his own something soft upon which to sprawl. That was Archie, never really understanding anything and always thinking of himself. Yet Archie was part of the pack now, so Riggs, other than resolving to keep the young dog in check, accepted the Labradoodle's presence.

Luna didn't come back to join them for a long time. Liam

had turned off the light and his breathing had slowed by the time Luna clicked her way down the hallway and launched herself lightly up onto the bed. She sniffed at Sabrina's pillow and then lay down on it with her back to Archie. Her mood matched Liam's.

Riggs wondered what was going on.

9

The next day, the dogs traveled with Liam to the place of all the hammering and sawing and the smell of fresh wood. Riggs thought of it as the loud house because the noise didn't cease until they were leaving.

The air temperature had gotten warmer and made the loud house more fragrant, and the sweat of the men mingled their odors with Liam's distinct smell, along with the clean, bright presence of freshly cut wood and other, unidentifiable, distinctly human-caused fragrances.

Liam led the dogs into the house, through a door, and down some wooden steps that rang with percussions as his work boots clomped down them. He told them they were good dogs and that they were to stay. "It's going to be a hot day today. It's better for you down here," Liam explained. He tossed out a couple of Luna's dog toys and some rubber rings. Archie, of course, tried to play with everything at once. Luna just sat and stared. Riggs watched mournfully as Liam ascended the steps and closed the door at the top, locking them down in the cool, shadowed basement.

When Riggs clicked his way up to that door and sniffed underneath it, he could smell Liam on the other side and was reassured that his person had not abandoned them. But nonetheless, he felt forlorn. Liam needed his dogs with him but instead had enclosed them in this place.

They weren't abandoned down there all day. A couple of times, Liam came down to let them out to run around in the backyard, which was baking under a hot sun. Riggs marked it carefully, mapping it out as his territory. When Archie trotted off and Liam called, Riggs ran to Archie and in no uncertain terms let him know that he needed to be back in the yard, regardless of the lack of fencing.

Archie, in his usual agreeable fashion, allowed himself to be herded, and there was an extent to which Riggs appreciated this behavior. Archie was the largest of the three of them, but thin and lanky. He was filling out, though. His curly hair had quickly come back, and as it did so, the desire to herd him around grew ever stronger inside Riggs—a breed-deep memory tickling him to round up a whole flock of woolly-looking creatures. There was just something about the way Archie looked and acted that made Riggs long to bring the other dog's life to order—in fact, it would be even better if there were more curly-haired canines to herd!

Riggs was anxious to obey their person because Liam was sad. All three dogs could sense it. He didn't talk to them nearly as much as he normally would.

The next afternoon, in a further deviation from usual behavior, Liam tied them up and crossed over a sidewalk to where a truck was parked that had two people inside peering out windows. As he spoke to those people, the Australian shepherd was distraught. Luna lay tiredly on the cement, and Archie busied himself trying to bite a flying insect that was circling their heads.

This was not right. Though he was within sight, Riggs felt as if Liam had gone far, far away when he abandoned them to venture over to the truck. Riggs wanted to go, too. He strained, but of course, the leash affixed to his collar held him fast. He twisted, pulling, then decided to back away from that leash. With his nose pointed directly down the line, his back legs applying all their strength, he felt the collar sliding up past his ears, and then, with a tug, he was free.

Luna raised her head and regarded this with alert eyes. He had the sense that she admired him for having figured out a human-designed puzzle. Riggs wheeled and ran to his sad person, his nails making very little sound on the cement. Liam started in surprise when Riggs nosed his leg.

"Riggs, what are you doing?"

Riggs felt the brief moment of happiness in his person, and that made the effort worthwhile.

Liam was not angry. He now held a fragrant-smelling meal of some kind in one hand, and with the other, he urged Riggs back across the street. Riggs, of course, stood still to allow that collar to be slid back over the top of his head. As long as he was doing what Liam wanted, Riggs was willing to put up with anything, even a bath. But nothing seemed to make Liam happy.

The third day, Liam showered whistling, and there was a brisk enthusiasm to the way he pulled on his clothes. The dogs, picking up his mood, were dancing at his feet. He let them out of the yard to do their business and fed them a breakfast that they polished off with gusto. Luna even pounced on a stuffed animal, the first time she had done so since Sabrina's abrupt departure, what seemed like forever ago.

"Do you want to go see Sabrina?" Liam asked them.

They heard the name and responded with joy. Maybe Archie didn't understand precisely what was being said, but he picked up on Luna's manic response and chased the little Jack Russell around the house, pretending to growl. Riggs tolerated it because Liam was so happy. In the truck, Liam told Archie, "Stop that noise," and for the first time, Archie seemed to associate that command with his barking. He didn't stop barking when he saw other dogs, but his glance back at Liam indicated he was making a connection, albeit slowly, between his behavior and Liam's chastisement.

Riggs knew where they were the moment the truck stopped. He and Luna had been here before. It was a vast, wonderful area

with a set of gates. Passing through the first gate, into a small
enclosure, and then through the second gate admitted them to a
place filled with wood chips and dog odors and, of course, many
dogs. Some slept in the shade, some sniffed at every newcomer,
and some dashed around in circles. People mostly sat at small
tables and talked and watched their dogs.

Archie took off at a gallop, his feet kicking up wood chips as
he pursued a small white dog, but Luna and Riggs were immediately focused on the woman sitting at one of the tables.

It was Sabrina.

"Dogs," she called.

Luna was almost irrepressibly joyous at this turn of events.
She rolled on her back, she licked Sabrina, she cried. Riggs was
a little less enthusiastic, however. In Riggs's mind, Sabrina had
somehow abandoned them. He didn't really understand how it
all worked; he just knew that after the day of filling boxes with
things, Sabrina stopped sleeping at the house and Liam became
sad. That Liam was happy now didn't give Riggs much confi-
dence. The two humans hugged and then awkwardly kissed at
first on the cheek and then on the lips, but briefly, with Sabrina
giving a small laugh when Liam attempted to prolong the embrace.

"Let's sit," she suggested.

Luna heard the word and sat, so Riggs did, too. Archie was
coursing back and forth on the other side of the park, seemingly
having forgotten about his pack forever.

"I got the job," Sabrina announced after a while, pride in her
voice.

Liam regarded her with a smile. "Well, I knew you would, of
course."

"You know what's really sad? I might make more in tips waiting tables than I make as a teacher. What does that tell you about
our country?"

Liam shrugged. "I don't know what it tells me. I just know that I'm happy to see you, Sabrina."

She smiled. "I'm happy to see you, too, Liam."

"When do you start work?"

"Tonight, back to waitressing. I don't know how I feel about it except I'm excited. It feels like I'm doing something again."

"That's excellent."

"What are you thinking? Why are you looking at me like that?" Sabrina demanded.

"Well," Liam nodded, looking guilty, "I'm just picturing, there you are, this beautiful waitress, and you're serving drinks to all these guys, and they're looking at you, and they're talking to you, and they're, like, asking you out. Proposing marriage."

"Oh my God, Liam!" Sabrina exclaimed with a laugh. "No. Not interested."

"Well, sure, you say that, but they'll come in and they'll be doctors, lawyers, astronauts . . ."

"Astronauts?" She laughed harder.

"Well, you know what I mean."

"Liam, that's not what's happening."

"What is happening? Wait—" Before she could answer, he held up a hand. "Sorry, no, that came off as argumentative. Can I rephrase the question, Your Honor?"

"Okay, sure."

"Okay. What would it take for you to come back home?"

Sabrina seemed to mull that one over. "Home," she finally repeated.

"Well, temporarily home, but then," Liam plunged on, "then we would move into the new place. I promise you, not going to sell this one, not for a long time. I'm going to landscape it. There's a house going up across the street. We're going to have neighbors. The whole vibe of the place, the street, is new and fun. I've already been talking to people about helping them decide on their new construction. I might spend the next ten years building houses on our own block."

Sabrina was watching him with a bemused expression. "Okay," she finally agreed noncommittally.

"That's what you wanted, though, right? I mean, stability. That's what I'm trying for now. No more playing it by ear, and I wouldn't have to go anywhere else like that time I spent three months in Grand Junction on that job. I would be right there, and we would see each other all day, every day we wanted. I mean, not all day, you have a job, but you can stay at the restaurant if you like, I know you're sick of teaching. I just—" He gave her a helpless look. "I just want you to be happy."

"You make me happy," she finally confessed.

"I do?" Liam's face lit up in a delighted, hopeful grin.

"I promised you I'd think. That's what I've been doing. And I've missed you, Liam. A lot. I think I've got it figured out. What we can do, I mean."

"Let's do it."

"You don't want to know what it is? What if I want to move to Peru?"

"I'll pack tonight."

"Okay, but seriously. When I got the waitressing job, it hit me—I need to feel like I've got an equal vote in my own life. A job's only part of it. I need you to be my partner. I get how you make a living, but it affects me every time you sell our home out from under us. You need to bring me into that, to all of your decisions. Let me have some control."

"I think I can manage that!" Liam told her with a grin.

"Plus, honestly, my sister and I haven't really gotten any better at living together than we were as kids. This situation—it can't last."

Liam was still smiling.

"But"—she sighed—"you know Marcy."

Liam's smile lost some of its buoyancy.

10

"I do know your sister, but what should I know in this particular context?" Liam asked after a pause.

Sabrina shrugged. "She let me move in, but then immediately, as usual, I got conscripted into the Marcy army. She's throwing a surprise birthday party for her husband July 1, and somehow I've become the party planner. She asked me if I could stay until then. I mean, what could I say?"

"So you can't move out for two weeks? How does that make any sense?"

"It's just how it's always been between us."

Liam thought about it, then nodded. "I've got a similar thing with my brother, Brad, only he wants to be my parent, protect me. Marcy wants you to be her slave."

"Okay, but she did let me move in with her on short notice."

"Of course. Nobody wants a slave who works remotely."

Liam and Sabrina were grinning at each other, and Luna and Riggs picked up a change in the energy between their two people. What had started as something odd, as if there were strain between them, something blocking them, seemed to have melted away.

Riggs sprawled down on the grass. He decided to remain next to Liam in case he was needed, and he saw Luna making the same decision about Sabrina.

Luna pressed her nose up against Sabrina's ankle and breathed in deeply. For Luna, this was it, this person's smell. It filled her nose and her heart. As long as Sabrina was there, she would be content.

There was an easy silence. "Do you want to know something funny? I was nervous about seeing you," Liam admitted.

"Me, too," Sabrina quickly confessed. "It's only been a few days, but, well . . ."

"They were a strange few days," Liam finished for her.

"I never said you shouldn't text or call."

"You said you needed space. I wasn't sure that texting every thirty seconds would fit the spirit of the request."

Sabrina smiled. "Thirty seconds, you're right. But ninety seconds would have been okay."

Liam laughed.

"Archie seems to have made some new friends," Sabrina observed.

At Archie's name, Riggs looked up in disapproval, finding Archie, who was racing around with several other dogs, mindlessly tracking back and forth, kicking up wood chips, and doing nothing of any service to Liam.

"I don't want to say that I'm betting everything on the new place, but I can't wait for you to see it." Liam turned a hopeful gaze on Sabrina.

Sabrina gave him a smile. "Okay. I want to see it."

"Of course, yes!" He jumped up.

She laughed. "Well, not now, but yes, I want to see it."

"I hate life without you, Sabrina. I hate it," Liam said urgently. "I feel like I did something really stupid, and I don't know what it is, but I want to do something un-stupid now to make up for it." That made her laugh again. "Hey, a lot of guys are worse. You're going to find that out now that you're slinging drinks to felons and drug lords."

"Oh, so we've gone from astronauts to drug lords? I have worked in a bar before, Liam. Are you forgetting that I put myself through college?"

"No, I get it. Yes, I mean, but let's face it, if . . ." He trailed off.

He gazed at her as if there was something he needed to say, so profound and important, he couldn't find the words.

What should have happened didn't happen. Riggs and Luna both felt it strongly and deeply. Sabrina should have accompanied them home from the dog park. That was the natural order of things. She belonged with the pack. She belonged with Liam. When Sabrina was there, Liam was happy. When Sabrina was gone, he was not. Making Liam happy was the purpose of the dogs, and thus Sabrina was at cross-purposes with the pack. This made Riggs very uneasy.

Luna missed Sabrina for her own reasons. Sabrina was simply the right person for Luna. But she also felt the empty wistfulness in Liam as he kissed Sabrina at her car and she drove away.

Liam left the dogs alone that afternoon. "Just for a few hours, I swear," he promised them. Riggs could tell, though, that Liam's thoughts were still back at the dog park, back with Sabrina.

A dog knows when a person possesses that essential something, that unconditional approval and love that so bonds a dog to a human. With Sabrina, Luna had found that purpose and that person. Riggs watched as Luna paced around the house, sniffing up the remnants of Sabrina in odors painted on furniture and the bedclothes. People vanished so rapidly from a place, their scents overwritten by other scents, and Riggs knew how much Luna was hurting and missing her person. It made Riggs very sensitive to the same raw need in Liam, and Riggs tried harder than usual to engage his person in play when he came home. Riggs even shook one of Luna's least objectionable stuffed animals, a skunk whose eyes had fallen out, but Liam did not rise to the bait.

Without Sabrina in the house, Liam spent far less time preparing meals. Often with a defeated slump to his shoulders, he would unwrap something and dig into it unenthusiastically. The dogs always watched attentively, believing everything Liam ate was worth sharing, but the gusto that Liam always displayed around meal preparation had vanished with Sabrina.

Riggs wanted her to come home.

One such evening, Liam sat on the couch and did not object when Luna and Riggs joined him. Archie elected to take up position in a dog bed at their feet.

"Oh, don't worry; she's coming back," he informed his dogs quietly.

Luna and Riggs both regarded him curiously. He was speaking to them, but not in a way that they recognized as having a command or a promise involved. They were just words.

"Sabrina belongs here."

Luna's ears twitched at Sabrina's name.

"Don't worry, dogs. This is a temporary screwup, but I've got a solution. A *permanent* solution."

He reached out and ran a hand up and down Riggs's chest. Riggs half closed his eyes with pleasure. There was something about Liam's touch that no other human had ever been able to duplicate.

"Don't worry," Liam repeated.

The dogs went on full alert when the doorbell rang. It didn't ring very often, and when it did, it was incumbent upon the dogs to alert every human in the room that there was something going on that needed their attention. Even when Liam shouted, "No barks!" they continued to signal because, well, it was the doorbell. Shaking his head and grinning, Liam walked over and opened the door.

The man who stepped inside was someone Riggs and Luna had met before, but not Archie. Archie, therefore, with his typical complete lack of suspicion, greeted the man as if he were a long-lost family member.

His name was Brad. There were certain ways in which Brad smelled a lot like Liam.

"Hey, brother," Brad greeted.

The two men came together and slapped each other almost painfully on the back, grinning. Brad had to reach up to do so. The dogs all noticed the smell of breads and sweets coming from Brad's clothing under the friendly, assaultive hug, and Archie registered that Brad's eyes and hair were darker than Liam's but that there was an underlying similarity to their odors.

"Come on out to the backyard," Liam invited.

The dogs eagerly followed the men out into the yard. Archie raced around as if he had never been there before. Luna watched suspiciously for squirrels. Riggs sat loyally with the two men, who opened bottles of a fragrant-smelling liquid and clinked the bottles together before taking long swallows.

"How's it going?" Brad asked after a moment. "You like being a bachelor again?"

Liam just gave him a skeptical look. "I've always been a bachelor," Liam reminded him.

"You know what I mean," Brad replied.

"No, actually not," Liam responded. "I don't like it at all."

"I get it. But I also get that Sabrina just moved out without warning."

"Not exactly without warning."

"Okay, sure, you walked in and all her belongings were in boxes and she 'warned' you that she was leaving. Look, I'm just watching out for you. You don't need somebody in your life who flakes on you like that."

Liam pondered this silently.

Brad smiled. "Oh, so in other news, I need to tell you, I got that job."

"The one in Germany?" Liam responded delightedly.

"Yes."

"Talk about burying the lede! That's fantastic. When do you go over there?"

"Probably in a week. I don't have it all planned out yet. There's a lot that needs to go into it."

"What's it like to think about living there?"

Brad raised his hand. "Well, not *living*. I'm not sure it's permanent. First, they have to like my work, and then I'd cut a longer-term deal, maybe for a year or so. But yeah, I'm looking forward to it."

"Looking forward to it," Liam repeated flatly. "Isn't this what you've worked for five years to accomplish? Why aren't you shooting off bottle rockets, drinking champagne, mooning the neighbors?"

"I knew there was a reason I don't come to your parties."

"Hell, Brad, this is huge! Congratulations!" They clinked their bottles together again. Riggs regarded the glass objects and wondered if one of them was planning to throw it. That seemed to be the attitude they were adopting, a fun, celebratory sense that they had toys in their hands. Riggs was not interested in chasing a glass bottle, but he supposed Archie would be agreeable.

After a long swallow, Liam regarded his brother with suspicion. "Okay, what is it?"

Brad shrugged. "It's just . . ." He gave Liam a sad smile. "I'll be an ocean away. It feels like I'm abandoning you or something."

"You are living your life," Liam responded firmly. "I want you to do this, Brad. I *insist*. You've worked so hard to get to this point. I would literally kill you if you didn't go!"

"You're going through a rough patch lately, though," Brad protested weakly.

Liam shook his head. "I'm in construction. The whole thing is a rough patch." His eyes narrowed. "Wait, you mean Sabrina?"

"She up and left you," Brad insisted. "You put on a brave face, but she broke your heart. I told you I didn't trust her, and I was right. Women like that, they only care about themselves."

Liam rolled his eyes. "So you think if you're here instead of Europe, you'll what, protect me from women?"

Brad grinned at that.

"Besides," Liam continued, "there's something that changes the formula."

Brad raised his eyes in encouragement.

Liam grinned at him. "I'm going to ask Sabrina to marry me."

11

Brad stared in shock, and Riggs watched him curiously. *"What?"* Brad sputtered.

Liam nodded. "Yeah, I've been thinking about it. Why should I wait? I'm never going to meet anyone better. And I've got this new house . . ." He trailed off at Brad's shaking of his head.

"This is *not* a good idea," Brad stated emphatically.

"What do you mean it's not a good idea?" Liam challenged. "Sabrina and I have been together for a couple of years. I love her. She's the love of my life, Brad."

"Don't you think this has got more to do with the house? You told me about it. It's perfect to raise a family, so naturally, you turn to Sabrina, because she's at hand, and think, *Okay, she's the one to bear the young.*"

"Oh, come on, that's not it. You make it sound like I'm opening a breeding facility or something."

"I'm just saying, man, you're not thinking straight. Maybe the whole reason she walked out on you was to force you to decide the only way to keep her is to marry her. That's just the sort of manipulation I'd expect from her."

"Careful."

"*You* be careful! Do you remember Mrs. Burris?"

"Why in the world are you bringing up our babysitter?"

"Just bear with me," Brad insisted.

"All right."

"When we were kids and our parents would leave us with Mrs. Burris, remember how you were always so happy to see the old bag, so eager to think that it was going to be different this time, that she was going to be nice, because she was nice around Mom and Dad? And she'd be kind, and happy, and laughing, and wonderful until the moment our parents drove down the driveway, and then she'd start with the yelling and the hitting."

"Are you implying that Sabrina's going to hit me?"

"No, stop. I'm just saying," Brad seethed, "that you don't see the bad in people, Liam. You trust them, the way you trusted Mrs. Burris. The way you trusted *Mom*."

"You're way off base here, Brad. Sabrina's nothing like either of those two women."

"Yes, she *is*. This is why I think I can't go to Germany!"

The two men stared angrily at each other.

"If you don't get on that plane and pursue your life's dream," Liam stated icily, "I will never get over my disappointment in you. You've been my big brother, more than that, and I appreciate it, but I don't want you staying here for me."

"Why do you want to get married to *her* of all people?" Brad challenged, unwilling to make peace just yet.

"You heard me say she's the love of my life, right?"

"Come on."

"I'm dead serious. These past few days have been even worse than the first few days. Seeing her at the dog park reminded me of how much I've lost with her gone. You know what she's doing now? She's working in a restaurant. She's being hit on by people like you all the time."

"People like me." Brad snorted.

"You know what I'm saying. Single guys. They just go into the place, they see this hot babe, they order a beer, next thing, they're buying her a ring."

"Did *you* buy a ring?" Brad parried shrewdly.

Liam shook his head. "Not yet. I've been looking at them,

though. The thing is, we never talked about it before, so I don't know what she likes. I think she said something about her sister's ring being beautiful. I thought I would go ask Marcy to show it to me."

"Yeah," Brad agreed sarcastically, "that won't tip anybody off if you show up at your ex-girlfriend's house and ask to see her sister's engagement ring."

"Okay, the plan needs some work," Liam admitted cheerfully. "I found one that I think's perfect. I'll go in tomorrow and get it. We can always return it if I'm off the mark. Oh, and she's not my ex-girlfriend. We're on a break, a temporary break."

"Yes, sure, that's what our parents said, that they would be gone temporarily. And then what happened?"

Liam didn't reply.

"Then what happened?" Brad repeated with more force. "They didn't come back. Ever. That's what happened."

That one caused both men to pause and look inward. Riggs stirred, concerned.

"Look," Liam continued after a moment, "I can't live my whole life by what happened in our family. I so appreciate that you stepped up and took care of me when we were abandoned, but your job is done. I'm a grown-up now. I can make grown-up decisions. Go. To. Germany."

Brad's expression was pained. "She's not good enough for you, Liam."

"Objection noted. Will you be my best man?"

Brad groaned and reached for a fresh beer.

The next evening, Liam was wrapping up trash when the phone rang. It trilled with a noise that Riggs had never really understood. It meant that he would soon be talking, though, and sure enough, he picked up the object that made the noise and pressed it to his face. His face split open in a grin, and both Riggs and Luna reacted to his abrupt change in mood, and then Archie, curious, came to join them.

"Sure, of course I can, Sabrina," he responded eagerly. "What happened?" He listened for a moment. "All right, yes, it's got to be something wrong with the motor. Did you check the circuit breaker? No, it's usually a panel either in the garage or the basement. I'll come over and take a look."

He set the phone back down and grinned at the dogs, who all wagged at him.

"She needs my help. Her sister's garage door opener crapped out and the car is in the garage and they need to get it out and they don't know how. All right. Okay."

He dashed back to his bedroom, and the dogs scampered after him, happy with his energy. Liam pulled on a different shirt and a clean pair of pants, ran into the bathroom, swigged some horrible-smelling stuff, and spat it into the sink—from that action, the dogs concluded it must have tasted as bad as it smelled.

"You guys will be okay. I'll feed you when I get back. I won't be gone long. I'll see if she'll come back with me, maybe for dinner or something. All right, guys? You're good dogs. I love you. You're good dogs. Bye."

Liam sprinted out the door, pulling it shut abruptly behind him. Riggs was not happy. Obviously, something had happened to drive a little chaos into Liam's life, and now Liam was gone before Riggs could fix it.

Luna had heard the word *Sabrina* and reacted to it, but that just made her more unhappy now that Liam was gone.

Archie tried to cheer Luna up by pawing at her face, but Luna ignored the younger dog and slouched over to her dog bed and curled up. Archie approached Riggs, wagging hopefully, and

Riggs went to his own bed. Their person was gone. There was nothing to do now but wait.

Liam pulled his truck into Marcy's driveway and jumped out. He sauntered up to the front door and pushed the bell. Marcy opened it. She was holding her stomach in an odd fashion.

"You okay?" Liam asked her.

"Hi, Liam. Yes, I'm fine. Didn't Sabrina tell you?"

"Tell me what?"

Marcy patted her stomach. "We're expecting."

"Oh, that's great. That's fantastic," Liam enthused.

In truth, he felt there was almost nobody less suited to having a child than Marcy. He found her to be irritable and brittle. The sisters were in many ways similar in appearance, but what Liam considered to be the clean, smooth lines of Sabrina's high cheekbones and white teeth somehow seemed menacing in Marcy. Where Sabrina's hair flowed long and beautifully, Marcy, her hair the same silky blond color, chopped it short as if impatient with brushing it. She moved in quick birdlike motions, and Liam often entertained the idea that she might turn and stab him with a beak.

"Sabrina, Liam's here," Marcy called over her shoulder. She stood back and opened the door wider. "Come on in."

"How's she doing?" Liam asked.

Marcy threw up her hands as if that question were almost too difficult to answer. Liam smiled as Sabrina came running down the stairs. She looked radiant. Her skin was newly tan, as if her life working in a restaurant meant she spent more time in the sun. He supposed that in the afternoons before her shift, she might lie out for a few minutes catching some rays. She slid into his arms so easily they both smiled. They kissed once and then again, and he only very reluctantly released her as she stepped back.

"Thank you so much for coming, Liam."

"Let's check the fuse box," he suggested.

The electrical panel was, as he predicted, in the garage, but when he examined it, none of the breakers had tripped. The unit was getting power, but pushing the button did absolutely nothing.

"Are we going to have to break down the door?" Sabrina asked anxiously. "Isn't there some way to open it?"

"Oh yes," Liam assured her.

He reached up and yanked on the disconnect rope and then easily raised the door manually. "There you go."

"Marcy, it's open," Sabrina advised loudly. She turned to Liam and lowered her voice. "She's six weeks pregnant and acts like it's six months."

Marcy came scurrying out. She appeared ungrateful, even annoyed that Liam had so easily rescued her car from its imprisonment.

"Okay. I'm running late, got to go," she informed them snappishly as if they were begging her to stay. She shot a disapproving look at Liam and then at Sabrina. "Just . . ." She shrugged, got in her car, and drove away.

"Just . . . find a different boyfriend," Liam finished for her.

Sabrina laughed.

"She really doesn't like me," he observed without bitterness.

"No, it's more like she doesn't like anybody," Sabrina suggested. "Can you fix the garage door motor or whatever?"

"I don't fix it," Liam corrected, "I replace it. We can go get one now, and I can put it in."

"Oh," Sabrina frowned. "I think maybe we'd better wait for Jim to get home. I wouldn't want to make that decision without him."

Liam shrugged. "All right, suit yourself. What do you want to do?"

Sabrina smiled. "Pizza?"

A couple of hours later, a mostly empty pizza box between

them, Sabrina and Liam were seated at an outdoor table in the backyard. Liam glanced behind him and saw that the five cats had each taken up position in separate windows and were all glaring at him.

"A lot of cats," he remarked.

Sabrina laughed. "It has taken some getting used to. How're the dogs?"

"They miss you," Liam told her.

Her smile faltered only a little.

Soon after that, they decided it would be less threatening for Marcy's husband, Jim, if Liam wasn't there when he returned home.

"He'll want to decide for himself about the motor," Sabrina reasoned.

They were just standing there underneath the garage door opener motor as if it were mistletoe, so Liam gathered her into his arms, and, telling himself to be gentle and not blow this moment, he pulled her in for a kiss. When they separated, they were smiling into each other's eyes.

The moment was perfect, and Liam reached into his pocket for the ring.

12

The ring, of course, was not in his pocket. He'd had it in his other pants, but the clothing change left him unprepared for what he wanted to do. He wondered if he should just go ahead without the ring, or if it would be better to wait, go home, and come back fully loaded with ammo. Tonight? Should he try to return tonight?

"When will I see you again?" he asked, trying not to sound plaintive.

"When do you want to see me again?" Sabrina replied flirtatiously.

"Ah, tomorrow morning."

She laughed. "I have to go to work in about an hour, and then I promised Marcy I'd help her decorate the nursery."

"That'll take years," Liam complained. "So I won't see you for a few days? You swear it's just because of your sister and nothing else?"

"Don't read anything into it, Liam. Right, I'm busy, but let's try to get together Sunday. I'm off, and you should take a break at least once a week. We'll do something fun. Oh! It's the summer solstice coming up—let's do something this weekend where we wind up on a rooftop deck."

He gave her a serious look. "There's something I want to talk to you about."

"All right." She smiled. "Sunday."

Four days from now.

"Deal."

Another kiss followed that conversation. When Liam slid into his pickup to head home, he cranked up the radio and sang along with the music. His brief examination of Marcy's ring had given him all the affirmation he needed—the one waiting back in his home pants was very similar, but different enough, he thought.

Liam was still smiling as he drove along the country highway. Everything was going so well.

He didn't really register the pair of headlights on the surface road parallel to the highway, off to his right but headed in the opposite direction, so that the headlights flashed in his face. The car was moving fast, really fast, high beams negligently stabbing Liam's eyes. He looked away, then back when he realized those headlights were now bobbing up and down—the speeding vehicle had left the road. "Whoa!" Liam exclaimed as the car slammed into the ditch. He lifted his foot off the accelerator, and then the car was hurtling out of the ditch, through the barbed wire fence, onto the highway, directly at Liam's truck. Liam desperately twisted his steering wheel, his cab flooding with light, feeling his tires lose their grip.

Liam gasped, but there was no time for anything else. The impact was brutal, punching the air out of him. The airbag slapped at Liam's face, and then his head registered a blow that knocked black bolts of lightning across his vision. He sensed the g-forces as his truck rolled and his neck burst in pain, but he was blind now, numb to sound and sight and even feeling, his body limp and dead.

He thought of Sabrina, of the kiss they just shared, of the way she had felt in his arms. Then he remembered, in one last flicker of consciousness, something else really important.

He had forgotten to feed his dogs.

Luna was the first of the three dogs to sense trouble. There was an open window in one of the back bedrooms through which evening noises and smells drifted in, and she had come to learn the pace of the night from them, gauging when Liam should be home. As the hours advanced, the noises reduced in quality, quantity, and sound level, until there was a silence, oppressive and worrisome, in that back room.

Where was Liam? Luna paced, and Riggs watched her and felt a rising anxiety himself. Something was happening; Liam was not here, and Luna was agitated about it. For Riggs, the obvious conclusion was that whatever was making Liam so sad lately was keeping him away. Further, Riggs understood, without really comprehending, that it had something to do with Sabrina. That made Riggs a little resentful toward Luna, who so favored Sabrina over their person, Liam. Archie just basically followed the other dogs around, not sure what they were doing, ready to play if asked, but also picking up on their distress.

Eventually, they all settled into a restless sleep in their dog beds.

When dawn came the next morning, lighting up the room, Archie was the first to awaken. With a yawn, he stretched and then padded over to the food bowls. He nudged each food bowl with his nose as if believing a minute adjustment in their positions would result in them miraculously becoming laden with morning dinner. He licked the inside of one and then turned his attention to the water bowl as a substitute. He lapped up water, and the sound awoke both other dogs.

Luna remained alert in her dog bed, but Riggs also stretched and made his way to the bowls. He, too, was disappointed that food had not somehow appeared during the night. He also drank water, noting as he did so that it was nearly gone. When Luna repeated the same process, following the example of the other two dogs, she had almost no water to drink, and she took the last of it.

Riggs looked to Luna as if expecting the smaller dog to explain the absence of their person. Luna's apprehension had increased to the level where she could not sit still; she paced relentlessly through the house. She kept returning to the back bedroom with the window open, lifting her nose, smelling for Liam. The window was far too high to contemplate climbing out, which would have been a radical choice for them anyway.

They paced, and today, there was no playing with toys, no attacking the stuffed livestock, no rolling on the floor and having fun. Even Archie was subdued, mimicking the mood of the other two. Perhaps to him, still not fully accustomed to the house's admittedly irregular routine, it did not seem unusual for Liam to be gone. It was true that, in the past, Liam had sometimes been out very late at night, but never without first making sure the dogs were fed their dinner. This abrupt change in procedure was upsetting to Luna and Riggs.

Before long, Archie was panting, not so much from anxiety but from the fact that it had become warmer in the house, and they still had no water. Each of them hopefully checked out the water bowl, trying to understand why it was still empty.

Riggs registered that he needed to squat in the yard. He began looking hopefully out the back slider, expecting that any moment the door might open itself, and then he could go out to relieve the increasing pressure inside. Luna seemed to understand, sniffing pointedly at the spot beneath Riggs's tail. It was Luna who went to the back bedroom first, squatting there and depositing a pile. Riggs gratefully followed her example, relieving the pressure and feeling like a really bad dog. It had been a long time since Riggs had done this in the house.

He remembered Liam's reaction when Archie squatted in front of the sliding door, how Liam would snatch up Archie before the poor dog had a chance to commence his business and run the dog out into the yard. Very often, Archie's confusion meant that, for several minutes, he didn't do anything but look around the fenced-in enclosure in bewilderment.

That was the proper way for a dog to be, Riggs knew, to go outside in the grass, to lift legs against the fence, and to squat in the yard in a place where Liam would reliably come and clean it up.

When Archie went back to add his pile to that of the other two dogs, the smell reminded him of being at the short end of that chain because now, throughout the house, there drifted the unmistakable odor of dogs having squatted. Archie kept looking to Riggs and Luna. They were the older dogs. They ought to understand that he was thirsty and needed to be fed. He pointedly pawed at his dinner bowl, gazing expectantly at Riggs. Riggs was in charge. Riggs should feed them.

Luna understood that whatever had gone so terribly wrong, it meant that there was no food and, more urgently, no water. Her nose eventually led her to the room with the bathtub, the dreaded bathtub. The scent of water was powerful in an elevated porcelain bowl with a lid, but that lid was shut. When Luna rose gracefully on her rear legs to probe at that lid, it was immovable. She dropped back down in frustration.

Riggs watched all of this from the doorway. He didn't really want to go into the room that he associated with a bath.

Luna began a process of revisiting that room throughout the day. Riggs eventually stopped following her. There was nothing to be gained, he realized, by sniffing at the rim of that bowl, despite the seductive smell of water just out of reach. It did nothing but increase his anxiety and frustration. Riggs did look to Luna, though, to figure something out. Luna was the dog Riggs could count on to unlatch the gate that had kept them separated from their person in the other room, the back bedroom where they had now squatted so effectively. Luna just understood more about the human world than Riggs could ever hope to.

When night fell, it came very gradually, but then it was dark. It had now been so long since they had eaten, so long since they'd had water, that they were compelled to think about almost nothing else.

They sniffed everywhere. A pantry door was promising, but

none of them could reach the knob, and even if they could, they weren't sure what to do about it. Riggs felt confident that Luna could get that door open and that there were bags of food in there, but Luna didn't seem to want to do so. Or perhaps she couldn't. When she and Riggs sniffed each other, Riggs could smell her desperation and knew if she could think of a way to get into the pantry, she would do so.

The night was long and sleepless, each dog turned inward to their own hunger and thirst. Riggs remembered swimming in a mountain stream with Liam, biting the water, drinking it in. Luna was remembering tackling the water sprinkler in the yard.

Archie's thoughts turned to his chain. This was so similar, the ache of hunger, the dry pain of thirst, the odors. This was what people did with their dogs, sometimes. Oddly, though he was the youngest dog of the three, Archie felt the least desperate. Eventually, he knew, humans would save them. It's what always happened.

The air was still except for the quiet panting of the three canines as they waited for Liam's return.

13

Light was barely probing the home the next morning when Luna walked to the kitchen and began sniffing with a purpose. Riggs and Archie followed hopefully. She seemed to have a plan, though nothing really happened for some time. Eventually, all her probing examinations took place around the cold box that held wonderful smells. When the door was open, those smells would come rushing out, and now Riggs could remember the succulent odors of meat and cheeses.

Could Luna get in there? Riggs didn't see how. There was a big handle on one side, but it was well up off the floor. Another handle, lower, ran parallel to the ground. That handle opened a drawer and food smells would flood out of there as well—much colder food smells, but food nonetheless. Riggs watched as Luna sniffed and registered the fact that the Jack Russell was mostly staring up at the big side handle on the cold box. Archie just sat and watched, patiently waiting for someone to solve his problems.

Riggs was panting, partly from thirst, but mostly from fear. This had never happened, and he had a deep sense that something awful was occurring. Perhaps Liam had left them. Perhaps whatever was making their person sad had caused him to abandon his dogs and go somewhere else, perhaps with other dogs, dogs who could manage to make him happy.

Riggs felt now that none of them had done as much as they needed to in order to keep Liam content. Luna gave too much attention to Sabrina instead of focusing solely on Liam. Archie was too dumb and puppylike to be of much value and had been squatting far too often in front of the sliding door. Even though it appeared to Riggs that this was happening less frequently, it still had set the stage for a disappointment in dog behavior that may have led to Liam going away and never coming back.

Both Archie and Riggs perked up when Luna abandoned her searching in the kitchen and returned to the room with the elevated water bowl and the bathtub. There was some sort of purpose, some sort of determination that compelled them to follow her yet again into that small room. Riggs was astounded when, without being forced to, Luna leaped up and over and into the porcelain bathtub. Why would any dog voluntarily enter such a place? Riggs had no idea what she was doing. Archie was even less sure, stuck on the threshold to the room, unwilling to commit to fully joining them.

Luna made her way, her nails clicking, to the dreaded water faucet from which all the baths flowed. There was a lever there, of course, but Riggs had no idea what it was for. He was somewhat astounded to see Luna leap up and thrust her paws and nose at it. It made no sense to him whatsoever. An odd sound began to fill the air as Luna continued her attack. It was a gurgling, high-pitched whine, very faint.

Then it happened: a tiny stream of water flowed out of the nozzle.

Luna's reaction to this stream was immediate. She lunged at it and bit at the stream, lapping up water. Riggs, intoxicated by the odor, rushed to the edge of the tub and stared at her. Luna was drinking water, and he was not. That is what he registered. She was in the tub, and he was not. There seemed to be a real association. With something approaching resignation, Riggs launched himself into the tub, landing and sliding and then making his way quickly down to the trickle of water where Luna was still drinking greedily. He thrust her face next to hers, and she graciously let him drink as well. The two dogs stayed there slaking their thirst for some time while Archie watched in uncomprehending envy.

At first, Riggs paid no attention to the younger dog, focused only on the blessed relief from having a source of water. When he finally had conquered his thirst, he turned and looked at Archie, who was sitting in distress, now inside the room, but barely. Archie stood up, wagged, stretched, and bowed, and then beseeched Riggs with an imploring look.

Riggs thought about it. What Archie needed to do was get in the bathtub, but he clearly had no sense that he could do so. Despite the fact that he had seen both Riggs and Luna jump in, he seemed absolutely perplexed, incapable of formulating a plan on his own.

Riggs pointedly climbed out of the tub, demonstrating, he felt, that by putting one's forepaws on the side of the tub and thrusting, a dog could clamber in and out. This didn't seem to register with Archie at all, who just wagged harder and gave another little cry. He wanted water so desperately—that much was obvious. He sniffed jealously at Riggs's lips but backed away when, after being given an exploratory lick, Riggs bared his teeth. Riggs was not going to regurgitate for Archie. Instead, after a moment, Riggs elected to push forward, crowding Archie into the small space between the elevated bowl and the lip of the bathtub. Luna was still licking up water but with much less urgency, and she watched this process curiously.

Backed into that corner now, Riggs made Archie very uncomfortable. The younger dog felt trapped and anxious. There was literally nowhere to go, and still Riggs pressed forward. Archie started to panic. Then Riggs nipped once at Archie's rear leg. Frantic to escape this inexplicable assault, Archie launched himself straight up and, in the process, cleared the lip of the bathtub. He fell as if thrown, landing on his face, rolling, but he was in. He went after that trickle of water, and Luna accommodated him.

Luna remained in the tub while Archie drank and drank. When the younger dog finally had his fill, Luna soared gracefully out of the bathtub onto the hard tile floor and clicked out of the room. Riggs watched Archie track this with confusion. Then Riggs left.

Archie was now alone in the tub. The water was wonderful, but he was no longer thirsty. He was hungry, and, even worse, he was alone in this place of anxiety. He needed to be with other dogs. He tried to picture what had happened, how both dogs had managed to get in and out of this odd container. His association with it was that he was lifted in and out by Liam, and that had been a very unpleasant experience, and yet, now here he was of his own volition. He wasn't even sure how such a thing was possible.

Archie thought about it. Then, scrambling, he attempted to climb out of the tub. The sides were slippery and his efforts fruitless. He repeated the process several times, sliding back with each attack.

Archie yipped plaintively, then cocked his head, listening for sounds of rescue.

Nothing.

His fear turned to panic, and he went after the side of the tub in a frenzy, leaping and clawing and landing rather painfully on the lip of the tub, but now he was half in and half out. When he toppled forward, he had escaped.

Archie turned and ran after the other dogs, who had reassembled themselves in the kitchen. They were still sitting and staring at the cold box. Archie didn't know what was in there and didn't know what they found so fascinating.

Luna focused on that side handle. She could recall so many times where Liam had casually reached up and pulled on it, and she had registered the wonderful smells flowing from the interior. It seemed to her it should be easy to pull on that handle if she could get to it. How could she do that?

It was frustration more than calculation that led her to leap into the air. As she did so, she tried to snatch at that handle with her mouth. She was unsuccessful, but as she fell, both of her rear paws landed on the lower handle. Now, she was within striking distance of the side handle, with her two back feet propped up on the drawer pull that ran parallel to the floor. She began to bite and tug and work at the side handle, barely able to get a grip, straining and pushing as hard as she could, and then something completely unexpected happened. With a lurch, her back legs fell away, the freezer drawer yawning open, and she dropped and landed directly onto a pile of frozen objects.

Riggs watched all this in astonishment. He'd not really understood much about what Luna had been attempting, but now she was literally inside the coldest part of the cold box, lying on top of what lay within. Their eyes met, Luna and Riggs exchanging information. This was a triumph of some kind. They just needed to understand what to do next.

Luna stood up, still in the cold box. Her paws were immediately aching from the temperatures, which normally, when given a winter's worth of time to adjust, shouldn't bother her so much, but this had been an abrupt change. Yet there were food smells in here, and she dug with her mouth at one of the packages. It was coated in plastic, but that didn't disguise the deliciousness of the chicken that lay within it. She bit and pulled and dug at that plastic until she could pull a chunk of chicken into her mouth. She began gnawing at it greedily, aware as she did so that both Archie and Riggs had pressed forward to watch her progress. Luna chewed that crunchy, frozen chicken and went for another piece.

The dogs sat expectantly, as if Liam had commanded them to do so. When Luna dipped her nose again into the frozen box, she smelled a delectable piece of meat. She pulled it out, and it was heavy. She looked at Riggs. Riggs's face was beseeching. Luna dropped the frozen beef to the floor, and Riggs jumped on it. Archie held back despite his obvious hunger because Riggs was in charge. Riggs ripped and pulled frantically at the packaging, eventually exposing enough of the red meat for him to get his teeth on. He lay on the floor and began licking and licking.

Luna, meanwhile, had excavated another small piece of chicken and had chewed it and swallowed it and was feeling slightly better. Her next foray gave her a plastic bag with the unmistakable smell of cooked turkey. That one, she pulled out and dropped on the floor for Archie. The three dogs fed, feeling remorseful, feeling like bad dogs, but compelled by their near starvation.

They overate, the food swelling their empty stomachs, and soon were visiting the back room. Luna and Riggs and perhaps even Archie knew that beyond the mess in the kitchen, beyond the purloined meats, what they had done on the floor back there would get them in serious trouble—so they reacted guiltily when, much later in the day, the front door rattled and swung open.

14

The dogs ran to meet the person on the threshold, barking with unrestrained relief, but it wasn't Liam. It was the man they knew of as Brad, which was good—Brad knew Liam. Brad would take them to Liam.

"Oh my God, you poor dogs," was the first thing Brad blurted.

They were frantic and would have jumped into the arms of a stranger, so when Brad extended his arms, they all swarmed onto him, smelling him, looking for signs of Liam.

"Oh man, oh man. Wow, it stinks in here," he observed.

After giving them affection, Brad strode to the rear slider and threw it open. The dogs dashed out into the yard, relieving themselves and feeling better about it than they had in some time. Riggs and Luna exchanged a glance, as if hopeful Brad wouldn't think to look inside the room down the hall.

Brad remained in the house for a long time. When the dogs trotted in to check on him, he had filled their bowls full of dog food, and nothing had ever tasted so wonderful. The fact that they were being fed by human hand meant they were not bad dogs after all.

"All right," Brad advised. "I got all that cleaned up. Man, I'm so sorry. No one even thought about you guys." Brad knelt and gave each one of them hugs and petted their fur, smiling sadly into their faces. "Poor dogs, things are going to be so different now. I'm so sorry." Brad went to the kitchen and sifted through some papers and then pulled out his phone, stabbing at it with an index finger. Riggs watched curiously. When Brad uttered the word *Sabrina*, Luna reacted, raising her head.

"Hey, it's Liam's brother, Brad. I know you know that, sorry, I'm not thinking straight. Listen, I have bad news. Liam's in the hospital."

The dogs were all watching him now.

"It was a car accident." Brad faltered for a moment, then plunged on. "They took him to Swedish Medical Center. Can you meet me there?"

When Brad put away his phone, he made to walk out the front door, then stopped himself. He turned back. "I'll come back soon, I promise," he told the dogs, who were quiet and apprehensive. They watched him close the door behind him and then looked at one another in anxious bewilderment.

What broke Sabrina was the view through the window into the ICU. Brad had already arrived and was wearing a mask identical to the one she was pausing to don, the male nurse who was escorting her waiting patiently while she fumbled with it.

"You okay?" he whispered concernedly.

No, she was not okay. The tube at Liam's throat was what made her not okay. She knew it was a ventilator because of her mom's final days. Marcy, with her typical lack of sentiment, had pronounced flatly that "once they're on a ventilator, it's over." Which had proven true, in their mother's case. But surely that couldn't be true for Liam!

Brad stirred as if he might embrace her when she approached, but appeared to think better of it. He stood silently by while Sabrina sobbed, half-suffocated by the mask over her mouth. "It's okay to touch him," he finally murmured.

Sabrina seized Liam's left hand, because only his left arm was free of tubes, and held it, willing him to respond with an acknowledging squeeze, but all his power, all his wonderful, assuring strength seemed drained from him, his fingers flaccid under her grip.

After what could have been minutes or hours, Brad tentatively reached out and touched her wrist. "We should talk," he suggested in the same low tones.

They found their way to an empty waiting room and stripped off their masks. Sabrina used a paper towel to wipe her wet face.

"I couldn't figure out why he wasn't texting back. I thought maybe he was mad at me," Sabrina lamented in a choked voice. "We've been having some problems."

Brad seemed to want to say something to this, then thought better of it. "I was camping. Out of cell range, naturally. I'm leaving soon and wanted to get my last taste of Colorado." His smile was bitter. "They kept calling me, but I didn't know it."

"Why didn't they call *me*?" Sabrina wanted to know.

"Because I'm the emergency contact number. Because it's always just been Liam and me," Brad replied, an odd tension in his voice.

Sabrina gave no sign of registering Brad's tone. "It was an accident? What happened?"

"A drunk veered onto the highway and hit Liam head-on. The drunk didn't make it."

"He *died*? What about Liam? Is he going to be okay? What do the doctors say?"

"There's no way to know, but . . . they told me he's in a coma, and the odds of him waking up are very slim. His injuries are just too severe."

Sabrina put a hand to her mouth, weeping again. Brad looked away uncomfortably, then back at her. "Are you with me, Sabrina?" Brad asked softly. "I know you aren't okay—God knows I'm not—but there's more to talk about. Can you do that?"

Sabrina shuddered, nodding, trying to regain control.

"So, we have, like, a real problem," Brad continued. "It's the dogs."

Sabrina raised her eyes.

Brad shook his head. "I can't take them. I was supposed to go to Germany the day after tomorrow. I explained, and they're giving me an extra week. By then . . . I guess by then, we'll know about Liam. But I have to *go*."

"You're going to leave," Sabrina challenged, "with Liam in the hospital?"

Brad's face contorted in anger. "Don't lecture me on leaving Liam. You don't know anything about the two of us."

Sabrina stared at Brad.

Brad paced agitatedly. "Did he ever tell you about how we grew up, about how our parents were both drug addicts? They kept disappearing. It was always my job to take care of him when they left, but I was a kid, too. I'm only four years older. We had to survive until they returned. Eventually, we went to live with an uncle, but he was . . ." Brad shook his head. "Uncle Dean had some mental problems. It was not a good situation for us. So then the state took us away, and they separated us, and I did everything I could to be reunited with Liam. I applied to be an adult when I was sixteen. Sixteen, Sabrina. I became a legal adult so I could take care of my brother. Do you understand how hard that was? So don't lecture me about going to Germany. They tell me Liam's not going to live. He might not even make it until tomorrow morning." Brad's expression was hard and unforgiving.

"No," Sabrina responded in a small voice, "Liam never told me any of that. I wonder if that's why he's so content when things are chaotic."

"Well," Brad responded, anger in his eyes, "let's not do a bunch of psychoanalyzing right now, okay?"

Sabrina lowered her gaze. "You're right. Sorry. This is all so much."

"So, yeah, of course I'll manage things for Liam. We have each other's power of attorney, just for situations like this. I've got to leave, though. It's a new job for me, something I've worked on for a long time."

"But surely this changes everything."

Brad nodded wearily. "It does . . . and it doesn't. The doctors tell me there are only three outcomes. The first is he passes before I leave."

Sabrina swallowed and shook her head, denying this possibility.

"The second is that he remains in this state for the rest of his life, which may not last long. And the third is he gets better. Which they keep telling me is the least likely. So whether I leave or not makes no difference, understand? And I'm not moving permanently, but I'll be in Germany most of the time, so I need you to take the dogs."

Sabrina's eyes widened. "No. I mean, I can't. I live with my sister, and she's got five cats."

"There are five cats?" Brad interrupted incredulously.

Sabrina shook her head impatiently. "It doesn't matter. It's my sister's house. I can't just invite the dogs."

"Could you go live at Liam's home with them?"

She shook her head again. "That doesn't make any sense. The place is sold. He was moving this month. The new people are coming. He and the dogs were going to stay with a friend. I don't even know who. He's got a new place, but I've never been there. He wanted to surprise me with it, so I don't even know where it is."

"He seemed to think the two of you were a lot closer than you apparently were," Brad observed softly.

Sabrina's eyes flared. "What's that supposed to mean?"

"Nothing. Except you know how he feels about the dogs. I'm surprised you're not putting more effort into helping them."

"Well, I'm not in a great position to do so, Brad. I quit my job last night."

"The waitress job?"

"I was a server, yes."

"Well, isn't that just typical. Have you ever stuck with a commitment in your life?"

"Screw you, Brad!" Sabrina hissed. "You don't know the first thing about it. My manager expected more from me than just work, especially after someone told him my boyfriend and I broke up. Okay? I didn't have a choice."

"I thought you and Liam were just on a temporary break," Brad objected. "That's what he thought, anyway. Were you ever honest with him?"

"Ever honest?" she repeated incredulously.

"Were you broken up or not?"

"That's none of your business. So yes, I don't have a job, Brad. I'll get one, and school starts in the fall, but right now, I'm living off my sister's generosity, and yes, she's got a lot of cats. Sorry." Sabrina spat this last word.

The two of them glared at each other. "All right, then. I've got a lot of things to solve with no help from you," Brad concluded, his voice rising. "I'll get Liam's crap moved out of his house and get an attorney to figure out how to close on the sale and I'll figure out what to do about the new place and I'll take care of my brother and I'll take care of his dogs!"

Brad's furious shouting drew attention. The same nurse poked his head in the room, concern and warning on his face. "Please keep it down," he admonished firmly.

Brad gave an ill-tempered nod.

"Maybe I can help," Sabrina finally offered.

Brad vehemently shook his head. "No, you know what? Liam and I have always been fine. It's other people who have messed up our lives. When you flaked on him, you broke his heart, Sabrina."

"I didn't *flake*!"

"Whatever. I'm going to go back in and be with my brother."

"I'm coming, too."

"Actually, you know what? I don't want you there with me. And if Liam's passing tonight, I don't want you in the room with him. Understand? I'll take care of everything. That's my job. But it's not my job to take care of *you*."

15

At least the three dogs weren't alone. Brad came to be with them and slept in Liam's bed. When, many days later, people arrived and began boxing things and hauling furniture out to a truck, Luna and Riggs paced nervously and actually felt better when they were finally sequestered behind the wooden accordion gate. They'd been through similar experiences before, but never without Liam in attendance, and having Brad close the gate gave the dogs a sense of human order being imposed.

Not for Archie, of course. New people meant new friends, and he was frustrated that all the activity was taking place on the other side of the gate. At one point, he nosed Luna expectantly, but she refused to be provoked into another jailbreak.

When the house fell silent and Brad opened the gate, the place was completely empty of furniture. Archie tore around the bare rooms manically, but Riggs and Luna remained right on Brad's heels as he wandered around, fiddling with cardboard cartons. They didn't trust any of this.

When the door opened, Brad started in surprise, but the dogs rushed forward in delight. Sabrina fell to her knees, arms wide, and they piled onto her. Luna whimpered and begged to be held.

"I thought we said five thirty," Brad greeted pointedly. "I was just leaving."

Sabrina stood. "Because I wanted to talk to you, Brad. Why won't you take my calls? Why only text?"

"Maybe I don't want to talk to *you*."

"I don't understand any of this."

"Oh," Brad agreed with a mirthless laugh, "I don't understand either, I promise you. But that's how life is."

Sabrina looked around for a place to sit. Brad gestured to the kitchen island, and she scooted up on it. He remained standing, his arms folded.

"The doctors won't tell me anything," Sabrina complained in a small voice.

"That's because I told them not to. They tell *me* that you're visiting twice a day."

"Of course!"

They were silent for a moment.

"You're still going to Germany?" she inquired.

"Yeah. I leave July 13. They've given me all the extensions they're going to give me. I either show up or I lose any chance of securing the contract."

"Any luck finding a place for the dogs?" Sabrina asked hopefully.

"No," Brad replied bluntly. "I'm taking them tomorrow to the shelter. They told me they'll do their best to adopt them out together as a pack."

"Adopt," Sabrina repeated, her face ashen.

"There's more. Liam's not improving. They tell me there's no hope."

Sabrina swallowed, her eyes tearing. It was one thing to infer a prognosis, it was another to hear it confirmed out loud.

"They suggest I should pull the feeding tube. Said it's a mercy."

Sabrina gasped. "You can't do *that*."

"My brother has a DNR," he pressed on stonily. "You know what that means? Do not resuscitate. He specifically said he doesn't want to be kept alive. You don't think I should honor his request?"

"*Brad*," Sabrina wailed in anguish.

Brad looked away. When he turned back, his eyes were softer. "It's just how it is, Sabrina."

It took her a long time to recover from that.

Finally, Brad cleared his throat. "You'd better say goodbye to the dogs. I'm not sure when you'll see them again. Or if."

"This can't be happening," she whispered.

"Please don't go see Liam again. I don't think it helps him."

Sabrina stared at Brad. "Why do you hate me so much?"

He looked weary. "I don't hate you. I don't hate anybody. But Liam's got a blind spot, had it since he was a kid. Always thinks the best of folks. He believed every promise our mom ever made. He'll have faith in the most unreliable people on the planet, because his heart is too big. If it weren't for me, he wouldn't have made it. I'm serious. I don't think he would have survived. I had to protect him from our parents and everybody else."

"I'm not unreliable, Brad."

"Your behavior suggests otherwise."

"Please."

"I'm going back to my place for a bit. Say goodbye to the dogs. Lock up when you leave."

Luna was pressed up against Sabrina's ankle as if intuiting what was happening. Archie found a kitchen sponge and was shaking it—the closest thing he could find to a dog toy in this oddly empty house. Riggs regarded Sabrina warily, feeling the waves of grief pouring off her.

Sabrina knelt and extended her arms, and her cheeks were wet, and the pain breaking inside of her made Luna whimper. Even Archie seemed to understand something very sad was happening. He abandoned the sponge and joined Luna. Riggs was drawn to the hug, pulled in by the strength of Sabrina's feelings.

"Oh, dogs . . . oh, dogs," Sabrina murmured. "I am so, so sorry.

I don't know what to do, but I can't take you with me right now. Not even for one night. It just wouldn't work." She gazed sadly into Luna's eyes. "This is all happening too fast. I don't even have time to think."

Dogs very often can't do anything to help a person stop being angry, but making sadness go away is usually something for which dogs feel uniquely well suited. Frustration rippled through the pack as if they were being bad dogs.

Sabrina picked up Luna and cuddled the little dog to her chest, Luna's tongue licking away the salt on Sabrina's cheeks. "Oh, Luna. I love you. I'm sorry this happened. But you dogs will have good homes now, I promise."

Sabrina broke down, unable to speak further. Riggs helplessly pawed at her knee, and Archie sprawled uncertainly on the floor.

Sabrina clung to the dogs for a long time, so long that Archie became restless, but Luna and Riggs seemed to know that whatever was going wrong in their world was continuing to have its cruel impact.

When she finally whispered goodbye for the last time and went out the door, the dogs could hear her lingering outside, her sobbing continuing until finally her car started and pulled away.

Brad spent the night with them, sleeping on the floor in a soft sack, the dogs finding places nearby. When morning came, Brad made coffee and looked around. "Well. That's it. The cleaners will be here in a while, and then I'm meeting the people for the closing." He focused on the dogs. "I guess we should get going, then."

Luna had to be carried to the car. She simply wouldn't voluntarily leave Liam's house. All three dogs piled somberly into the back seat, sniffing each other in confusion and upset. Something was happening, and obviously they did not understand what, but the emotions were very clear, raw, and painful.

When Brad sat in the front seat and the car began moving,

Luna stood on her back legs and watched out the back window, focused on the house where they'd last seen Sabrina.

Sabrina knew the people in the ICU now, well enough to smile and nod at them, and the woman in charge of the operation, Vivian, had always been pleasant. That's why Sabrina slowed as she approached to check in, seeing something in Vivian's dark eyes and pursed lips that warned of a problem.

"Hi, Vivian," Sabrina greeted cautiously.

"Sabrina," Vivian replied, the word coming out heavily. Sabrina's stomach dropped, and she clutched it involuntarily.

"Did something . . . Did Liam . . . ?"

Vivian gravely shook her head. "His brother called yesterday, right after you left. We're not allowed to admit you as a visitor anymore."

"But I don't understand."

Vivian had the sort of broad, jowly face that transmitted a motherly concern. "It's the law, hon. Privacy. Brad says you can't visit."

"But Liam and I *lived* together," Sabrina protested wildly.

"I understand." Vivian looked like she *did* understand. Her eyes were pained. Sabrina had the thought that if she needed a hug, Vivian would offer it.

But Vivian would also block her access to Liam. That, too, was clear. "But I can't let you go back there anymore, Sabrina. I'm truly sorry."

"But he's okay. Tell me that, at least."

Vivian took in a deep breath, then shook her head. "I'm not allowed to say."

Sabrina had cried enough in the past few weeks to recognize the symptoms of another meltdown. She closed her eyes and stood motionless for a moment, then nodded. "It's not your fault, Vivian. His brother . . . we don't get along. But this is childish."

"Thanks for understanding," Vivian replied, looking relieved.

In her car in the parking lot, Sabrina tried calling Brad. It rolled to voicemail. Then she texted.

> Why won't you let me see Liam?

There was no reply.

> Brad please let me see Liam

She sat and gazed at the phone, waiting for the three little dots to indicate a reply was coming. Nothing.

Anyone watching security footage that afternoon would have seen a young blond woman in the front seat of her car, pounding her steering wheel with her fists and screaming.

When the rage and the pain and the grief were all vented, her hands ached, but her resolve had hardened.

They could not keep her from seeing Liam.

Only Archie was excited about the car ride. It was a strange vehicle, one the dogs had never been in before. They were in the back, but only Archie raced back and forth, trying to look out each side window. The other two dogs were subdued, watching Brad, who flexed and unflexed his hands on the wheel, radiating deep grief. Something bad was going on.

As far as Riggs was concerned, the logical conclusion of this day would be reuniting with Liam. Brad had almost never been in their presence without Liam, so this seemed a reasonable expectation. But it was not to be so.

Brad pulled up in front of a nondescript building along a heavily cemented area with many cars that were not moving. When Riggs was allowed out, his reaction was the same as Archie's, to lift a leg against a well-tagged fire hydrant nearby. Once they had done that, though, they returned in concern to Brad, who was calling Luna's name.

The Jack Russell did not want to get out of the car.

Eventually, Brad reached in and cradled Luna much the way Sabrina had held her the night before. "It's okay, Luna," Brad murmured. Luna heard the comforting words and her name but took nothing from it but a deepening sense of foreboding.

Riggs and Archie followed Brad through a glass door into a room that was so redolent with the smell of dogs and cats that it caused Luna's nose to wrinkle. Archie, of course, was energized. It was a new place. New places were exciting, and new places with animal smells were doubly exciting. Riggs, though, was reacting to Luna. Her suspicious manner led him to believe that she understood something about this place not apparent to the male dogs.

Two women came out from behind a counter. "My name's Mrs. Kepler," greeted the smaller of the two. She had white hair, something Luna had never really noticed on a person before. Her smells, Luna noted, were of breakfast, and the friendly hand that was extended wafted a cinnamon spice.

"I'm Teme," added the other one. "Teme Ring." She was taller and thinner and younger than Mrs. Kepler by a significant degree. Her hair was the same color as some of the mottled patches on Riggs's back, and she smelled like cooked vegetables.

"Who have we here?" Mrs. Kepler asked cheerfully.

16

Archie reacted to the woman's crooning tone by throwing himself onto his stomach and crawling forward, his tail beating the floor. A faint whiff of urine came to Luna's nose. Archie was so excited, he'd leaked a little. The humans didn't seem to notice.

"These are my brother's dogs," Brad replied in a choked voice. Something about his inflection caused the other two humans to regard him warily. Brad closed his eyes momentarily. "Liam was in a car accident. A car veered onto the highway and into oncoming traffic. The other driver was killed."

"Oh no," Mrs. Kepler replied softly.

Brad nodded. "My brother's in a coma. He has"—Brad hesitated—"head injuries. He's not expected to recover."

"I see," Mrs. Kepler murmured.

Teme knelt and extended her hand. Archie went to her, but Riggs held back, mimicking Luna's reticence.

"This is a surrender, then," Mrs. Kepler speculated.

Brad nodded again. "I've been working a couple of years on a contract. I'm in mechanical design, and I have to go to Germany. I'll be there for three months or longer." He shrugged. "Could be as long as a year. Or . . . forever. Obviously, I can't take the dogs with me."

"Obviously," Teme replied supportively.

"It's so sudden. There's no one else who can take them on such short notice." Brad nodded then, a quick gesture to indicate he understood his own words, even if they hadn't convinced him he was making the right decision. He brought in a deep breath. "Am

I doing the right thing? Should I not go? Everything is happening so damn quickly, there's no time to even *think*."

Mrs. Kepler's smile was sad. "I can tell you want to do the right thing for your brother's dogs, and we will find them new homes where they'll be happy, I promise. Obviously, we're not a boarding facility. We can't just keep them here while waiting for your plans to settle—that would be cruel, under the circumstances—but we will do our best, and I am sure they'll be fine. We do understand what you're going through," Mrs. Kepler finished.

The sadness inside Brad was remarkably similar to the sharp pain in Sabrina. Riggs raised his head, regarding Brad, and for the first time contemplated that perhaps something was significantly wrong with Liam. Perhaps the reason why Liam had not come home was what lay behind Sabrina's sadness and now Brad's. Riggs couldn't fathom what that could be, though. He looked to Luna, always quicker, always smarter, to see if she had any reaction, but she was gazing up at Mrs. Kepler with a solemn expression.

Riggs, Luna, and now Archie belonged with Liam. There wasn't much about the world that Riggs understood, but he understood that much. Yet here they were, without him.

A man wandered out of a back room, moving carefully. He said his name was Noah Reed. Brad called him Mr. Reed, so that's how Luna thought of him. Mr. Reed put down very gentle hands that smelled delightfully of meaty food. Luna could not help but sniff them, and then, with a resignation that Riggs both saw and felt, Luna allowed herself to be scooped up by this old man, who moved slowly and nonthreateningly and wore a steady smile on his face. His face wrinkled as he grinned, and above the wrinkles were wisps of hair the same color as Mrs. Kepler's. "What is your name?" he asked the little Jack Russell.

"That's Luna," Brad volunteered.

"Luna." The man's soft brown eyes regarded the dog in his

arms. "I will take good care of you, Luna. We'll find you a good home. People love Jack Russell terriers."

When the man opened the door and carried Luna through it, Riggs alerted, and the glance he exchanged with the Jack Russell was full of alarm. This separation of the pack was not something expected or welcome. It felt dangerous. Riggs snapped his gaze to Teme and Mrs. Kepler. They seemed nice, but they had taken Luna away, or at least participated in Luna's removal. Riggs took a careful, unnoticed step back. He turned and looked at the glass door through which they'd come. The shadows were growing long in the parking lot, seeming almost to beckon the little Aussie. If someone came to that door and opened it, Riggs resolved to break through to freedom. He pictured doing it, felt the afternoon sun on his back, the cement under his pads as he ran and found Liam and ended this horrible ordeal.

Brad stood and wrote things down with a pen, filling out forms while Teme took a loop of rope and slipped it over Archie's willing head. The only moment of hesitation was at that same door, where Archie suddenly turned back to glance at Riggs.

Riggs knew what Archie was wondering. Was this the last time they would see each other? Were they now all going into some mysterious new part of life where the pack was separated?

Brad dropped to his knees and held Riggs's face in his hands and stared into his eyes. "I'm so sorry, buddy. Sometimes these things just happen in life. I wish I could tell you it's all going to be better, but I think it's not. I think it's going to be worse for a while, but you'll find a home. You'll learn to love the new people. I know, though . . ." His voice roughened, and he wiped hastily at his eyes. "I know you'll never forget Liam, and you shouldn't. He was . . . He is a very good man."

Riggs had felt these goodbye feelings from other people enough in his life to appreciate that Brad was going away. To find Liam and bring him here? It didn't appear so.

Riggs glanced back at the glass door. If Brad left, he would clearly have to open that door. But, Riggs realized, dashing through it to freedom would mean abandoning the other members of his pack.

Brad stood back up. "Thank you," he told Mrs. Kepler. "I so appreciate it."

Mrs. Kepler put a loop around Riggs's neck, which he accepted with despondence. There were no other choices available.

"These dogs will be fine," she reassured Brad. "You can tell they've been raised with love. That's so important."

Riggs turned away from Brad and, without protest, kept the leash limp as he followed Mrs. Kepler through the same door that had claimed Archie and Luna. He registered the abrupt change—a change in noise level, in the overwhelming smells of canines, of the air becoming moist and warm from the panting of all the dogs. As he tracked the woman down the center of the aisle, he ignored as best as he could the reactions of the caged dogs on either side of him: the ones who charged the gates, the ones who lay sullen and scared, the ones who paced and ignored him in return.

He knew where he was being taken because he spotted Archie and Luna in their own pens, with an empty kennel between them. Archie leaped and twirled, excited to be reunited with Riggs, while Luna solemnly gazed with what felt like silent reproach.

"There you go, Riggs," Mrs. Kepler invited soothingly, the gate open. Riggs padded in, the concrete cool underfoot, and took note of the clean-smelling bed in the back and the bowl of fresh water.

Archie was celebrating their arrival at this alien place, barking back at the vocalizations and putting his paws up on the cage walls, but Riggs and Luna retreated to their respective beds and curled up, intimidated and subdued.

Riggs could only hope that Liam would know how to find them.

Swedish Medical Center was a hospital, not a secret, high-security facility. While it was true Vivian and her peers appeared formidable as they maintained sentry duty at the reception desk, Sabrina had spotted a service elevator down the hallway from Liam's room.

Sabrina put her plan into action a few days after Brad banished her from the place, summoning up her nerve and finding her way to that service elevator on a lower floor. It was a simple matter to push the button directly below the EMPLOYEES ONLY sign and wait for the empty elevator to yawn open and whisk her up to Liam's floor. Alarms did not ring, and she was not met with a hail of gunfire.

Her heart was beating loudly because she felt like a burglar, but there was no one in the hallway to challenge her. She reminded herself that she was doing nothing wrong—it was Brad who was wrong, Brad who was doing this. He had no right to keep her from Liam, and she would visit every day if she wanted!

Steeled with resolve, she padded swiftly to Liam's room, pausing automatically to take a surgical mask from the bin in the hallway and slip it on. As she did so, she glanced through the small window, and what she saw felt like a physical gut punch, her breath leaving her lungs in a gasp.

Liam lay face up in his bed as usual. Most of his lower body was hidden by the window frame, but his head was in clear view.

It was covered with a sheet.

Sabrina gripped the window frame to keep from collapsing. She focused on his chest, willing it to rise and fall, knowing it was futile, knowing that there was only one known cause of such stillness.

Her sobs hacked at her insides, so painful it was as if she were breaking in half. She reached up and yanked the mask away from her mouth, pulling in choked breaths, trying to breathe past the agony.

The person who appeared at her elbow was a stranger, garbed in nurse blue, brown eyes warm with sympathy. "Hello?" he murmured to Sabrina. He lifted a hand as if to touch her. He was young, his name tag said *Garcia*, and he seemed unsure.

Sabrina was too stricken to talk.

"Did you know him?"

Sabrina nodded. The man's face was soft and caring. "I'm so sorry for your loss," he murmured. "Is there anything I can do to help?"

She mutely shook her head. No. There was nothing anyone could ever do.

She knew she was being rude, but without saying anything, she pushed herself away from the wall, staggering as if on a boat at sea, somehow finding the strength to pass by reception. Vivian was not there, no one was there, so no one saw Sabrina fall into the elevator and collapse in the corner, hoarsely screaming in anguish.

17

Luna, Archie, and Riggs understood that, at least for now, they lived in cages, separated from one another, and that Mr. Reed would take them out into the yard a few times a day and would put them back in approximately the same pens. Luna was now in the middle, so Riggs could touch her nose with his. Archie on the other side would do the same, and when they were not outside together, that was how Riggs could keep track of Archie's mood as well as his sister dog's. Luna curled up on her bed as if guarding it from intruders and would only deign to get out of it to squat in the corner near the drain, or to eat the food and drink the water that was set inside their cages. Mostly it was Teme and Mr. Reed who came around to take care of them. Riggs found himself liking both of them even though they were not Liam.

Mr. Reed moved so slowly down the hallway with the food that often a cry of frustration would emerge from Riggs's lips. Archie, on the other side of Luna, would yip and twist excitedly, not that any of their noises could be heard over the constant squalling of dogs in distress. Some of the animals here were as heartbroken as Luna, but whereas she took it all in silently, others were far more vocal. The barking and crying was ceaseless, and all the dogs were tense and afraid.

Riggs found himself thinking of Luna's daily assault on the basket of stuffed toys. What had always seemed a provocation now, on reflection, was an endearing ritual. When he lay in his bed, his eyes squeezed shut, the memory he summoned to block out all the barking was Luna's energetic attacks on her stuffed animals.

Within two days of having arrived, a man came to meet Archie. Archie greeted him as if they had known each other the dog's whole life. There was lots of petting and bowing and licking. Riggs watched this warily, while Luna could not even be bothered to open her eyes. It seemed that the man was here just to see Archie and not the rest of the pack.

Mrs. Kepler stood next to him and talked about Archie. "He's obviously a Labradoodle. We think maybe eight months old. He's been chipped with the former owner's information, but we believe, we've been told anyway, that his owner was killed in a car accident, so we're looking to find them new homes. Best would be someone who could take all three of them."

"Oh, I couldn't do that." The man chuckled. "But this little guy is so cute. Let me check with my cousin. I live with her temporarily, but if she's good with it, I'm good with it."

Mrs. Kepler nodded patiently. "That's nice. We've had several other people interested. You're the first to physically come in, but I have to say we're looking for a permanent solution. If you think you're going to move, perhaps it would be best to get that done first and then come back in."

"Sure, but if there's other people interested," the man objected mildly. He frowned, calculating, not wanting to lose the deal, then shrugged in resignation.

He was nothing like Liam, Riggs decided. His hair was longer, he was much thinner, and he smelled dry, not like the pungent fragrances that came off Liam's hands but rather with a bland, crisp odor that Riggs associated with paper. The man departed, but another family came, this one with three little girls and a man and a woman. They visited Archie as well. They also stopped and poked their fingers through the cage at Riggs. Riggs glowered at them, and they withdrew their fingers.

Riggs tracked Luna's sullen mood. She watched everything happening as if it had nothing to do with her, and Riggs thought he understood why. She was waiting for Sabrina or Liam or both.

Nobody else was going to cajole her off her bed and over to the cage door.

Riggs tried to understand what was happening through her eyes. Luna always understood situations faster than Riggs did. For Riggs, this place was an unwelcome, even catastrophic, change, and something needed to be done to have everything go back to the ordered and understood nature of their lives before the night that Liam didn't come home. For Luna, there seemed to be another grim purpose afoot, some deliberate plan to keep them away from their people. Riggs decided he would just do what Luna did, so he'd lie on his bed and watch as the flow of people loved and kissed Archie.

Mr. Reed always gestured toward Luna and Riggs. "There's a lot of interest in this pup, but these three dogs came in together. I think we would give preference to anyone who wanted to take all of them."

No one said yes to this.

Brad awkwardly made his way through the protocol of carefully scrubbing his hands and then putting on foot covers, a gown, rubber gloves, a mask, and a hat. This new place was far more scrupulous than even the ICU at the hospital. Thus attired, he was allowed entry into the stark yellow room to be with his brother.

Liam lay face up, inert on the pillow, his jaws covered with a mask, tubes in his arms, and low beeps and hummings filling the room with a sterile background sound. At first, Brad stood against the blinds as if being held captive, his shadow across the room and onto Liam. His arms folded, unable to or unwilling to approach his comatose brother, Brad remained completely silent for a while, working to overcome his tortured feelings of loss and grief. Several times, he braced himself, like a person getting ready to leap off the high dive, and each time, he blinked and shook his head, wanting to retreat, to escape. But there was no retreat, there was no escape.

Brad finally stepped forward. He put gloved fingers on the blanket, finding and holding Liam's limp hand. "Liam," Brad croaked, "this is it. I have to go. It's what you told me I had to do. Go to Germany, I mean. I can't promise when I'll be back. It's not up to me." Brad shrugged. "I'm so sorry this happened to you. I feel like my whole life I was supposed to protect you, but now there's nothing I can do. Well"—he gestured toward the door—"except I told them, no way are you going to turn off the machines. No way, stop feeding. Stop feeding? No. Give you every chance. And this place is a lot better than the hospital." Brad glanced around. The small room had a painting of a sailboat hanging on the wall. It looked like something you'd see in a cheap motel room.

"I've been doing a lot of reading about comas," he continued. "Some people make it to the other side, get better, sometimes without the doctors fully understanding why, and I want that person to be you. If there's anybody who can do it, it's you." Brad's face crumpled in agony, and he put his palms up and over his eyes and let the racking sobs beat at him from within. When he could finally catch a breath, he looked at the ceiling as if reading words written there.

"I've always been so proud of you, little brother. When we were younger and Mom and Dad vanished on us, you were always the optimistic one. When those people from family services came and took us out of the house, I wanted to fight, I wanted to hit them, and I couldn't bear the thought of abandoning the last place Mom and Dad had left us, in case they came looking and we were gone, but you said everything was going to be okay. You were my little brother, but you assured *me*; you propped me up and kept me strong. That's why everyone likes you, Liam. You go through life and people are drawn to you.

"That's why"—Brad gave a little laugh—"here in a time when

housing construction is being taken over by huge corporations everywhere in the world, you make a success at being independent, keeping your customers happy by just hiring the best people because they want to be with you, want to work for you.

"Mom always said you were like a light attracting the moths. Well, those moths are the people. The people who love you, Liam." Brad was silent for a long moment, visibly forcing himself under control. "So this might be goodbye until the next life. I've never talked to God as much as I have since the day of your accident. Am I doing the right thing? Should I stay? But they tell me this could go on for years, or days, or even just a few hours, though you're stable now, and this facility is designed for patients just like you. Everyone assures me there's no reason for me to come every day. You don't know I'm here, they say. They'll keep moving your limbs and turning you and helping you, and I'd just be in the way. The therapist told me I can't let the accident destroy everything, that if you did wake up and found out I never went to Germany, it would break your heart. So everybody who thinks they get a vote is telling me to go." Brad shook his head in resignation. "I tried asking God for a sign, you know, like the Clash—should I stay or should I go? I got nothing. So now when I pray, I'm just begging, 'Please, please let my brother live.' You're more important to me than anybody else has ever been. I can't imagine what my life will be without you, Liam. I just can't even describe it to myself. I think maybe it helps that I'm going to a new country where I don't speak the language worth a damn because it means everything will be so new and different. I won't be reminded of you at every street corner, every restaurant. Hell, even the beer is different." Brad barked out a short, mirthless laugh.

"I guess the only thing that will really strike me is when I see somebody with too many dogs." Brad gave a wry smile, but it quickly dropped off his face. "So yes, Sabrina couldn't take the dogs. You know, I had to . . . I had to take them to a shelter, but they'll find good homes, and I believe like in that book that we both read when we were younger that our dogs will return to find us, either in this life or the next one. It wouldn't be heaven without them."

Brad guiltily lifted his mask off his nose and hastily drew a sleeve across it before dropping it back into place. "This could be goodbye forever, Liam. Baby brother. Best friend. Only family I got left. I love you."

18

Yet another family came to the place of all the barking. There was a man, a woman, and a boy.

The boy ran to Archie's cage and announced, "This is the dog. This is the dog." He stood and gestured impatiently for Teme to open the door.

Teme nodded to the two adults. "We have to have signed permission from your parents first."

The boy scowled. As he did so, he raised his hand and pushed a flop of black hair out of his dark eyes. The hair immediately fell back. It reminded Riggs of the way Archie's curls sometimes seemed to completely obscure the dog's vision.

"I'm sixteen," the boy stated emphatically.

"Right," Teme responded blandly. She passed over a clipboard and the woman accepted it.

"This is Darren," the woman advised as she scrawled with a pen on the clipboard. "He's not legally Theo's stepfather, so does he need to sign?"

"Well, but we're married . . ." Darren objected mildly. "That makes me the stepfather."

The woman and Theo both shook their heads. "Not legally," the woman insisted.

Teme shrugged, returning to the question. "I don't know. I think as long as you've got one adult signature, it's good enough." Teme opened the cage door, and Archie came rushing out, going straight to the boy named Theo.

Archie jumped on Theo, and the boy let himself be tackled

to the ground, laughing. "I've always wanted a dog," he declared delightedly.

"Well, hey, are you forgetting Brody?" the woman asked.

The boy shook his head. "That wasn't my dog. That was your dog. And he died a long time ago."

"Well, two years," the woman corrected.

"What do you think, son?" the man asked the boy, who was still sprawled on the floor.

The boy darted a quick, hostile look at the man. "I think, Darren," the boy replied deliberately, "this is the dog I want. See how he came to me?"

Riggs watched in mild disgust as Archie reacted to Theo the way he reacted to everybody, with heedless, indiscriminate affection.

"A lot of responsibility goes into taking care of a dog," Darren observed neutrally.

Theo returned this bit of advice with a sullen glare. "I know that," he retorted impatiently. He looked to the woman. "What do you think, Mom?"

"I think whatever you want," the woman, Mom, replied. "It's going to be your dog, after all."

"What do you think, Archie?" the boy asked. "Do you want to come live with me?"

"You'll have to take care of this dog," the man insisted. "That means giving him food and water. That means taking him for walks. That especially means keeping the yard clean when he squats and does his business."

"Yeah," the boy replied vacantly. "Sure."

"You think you're ready for that?" the man probed.

The woman turned on him. "Darren," she chided, "he's sixteen."

"He is sixteen," the man responded agreeably, "but he doesn't even have a driver's license."

The boy darted an embarrassed look at Teme before responding. "None of my friends have driver's licenses," he snapped.

"All right," Darren acknowledged, still addressing Mom, "but he's not really taking care of the chores he does have."

"Yeah, but you said I could have a dog, Mom," the boy interjected in offended tones, ignoring the man.

The woman turned. "Darren, I think this would be a great way to teach responsibility, don't you?"

The man raised an eyebrow. "Sure," he agreed slowly, "sort of like how having a baby teaches someone responsibility, right?"

The woman scowled. "Whatever point you think you are making doesn't apply here."

The boy stood, and Archie gazed up at him adoringly. "Let's go," the boy suggested.

"You're next in line, but there are other families who are interested in Archie, so if it doesn't work out for you, please let us know and bring him back," Teme requested. "Labradoodle puppies are very much in demand."

"Well, he hardly seems like a puppy," Mom objected.

"He's less than a year old, and, in Labradoodle time, that makes him pretty much a puppy," Teme responded.

"We had discussed getting an older dog," the man ventured.

"Yes, but now I want this one," the boy answered emphatically.

Luna and Riggs watched as the family walked down the hallway with Teme and Archie. When they passed through the door and it shut, the smell of their fellow pack mate immediately began to leave the room. Riggs turned and met Luna's gaze. Something had happened, but Riggs didn't understand.

Luna did, though. Luna understood that Archie was irrepressibly affectionate and trusting. Instead of waiting for their real people to come back, Archie fell instantly in love with everyone.

Yet this particular family had seemed especially onerous to Luna. She had felt the real tension between the three of them, and it was clear that the boy wanted Archie to go with him but that the man wasn't so sure.

Luna resolved not to be enthusiastic about any visiting families. She would not act as if it would be wonderful if they would all leave together. And she would never, she decided as she regarded her brother dog, abandon Riggs.

Riggs gazed back at her as if he understood what she was thinking.

The first few days Archie was in his new home were so much fun the young dog almost forgot about life with Liam and the dog pack. The boy, Theo, gave him constant attention. They played in his room and in the backyard. Theo threw a ball, and Archie joyously pursued it and brought it back to him for another toss. The boy fed him and watered him on a regular basis, setting it out for him on the floor in the kitchen. Archie needed to go out into the backyard frequently to maintain the sort of biological discipline Riggs and Liam had seemed to want from him, and Theo cheerfully accommodated this need. Apparently, this was what people desired from dogs, though always before it had seemed most sensible to enjoy having fun and only stop to squat when the need was immediate.

After that initial time period, Theo started coming home in the afternoon, fixing himself something to eat, and then sitting on the couch to look at his phone. Archie was no longer the center of Theo's world, which meant that the dog wasn't getting let outside as much as he needed. Even when Archie pointedly stepped over to the sliding window and scratched, the boy didn't so much as look up. When Archie finally squatted on the floor, something that had always in his life led to doors being flung open, the boy shouted at him and smacked

him across his butt with an open palm. Chagrined and terrified, Archie retreated, urine still dribbling from him, and the
boy became even angrier. He did finally throw open the sliding
door, and Archie ran guiltily out into the warm sun. There was,
he was sure, a lesson he was supposed to have learned, though
he wasn't altogether sure what it was.

Later that evening, the man slumped into the house. That's
how he always arrived, as if carrying something invisible across
his shoulders. Archie now knew his name was Darren, that he
wasn't around very much but that he lived with Mom and Theo.

Darren walked into the kitchen, sighing. "Tough day today,"
he murmured.

Mom looked pointedly at her wrist. "Theo and I ate dinner
more than an hour ago."

The man settled tiredly into his chair, and Archie padded over
to sniff his hand. "There you are. Hi, Archie," Darren crooned,
stroking him. Some of the heaviness seemed to lift off him.

"Archie had an accident in the house today. It was all over. I
had to mop it up and spray Lysol," Mom complained.

"Huh," the man grunted. He looked up. "Where was Theo?"

The woman looked away and then back. "Is that what this
is going to be? Every time the dog does something wrong, you
blame my son?"

Darren wearily shook his head. "I'm just remembering the guitar lessons that he did for like a month. Now that guitar just sits
in his closet. Or the time I put up the basketball hoop and we
gave him those ridiculously expensive shoes and a new basketball
and then he went out and dribbled around for a while, and now
the basketball's in the closet next to the guitar."

"What's your point?" the woman asked sharply.

"I just think that we might be indulging Theo too much. That
the boy needs to learn—"

The woman held up a hand to interrupt him. "You have no

idea what it was like to raise him after his father abandoned us, and I will not stand here and listen to you criticize my parenting."

"I'm not criticizing," Darren responded with gentle defensiveness. "I just think if it's going to be his dog, Theo should clean up the dog's messes, and not you."

"Well, good luck with that," the woman spat. She stalked out of the kitchen. Archie watched attentively as Darren went to the refrigerator and pulled out something that crinkled. Crinkly noises were always a good sign.

The man sat wearily. "All right, Archie. Have you been fed yet?" The man glanced into Archie's bowl. "You don't have any water either." Before he had taken a bite himself, Darren eased back up out of his chair, went to the sink, filled Archie's water bowl, and then set a bowl of glorious food next to it.

Archie loved Darren.

A day later, when Archie's boredom could not be worse, he found a dry toy and chewed it contentedly. Once he started gnawing at the thing, he couldn't stop himself. Every time he pulled with his teeth and a satisfying tearing noise met his efforts, some part of Archie celebrated, even as another small part thought he might be doing something bad. Being a bad dog was not something Archie wanted, but it wasn't always clear how his actions might be interpreted by humans.

It was clear this time, though.

Archie had forgotten about the dry toy and left its pieces scattered around the room. He was sound asleep on Theo's bed when Theo came running in, dumped a bag that landed heavily on the floor, turned, and started to run out. Then he stopped, swiveled, and stared.

"What did you *do*, Archie?" he screamed.

That was a tone no dog could misunderstand. Archie slid guiltily off the bed, hit the floor, and trotted quickly in a fast retreat out of the room. Theo pursued.

"You are a bad dog, bad dog!" Theo yelled angrily. In the

kitchen, Archie ran to the door and gave Mom a pleading look. She was talking on the phone and turned away from him. Archie was afraid of Theo, afraid of his anger, and cringed away from it as Theo came across the kitchen floor. The boy drew back his foot for a kick.

Archie cowered, blinking, trying to shrink away from what was coming.

19

Theo's fury affected his aim. Archie darted aside as the foot swiftly descended, and it smacked audibly against the sliding door where Archie had been cowering a moment before.

"Hey!" Mom yelled. "What do you think you're doing?"

"The damn dog ripped up my sketchbook," Theo replied tersely.

The mom fixed him with an angry look. "Well, I'm on the phone," she snapped.

With an elaborate shrug and roll of his eyes, Theo reached down, snagged the handle of the slider, and flung it open so violently it made a loud bang. "Get out there!" he bellowed at Archie.

"Hey!" Mom shouted again. "Would you do that somewhere else?"

"Would I open the door to the backyard somewhere else? Like where, the bathroom?" Theo demanded.

Mom rolled her eyes.

Archie darted out into the yard for whatever safety could be had in the fenced-in enclosure. He registered the sound of the slider closing, and then he was alone.

Archie found shade and curled up in it, hoping Theo would stop being angry soon. As long as the boy was angry, Archie felt like a bad dog.

That night, Darren came out into the yard and whistled softly. Archie trotted to him willingly. It was dark now, and the day had given up a lot of heat. A joyous time to be outside, but Archie had been wallowing in grief from having been such a bad dog that he couldn't enjoy it. Darren, though, seemed forgiving, and let him in the house. Archie trotted immediately to the water bowl and lapped and lapped greedily. It reminded him of that first drink in the area of baths when Luna had figured out how to provide water for the pack—he was that thirsty.

Mom and Theo were in the kitchen. Mom was picking up dishes and carrying them to the sink, and Theo was looking at his phone.

"How long has the dog been out there without water?" Darren demanded.

Theo looked up with a scowl. "He's being punished."

Darren glanced at Mom, who shrugged, and then back at Theo. "You don't punish a dog by denying him water," Darren lectured sternly.

"That's not what I was doing," Theo responded evenly. "He chewed up my sketchbook. I mean, totally destroyed it. All of my graphic novel ideas were in there. I was going to submit them in English for extra credit this fall."

"So you believe that by putting him out in the yard without water that you have taught Archie never to have anything to do with high school English again," Darren summarized. Theo gave him a blank look. "Hey," Darren finally said, making a deliberate attempt to lighten the mood, "at least now you get to say that your dog literally ate your homework." Darren shrugged and smiled. "It's like a slacker's dream come true."

"I don't have to listen to this," Theo stormed. He stood up and stomped out of the room. Archie watched him depart, confused.

Mom turned to Darren. "You're going to have to apologize," she fumed.

"Apologize? Apologize for what, exactly?"

"It was a *graphic novel*. How would you feel if you wrote a whole book and it got destroyed?"

"What? I saw the thing. It was three pages of incomprehensible text and what looked like space walruses attacking naked women. It wasn't a *novel*."

"You have unrealistic expectations. He's just a boy, Darren. You're always so hard on him."

"He said he'd take care of Archie, and I'm holding him to his word."

"His word," Mom sneered. "That's all you care about."

"When I was sixteen . . ." Darren began.

"Oh, for God's sake," Mom snapped. She abruptly left the room.

Now it was just Darren and Archie, which was how Archie preferred it.

Two days after Archie left, a family came to see Luna at the shelter—two boys and a woman. The woman seemed uncertain. Luna glared at them while Teme opened the cage door.

"Come on, Luna, come on out," Teme called in a singsongy voice.

Luna liked Teme. Luna liked everyone here, in fact, but she had concluded that being too friendly would mean being led off like Archie, never to return, never to rejoin the dog pack.

"What's wrong with this dog?" the woman finally asked pensively.

Teme wore a sad expression. "We think Luna just hasn't been socialized properly. The problem is we don't have the staff to do that here. It takes time and money, something we don't have."

"Well, so what happens next to Luna?" the woman asked. Teme's sadness deepened—Riggs and Luna could both feel it. Riggs had retreated to his bed, safe from this particular family, mimicking Luna's aloof actions so that he did not wind up like Archie.

"So, this is not a no-kill shelter," Teme finally explained apologetically. "We have to make room for new dogs and cats. And that means the ones that are not adoptable have a time limit on how long they can be here. It's sad, but there are just so many abandoned dogs, because when they're not spayed and neutered, they start having litters and there's only so many puppies the city can process. Plus puppies are always the ones that go first. Luna is only a few years old, practically a puppy, but she just doesn't seem to like people. It means less interest than if she were eight weeks or something."

"You're saying Luna will be put down?"

Teme's expression was regretful. "At some point, yes."

"I've just never seen a Jack Russell terrier so still," the woman remarked. "They're usually running around like crazy."

"I know, and Luna's smart and really kind and gentle, but it takes a long time for her to warm up to somebody."

"All right, well," the woman turned to Teme, "who else have you got?"

After some time, the smells of that particular family left the room, accompanied by the odor of a particularly odd-looking dog that Riggs had glimpsed occasionally in the yard. The dog was long and shaggy, even shorter than Luna, but with a fluffy tail. The family seemed delighted to lead the dog away, and as their odors vanished, Riggs entertained the idea that perhaps it wasn't always a bad thing to be taken from this place. If you didn't have a Liam in your life, going off with another family seemed a good choice.

Riggs regarded Luna, who looked away and lay down with a groan. Did Luna remember Liam's backyard and walks with Liam and sleeping on Liam's bed? Did Luna remember Sabrina being with them? Riggs hoped so. It was the only chance he had of keeping together what was left of the pack.

Archie had a new life. Instead of sleeping on Theo's bed, Archie began each night outside in the yard. As the sun faded, so would

Archie's hopes of being let back into the house. It was only when Darren arrived home that things changed. It was Darren who would admit Archie into the house, often just moments after Archie heard Darren's car pull into the driveway. Inside, there very often would be a conversation containing a delectable word: *dinner.*

"Did you give the dog his dinner?" Darren would ask Theo.

Theo would shrug. "Not yet."

Sometimes this made Darren angry. "It's ten o'clock, Theo," he pointed out with irritation on one such occasion. "You should have fed him hours ago."

"I'm busy, *Darren*," Theo snapped back.

In the mornings, the sun had barely begun to lighten the sky when Darren would leave. He always made a point of giving Archie a friendly pat on the head before shutting the front door behind him. Once Theo was awake, Archie might or might not be given a morning dinner. The back door was slid open, and, with a gesture from Theo, Archie was consigned to the fenced-in backyard. Often, but not always, a water bowl awaited him out there.

There wasn't much to do in the backyard. Squirrels and birds had long learned to keep their distance from the fierce predator patrolling the grounds. There were a few trees to sniff, and Archie always took careful pains to mark all of these, but then there wasn't much else to occupy his attention. Over time, his feces began to pile up along the back fence. The odor reminded Archie of when he lived on a chain with a man named Face.

This was, Archie concluded, what people did. They loved dogs at first, but then eventually, dogs wound up alone, smelling their own waste, waiting impatiently for something good to happen. It was that way with Face, it was that way with Liam.

Though Archie was, of course, not aware of the days of the week, it was every Saturday when things changed. On those days, after waking up on Darren's bed, a leash would be snapped into Archie's collar, and they would be off together on a glorious walk. There were other dogs and other people to meet. There was an occasional squirrel to lunge at, with only Darren's hand upon the leash restraining him from catching the arrogant little animals.

Behind Darren was a small cart, which Archie learned to stay away from lest his leash get tangled. After a fairly long walk, Archie was eventually tied up at a pole near a bustling group of people and wonderfully vivid food smells. He would watch as Darren disappeared into the crowds and would wait patiently for the man to return with his cart now laden with fresh plants. Archie even learned the name of this place: Farmers Market. It meant a wonderful day.

People always approached Archie at the Farmers Market. They petted him and loved him and occasionally fed him an illicit treat of some kind. It was the high point of his life now, almost as good as being with Liam and the pack. Archie would dream about it during the week, lying out on his yard, waiting for that one special day. "Let's go to the Farmers Market," Darren would say, and then Archie's life would temporarily be better.

Darren often arrived home after Theo and Mom had eaten, but on Farmers Market days, the family sat together at the table. Archie always positioned himself to be within food-dropping distance of Darren's plate.

"Maybe," Darren ventured into a long silence, "we should think about returning Archie to the shelter."

Theo's eyes bulged. "Give up my dog?" he demanded.

"You're just so busy doing . . ." Darren trailed off with a gesture, unsure what, exactly, Theo was doing.

"Nice," Mom pronounced caustically. "You're the one always talking about how important it is to keep promises."

Darren's eyes drifted to Archie's. "Right. I'm just not sure we're keeping our promise to the dog."

20

A few days after the family came to visit Luna, Riggs was adopted by a very nice woman and a very reluctant man.

"He's got to be good with children," the man warned Mrs. Kepler. "We've got four boys. The oldest is only nine. The youngest is three."

"Oh my," Mrs. Kepler replied. She and the nice woman exchanged a meaningful look.

"It's a handful," the woman admitted with a soft laugh.

"This dog good with kids?" the man pressed.

"We don't know. We should arrange for you to come in with your children and meet Riggs in a private setting."

"I grew up with Australian shepherds," the nice woman informed Mrs. Kepler. "They're wonderful."

"Yes, they are."

Riggs was unsurprised when the family left, despite the woman's intense interest in him. He felt comfortable that he had so thoroughly incorporated Luna's almost hostile rebuff of people arriving to poke their fingers through the cage, to let him out, and try to pet him that he knew he would not be going anywhere until Liam arrived.

He was shocked when the woman returned and he was led into a room where the sullen man was attending to four young boys. They were instantly on Riggs, petting, wrestling, rolling on the floor with him, so energetic that he couldn't resist playing.

When Mrs. Kepler led him back to his cage, he was in good spirits, evading Luna's eyes, which seemed accusatory. When within moments he was led back out again and this time placed into an automobile with the adults and their children, he was astounded.

Luna had been left behind. Because of Archie, Riggs felt he understood what was happening and thought his pack mate probably did as well. At the door, he had turned back, and their eyes had met. Luna's gaze was as unreadable as it always seemed to be, but Riggs felt torn and sad.

The four boys swarmed with energy, racing around and shrieking and yelling, hitting each other and rolling together in the ground, throwing things, and just bringing mayhem to the house. Riggs tried to ignore the chaos, though it gnawed at his instincts, and instead focus on the fun things about this family. The boys threw objects—balls and other toys—which Riggs loved to pursue. The boys' constant running and yelling was a form of both irritation and excitement. Often, all of them would be together in the backyard, where an ankle-deep pool invited splashing. Riggs liked to cool off there after spending time chasing one or more of the boys under the hot sun.

Riggs contemplated his new life. Was he supposed to accept this? He just could not forget the expression on Luna's face when he was led down the hall to be with this rambunctious family. Luna was still back there somewhere, back in that place, but Riggs had been granted a reprieve—if this crazy, helter-skelter family could be considered a reprieve.

Over time, Riggs began to learn about this family. The woman stayed home with the children, but the man left most mornings and did not come back until around the time that the smell of dinner began to waft through the house. The woman was ceaselessly in motion. She was continually striding back and forth to a room where machines made loud noises and from which she emerged lugging baskets of clothes that she would sit on the couch and play with. At frequent and short intervals, she'd check on her children—the boys had an ongoing game of mild violence happening in the backyard, resulting in occasional tears and shrieks.

The yard was large, grassy, and full of trees. A high wooden fence on one side separated them from the noise and smells of people jumping into water, and through the gap in the fence slats, Riggs could see a deep in-ground pool with inviting, though sharp smelling, water.

Riggs began to understand that deep inside the woman, whose name was Mommy, was a real fatigue, a weariness brought on by the demands of her life. Riggs thought that perhaps her tiredness had to do with the children. She was audibly exhausted when she spoke to them.

It was impossible to learn the boys' names, because they changed all the time, from Tim to Timmy to Butthead to Stupid to Tattletale. To Riggs, they were all basically the same loud, rambunctious, yelling, kinetic child, with similar scents and diets and voices. They often yelled for Mommy, who was not unhappy at the demanding calls, but she carried a heavy weight that bore down on her.

The man, whose name was Daddy, wasn't very pleasant. He often came home and snapped commands at the boys, who mostly ignored them.

Riggs's favorite time was when the boys were in their beds with Mommy sitting and holding a dry toy that had audibly rustling papers inside them, talking to the boys in a quiet voice while they drifted off to sleep. Then Riggs would be alone in the house with Mommy and Daddy, who preferred to sit by themselves, occasionally murmuring. Riggs slept on a dog bed in the living room, and the separation from the wearying humans actually felt good to him.

He began eyeing the front door because it seemed to him that sometimes it yawned open with someone, usually Mommy or Daddy, in the doorway, and a clever dog could squirm past them. Riggs began to think about this. What would it be like to be out that front door without a leash? How would it feel, and where would he go?

Riggs raised his nose. He couldn't smell Liam anywhere, but

he had a general sense of which way lay home and which direction would take him to the house of loud banging noises. An escape out that door might very well lead him back to his person, and perhaps upon arriving, Archie and Luna would be there to greet him. The dogs would be fed and watered. They would be back with Liam, and eventually, perhaps Sabrina would come, too.

This became Riggs's fixation. He would get out that door.

Though of course she had no sense of dates, starting the first of August, Luna was taken on regular walks with several other dogs, an ever-changing pack. It was a bit miserable. The dogs were on leashes, unfamiliar with each other, unsure how to behave. Some of them were wanting to stop and sniff; some were wanting to charge far ahead of Teme, their nails digging at the cement; and some of them, like Luna, were content to gravely trot along, doing their business when necessary, occasionally examining where a male dog had lifted his leg, but for the most part, enduring the trek until they returned back to the cages.

Sometimes Mrs. Kepler walked with Teme, and they would talk.

Luna was sensitive to hearing her name, so she knew that sometimes she would be the topic of discussion.

"Luna was barking again all night," Mrs. Kepler remarked at one point.

"I know. Noah told me," Teme agreed. "She's fine, though. Look. She gets along great with the other dogs."

"The problem isn't dogs," Mrs. Kepler corrected. "The problem is people. Luna just does not like people. Well, she seems to have warmed up to me a little bit. You, too."

"Of course." Teme smiled. "I'd adopt all of them if I could."

"I know." Mrs. Kepler sighed. "It took me a long time to get past that feeling, but what you do here is so important. Helping lost dogs and cats find new homes. It's emotionally painful work, but if we didn't do it, no one would."

There was a silence between the people as the dogs moved along, sniffing everything wildly, trying to remember what it felt like to be on the outside before they had to go back to their cages.

"Well, Teme, I don't know if Noah told you, but we have a truckload of rescued dogs coming in a week from Friday."

Teme raised her eyebrows. "Oh?"

Mrs. Kepler nodded. "Yes, a puppy mill finally agreed to shut down operations. We get all of their dogs. They're going to be in rough shape, some of them. That's just how these things are. You'll see."

Teme smiled brightly. "I'll do what I can, Mrs. Kepler."

"Of course, dear, but I'm speaking very specifically about Luna."

Luna glanced up at her name, seeing a strange expression pass across Teme's face.

"What do you mean?"

"It's time now to consider what we have to do with Luna. These dogs will take up every available space to rescue them. We need to make room, and it does not appear anyone will ever want to take Luna home."

"What are you saying?" Teme asked innocently, but the look on her face indicated she knew exactly what Mrs. Kepler was saying.

"We have until then, Friday the twenty-third, and then if no family has adopted Luna, I'm afraid it will be her time to go."

Teme looked away. The sadness inside her reminded Luna of when Sabrina had knelt on the floor and kissed her and then held her. Something was happening, and Luna understood that somehow she was in the middle of it. "That's just ten days," Teme protested.

"I know, dear. But she's taking up a place that could be used for another dog."

"I want to try to save Luna. Is that okay?"

"Of course. That's our mission."

"I'll see what I can do," Teme finally murmured.

Riggs understood that Mommy was unhappy. He understood that she was having a day when the children's shrill voices landed on her like small percussions. She flinched from the verbal assault. She was so tired, radiating a dull weariness. She stopped several times and just stared off into space. Watching her with concern, Riggs felt responsible. He felt it was somehow his job to help Mommy gain control over her children. They were out in the yard running around with sticks that sported plastic hooks affixed to the ends. They were whacking at a light-colored ball and each other with the sticks, shrieking and yelling.

Mommy had gone inside, leaving the mayhem to play itself out, and Riggs decided enough was enough. He went after the youngest one first, growling a little, coursing back and forth while the child, eyes wide, dropped his stick and backed away. The next one was the oldest who, as he came pounding by, waving his stick, received a quick nip at a fold in his pants. The boy howled, and the little bite achieved exactly what Riggs had intended. The children stopped dashing about and stared at him in wonder. Riggs moved sideways to herd the third oldest toward the group, but they were coming together nicely, assembled in a tight little pack. Riggs regarded them with satisfaction. This was ordered.

"*Mommy*," the youngest one wailed.

"Mom!" two of the children yelled together, their voices in unison. The slider opened behind them. They all heard it. Riggs turned and glanced over his shoulder, proud at the way he had brought discipline to the unruly chaos.

"Riggs just bit us!" the oldest child yelled.

"Riggs!" Mommy blurted, her voice full of anguish. Riggs

didn't understand what had happened, but he went obediently to Mommy. He expected praise, but instead the woman spoke sternly to him. The children trooped inside. When Riggs made to follow, Mom blocked his way.

"No, Riggs," she told him. She slid the door shut in his face, and he stood peering at the people on the other side of the glass, not understanding.

21

Teme was sitting at her computer when Mr. Reed eased up to her. "I could use some help cleaning the cat cages," he remarked. "You look busy, though."

Teme nodded. "I'm on a Jack Russell website looking for someone to adopt Luna."

Mr. Reed nodded thoughtfully. "Not exactly sure what that means, but okay."

Teme glanced up at him solemnly. "In just ten days, Mrs. Kepler said we're putting Luna down."

"Oh." Mr. Reed nodded. "Yeah, I heard that."

"I can't let that happen."

"Teme," Mr. Reed began patiently.

Teme was shaking her head. "No. I mean, I understand. I know we're not no-kill, and sometimes what we've had to do here, I've felt like they were going to a better place. Some of them come in here so damaged, it's a mercy to put them down, but Luna's not like that. When she's on a walk, she's fine with the other dogs. She doesn't act aggressively toward people; she just doesn't run up to love them the way some dogs do. She'd get along great in a family if they would spend time with her."

"Exactly," Mr. Reed concurred. "It takes time. And we don't have that kind of time. We do the best we can, Teme."

Teme turned back to the computer. "Just give me another hour here, and then I'll come help you with the cat cages."

"Sure," Mr. Reed agreed. He put out a hand and patted Teme's shoulder. "I know how hard this is."

Mommy seemed to forgive Riggs for whatever it was he had done wrong, but Daddy was furious. Riggs could hear him yelling in the house, and the dog's name floated to the surface of those shouts. Then the sliding door opened with a loud thump as it hit the other side of the frame, and Mommy and Daddy came out into the yard.

Daddy pointed. "You are a bad dog, Riggs," he scolded.

Riggs lowered his ears. He knew what those words meant, though he did not know exactly what it was he was supposed to have done.

The man turned to Mommy. "Okay. He's staying away from the kids until he learns to behave himself."

"Well," Mommy responded reasonably, "we don't even really know what happened."

"My kids would never lie to me," Daddy responded sharply. "This dog attacked them. I'll let you keep him for now, but if it happens again"—he shook his head—"that's it."

Archie lay in the backyard of his home. The moon in the sky, the air still, the house quiet. Darren had yet to come home, and Archie waited patiently. This was his life now. This was what people wanted for Archie, to be left isolated and alone nearly all the time. Only occasionally would Darren come out to love him. Archie thought wistfully of being on the end of the short chain back when he lived with Face. Then Liam had come, and Liam had taken him to a wonderful home. Archie closed his eyes with a sigh and waited for Liam to reappear.

The days were hot, and Riggs found a place of shade in the back-yard and lay there most of the time. It was pretty quiet during the day. Through the open slider, he could see and smell the children racing around in the house. All the windows in the home were open as well, allowing Riggs to hear the shrieking and the crying and the yelling.

Sometimes the family would be gone all day and even part of the night. Riggs actually looked forward to that. His experience with the children was that they caused real stress for both of the adults, who then took out their anger on Riggs, especially Daddy, or at least that's how it felt.

One afternoon when the people had left the house and its emptiness seemed to drift out into the yard through the open slider, Riggs saw three older children, all boys from next door, scale his fence. He raised his head, and they pointed at him.

"Think he bites?" one boy asked.

"We'll find out!" hooted another.

Their wet hair was pasted to their skulls, and a strong chemical tang clung to their skins—they had been swimming in their in-ground pool, a constant activity in this heat.

They dropped to the ground on Riggs's side of the fence and crouched tensely. He contemplated going to greet them, but that would mean standing up from his shady spot. He watched as they relaxed, apparently believing he was harmless. They scurried as a group to the woodpile stacked up against the house and picked their way to the top of it. From there, they hoisted themselves one by one to the top of the garage roof.

Riggs thought perhaps they were intending to crab sideways along the roof and enter the wide-open second-story window, but that's not what they intended at all. Instead, they gathered themselves at the peak of the roof closest to their own yard.

Riggs contemplated their swimming pool. The sounds of children splashing and playing and laughing seemed to invite him to take a plunge, but no one had let him into that yard yet. He imagined the feel of the cool water as he paddled through it and for the first time wondered why humans built fences. Wouldn't things be more friendly if dogs and people could pass from yard to yard unimpeded?

The older children on the roof were excited—it showed up in their grins and the way they kept pacing the crest of the roofline. Finally, they all backed away from the fence.

With a shout, the first boy bolted, dashing forward along the spine of the roof and hurtling himself into the air, limbs flailing. He easily cleared the fence, and the loud splash told Riggs the boy had decisively hit his target. Riggs watched as the remaining children ran the length of the roof and leaped into space. There was a real air of delinquency in these jumps, and Riggs had a feeling they were doing something they were not supposed to do. A human version of bad dog behavior.

After several more jumps, the boys went quiet. Curious, Riggs made his way over to the fence and peered between the slats. The water in the pool was calm, and the trail of wet footprints led to the back door of their house.

Later, the children from Riggs's own house came into the yard, shooting a wary glance at Riggs. Lonely and yearning for friends, Riggs eased up from his spot and went to greet them, and received in return from the oldest of the children a tentatively offered hand, which he sniffed, but there was a definite sense by the children that Riggs wasn't really their dog. Only the woman of the house, Mommy, seemed to care about Riggs. She was the one who fed him. She took him on occasional walks, and she always spoke kindly to him. The man, Daddy, wanted nothing to do with Riggs and communicated it with scowls and sharp gestures whenever Riggs approached him, so Riggs didn't approach him at all.

The oldest child of the family passed in and out the side gate of the backyard quite a bit, and one day Riggs sat up, remembering a different gate, remembering Luna and how she had somehow been able to open the enclosure with her nose and paws. She had focused on the place where the people put their hands. Riggs watched the boy and observed where his fingers touched metal, and then the gate eased shut behind him. That was how the boy entered and exited the yard. Riggs stood, yawned, stretched, and made his way through the brutal sunshine to the gate. He sat and examined it. There was nothing for him to understand. There was wood, and then there was metal. He tentatively stood up on his back legs and sniffed. There was the clear scent of more than one human hand on the metal. What did that mean?

The next day, Mommy came into the backyard smiling, followed by a fit woman with light-colored hair and strikingly tan arms and legs. The woman was immediately very friendly toward Riggs.

"Riggs, this is Alysson. She's going to be your dog walker."

"Hi, Riggs!" the woman greeted cheerfully.

There were treats in a little pouch on the woman's hip. She extended one to Riggs, who took it without hesitation. There was a really strong scent of dogs clinging to this woman, painting her sun-drenched skin. She was nice, she was friendly, and when she put a leash into his collar, he accepted that she wanted him to go with her. He followed her willingly through the gate, noticing that she touched it the same way the boy did, her hand going to that one metal area, and then they were out walking.

They walked quite a distance, and during their trip, the woman stopped and another dog was handed to her through an open doorway via a leash. This was a big, gentle dog, mostly white, but with patches of black fur gone gray with age. His name was Ugo. His rheumy eyes suggested a wisdom as he sniffed Riggs down the length of his body, and when he lifted his leg, Riggs detected fish in his diet. Ugo would glance at squirrels with a disinterest born of a lifetime of unsuccessful pursuit, and he had affection for every human hand offered his way. He was a good companion for Riggs, and the woman, whose name Riggs came to understand was Alysson, spoke kindly to both dogs. They usually made their way toward the scent of water, and the trees became more abundant overhead, providing welcome shade from the sun.

The same thing happened the next day, and that set a new pattern. Almost every day, Riggs would be taken for a walk by Alysson, which was pretty much the extent of his human interaction. The children of the house stayed away from him, either because they were wary or just didn't like the heat of the days, and Mommy fed him and Daddy ignored him, and that was how his life went.

One evening, the children played in the yard and Riggs watched, holding back the impulse to try to corral them into an ordered group because it seemed that this was not something that Mommy and Daddy wanted.

"I still don't trust the dog," Daddy observed.

Riggs's ears flickered at the word *dog*.

"He's fine," Mommy assured Daddy. "He's getting used to the kids. I think he was just really nervous when he first arrived."

"Can't take the chance," the man grunted. "You need to fix this."

22

Luna's senses were bombarded with the odors of other dogs and the sounds of their voices, and yet, even in this crowded room, Luna was alone. This wasn't a dog pack, this was a place of complete and utter isolation, away from Liam, away from Sabrina. Archie had left long ago, and now Riggs was gone. In his place was a large, sleepy dog with pointed ears and a quivering nose who seemed friendly toward Luna, but Luna was not interested in making friends with this dog. Luna had figured out what happened here: dogs came, they barked, they cried, people then came in to play with them and talk to them, and then the dogs left. Then the cage would be filled with a different dog, and the cycle would start again. Only Luna was constant; she never went anywhere. She was never visited by anybody except the three people she had come to regard as the family that lived here—Teme, Mrs. Kepler, and Mr. Reed.

On the other side of Luna, in the cage where Archie had lived so briefly, were two small dogs who were from the same litter and who nosed each other constantly as they scampered back and forth. They were young and played with each other all day, and they eyed Luna as if inviting her to somehow squeeze her way between the wires into their enclosure. It was impossible to do this, but the dogs kept giving her welcoming glances anyway.

There was a definite change when the door opened one day and Teme walked in. There was a sense of something happening, and Luna lifted her head alertly. Two people followed in behind Teme down the hallway. At their feet was a dog very much like Luna. There was an instant passing of recognition when the two

Jack Russell terriers spotted each other. It was the sort of glance reserved for dogs of similar breeds, and Luna wagged the tip of her tail.

The couple was friendly, older than Liam, but smiling. The woman wore her hair piled up on top of her head in a gray knot while the man elected to have not much hair at all. Their attention was less on Luna and more on the little dog at their feet, whose shoulders and ears indicated he was cowed. Luna understood how the little dog felt. It was very intimidating to come into this place with all these smells and all these sounds. Now accustomed to all the racket, Luna could ignore it, even sleep through it, but it was far from comfortable, and this new dog felt scared and astray.

"Luna," Teme called in a singsongy voice, "this is—" She pointed to the man and paused.

"Nolly," the man offered.

"Nolly and Winnie. I'm Winnie," the woman added, and they giggled.

"This, of course, is Badger," the man introduced, pointing to his dog but looking at Luna.

Luna understood that they were talking to her. They were standing at the door to her cage, and Badger was right there, too, his eyes darting around, not really focused on Luna at all. Were they planning to put Badger in the cage with Luna? She considered what that would be like to have a dog in this enclosure with her. It was not something she wanted. It was different for the two littermates—they depended on each other. All the dogs Luna depended upon were gone.

"Okay. Luna, come. Come on out," Teme invited.

She opened the door and stood expectantly. Luna liked Teme and wanted to please her. It had become more and more difficult for Luna to maintain an aloof distance to this woman in particular. Mr. Reed was old and bent and seemed content to slowly do not much of anything. Mrs. Kepler was always scurrying around, always busy, and never really took time to try to cajole Luna into play or socializing, but Teme was patient and kind and had treats. So, despite her misgivings, Luna rose off her thin dog bed and padded silently over to the open cage door.

Luna's approach drew the other dog's attention. He looked at Luna but then dismissed her, still craning his neck, trying to smell and see everything at once.

"So far so good," the man observed approvingly. "How 'bout it, Badger? Wouldn't it be great to have a girlfriend?"

Badger, Luna decided, was the male dog's name.

The woman turned to Teme. "Badger's not exactly dog-friendly, but if these two get along . . ."

"I grew up with Jack Russell terriers," the man interrupted. "They're the greatest dog on the planet. Smart, too. People say poodles are smart, but my money's on a Jack Russell."

"Yes, well . . ." Winnie smiled sadly. "Badger's just been something of a handful."

"Oh, they're a handful"—the man chuckled—"but that's the point. Got so much energy you can't believe it. People claim beagles have all the energy, but they don't know Jack Russells."

"Why don't we take them outside?" Teme suggested. "See how they get along out in the yard."

When she opened the door at the back of the hallway and let them out into the yard, the sun was very prominent, bearing down on them strong and hot. The barking was audible but not nearly as loud out here, yet this place was no less intimidating to the new Jack Russell terrier. Badger seemed taken aback at the number of male and female dog scents that had been dribbled into the grass. He immediately put his nose to them, lifting his leg at one point but almost with a lack of enthusiasm that came from realizing the enormity of the task of trying to overmark all the places where the male dogs had been.

Luna decided to be friendly and sniffed where Badger had marked, but Badger ignored her.

"They're getting along," the woman announced.

"Well, come on, let's take them off leash and see," the man suggested.

"Sure," Teme replied. She knelt and unsnapped a leash. "Okay. Luna, why don't you play with Badger?"

Luna gazed up at Teme's questioning tone, not sure what was being asked. Badger didn't respond to Teme's voice at all. Luna thought Badger was not friendly, but not unfriendly. He was mostly still intimidated by this place. Luna felt a little bad for the other dog, remembering what it was like to arrive here for the first time. Badger would get used to it, though, once he was here long enough.

"Looks good to me, too, Winnie," the man declared when Luna made a tentative move to sniff politely at Badger's butt. Badger turned away from Luna dismissively, busy investigating the yard.

"Last time we tried something like this," the woman explained, "Badger went right after the other dog. Poor thing was terrified."

"It was a puppy, too," the man lamented. "We thought, you know, a young dog."

"Well, Luna's not a puppy, she's a couple of years old, but she's very sparky and very smart," Teme responded brightly.

The man looked at Winnie. "Well, what do you think?"

Winnie shrugged. "I'm not sure."

There was a long silence. Teme cleared her throat. "Well, today's Luna's last day, as I explained, and you're the only people who have shown an interest. Jack Russell terriers are not as popular in Colorado as they are other places because they're, well . . ."

"Easily hunted," the man concluded for Teme.

She nodded. "Exactly. I mean, the only place I could think a small dog like Luna could survive for very long would be the city, not out in the suburbs where the coyotes are roaming."

Winnie and Nolly were silent. Badger continued to ignore Luna, and Luna's eyes were on Teme.

Teme's smile trembled. "As I said, you're her only hope."

There was an air of indecisiveness between Winnie and Nolly.

Luna tried to understand what was happening. Whatever it was, it clearly had something to do with her. She was sure of it. Was she going to be living with this Badger dog in her cage or not? That seemed to be what the humans were contemplating. Badger gazed glumly at Luna, perhaps contemplating it, too.

"All right, let's do it," the man declared decisively. "They're not exactly best friends yet, but they're not fighting."

"Right, and they'll get used to each other, don't you think?" the woman asked Teme.

Teme nodded eagerly. "I really do. I really believe it."

As they passed from the yard back into the big room with all the dog smells, Luna caught Badger staring at her. He seemed hostile.

The next morning, Alysson came fairly early in the day. There was no set pattern to when she might arrive, but Riggs preferred it when she was there in the morning or the evening because the weather would turn cool. He walked with her again, and they took a very similar route, this time not picking up any other dogs at all—which was unusual—but just walking along the street. Alysson was kind and waited patiently for Riggs to sniff and make his mark.

The scent of water ahead of them grew stronger. They passed under the trees. Soon they came to a place where there was more traffic and more pavement, and the woman moved confidently.

And that's when Riggs smelled Archie.

Archie had come to love the Farmers Market. The smells were wonderful, and sometimes Darren would bring him a small piece of cheese. Other dogs visited Archie as he danced at the end of his rope, and people always stopped to pet him and smile. It made Archie feel loved, such a contrast to the days he spent in the yard by himself. This day, Darren bought some fragrant meat and led Archie to a table under an umbrella, and they sat. The man un-wrapped some delightfully crinkly paper and pulled something delectable out and began chewing on it. He slipped Archie a piece. Chicken!

"Here you go, Archie. I'm sorry, boy. I'm sorry I don't see you as much as I used to. Well, they call it *separation*. Not that you know what that means, but it means that Linda and I are not going to make it. We're going to get a divorce. Writing's been on the wall since the beginning, honestly."

Archie listened to all this, paying attention, waiting to hear the part where more chicken would be handed over.

"I don't have a yard right now. I've moved into a temporary place, but I'll find one, and then you can come live with me, okay, Archie? I know I'm gone a lot, but I'll figure something out. I can't exactly bring you to work, but we'll still see each other on Saturdays, and maybe I can cut back on my hours." The man shrugged. "Or maybe I'm being foolish and I should take you back to the shelter. I don't know. I am really fond of you, Archie. You're a good dog."

Good dog often meant chicken, so Archie sat attentively.

"I'd really miss you, but am I being fair to you?"

Archie snapped his head around. A distinctive odor had just reached his nose.

Riggs.

23

Darren saw Archie twist away from both the table and the food upon it—a very un-Archie thing to do. "What is it, Archie?" he asked.

Archie was frantically pointing his nose in different directions, trying to pin down where this scent was coming from. There. Riggs was being walked by a tall, thin woman, and Riggs was staring at Archie.

Archie stared back, wagging.

"Do you know that woman?" Darren asked curiously. As if hearing him, the woman glanced over, briefly met Darren's gaze, and then turned away.

Archie watched in frustration as Riggs vanished up the street.

In the car the day before, with the people Luna now knew of as Winnie and Nolly in the front seats, leaving Teme behind in the building with all the dogs, Luna sensed a change coming over Badger. Luna was in a crate in the back seat. Badger was free on the middle seat. Away from all the intimidating noise, Badger was no longer frightened. His muscles relaxed. He stopped panting.

As the fear dissipated, Badger first seemed puzzled, then hostile. He put his paws on the back of the seat and lifted himself to stare through the front of the crate at Luna.

"Get down, Badger. Get down," Winnie urged.

Badger reacted to this by dropping down to all fours and

vanishing from Luna's sight, but the hostility remained, as if he were still standing on his back legs and glaring at her.

Luna knew something bad was going to happen.

The car took them to a small house that reminded Luna a little bit of the home where Liam and Sabrina lived. Badger was off leash, but Luna was kept on the rope all the way into the house. Badger immediately ran to his dog bed and jumped on a squeaky toy. Then, holding the squeaky toy in his mouth, he fixed Luna with a challenging stare.

Luna knew exactly what was happening. Badger was declaring that this toy was his. If Luna wanted to play with that toy, she would have to go get it, and Badger would not let such an action remain unpunished.

Luna did nothing about the toy. She followed closely at Winnie's heels as the woman guided her into the kitchen.

"Okay, Luna, are you hungry?"

There was a snap as she did something that threw delightful dog food odors into the air. Luna watched with interest as Winnie filled two bowls and set them down on the floor. Luna scurried to the closest bowl and dug her face into it, quickly gulping down the food, eyeing Badger, who attacked his own meal while keeping his eyes on Luna.

Luna finished and backed away. Badger suspiciously inspected her bowl, but she ignored this and certainly didn't go near Badger's.

"Badger looks upset," Winnie noted after some time had passed.

"Let's keep them separated tonight," Nolly suggested, which was how Luna came to spend the first night on a rug in the garage.

Back in the house the next day, after morning dinner was fed to the dogs, Badger seemed content to curl up in his bed, but then as Luna sniffed along the baseboards of the living room, trying to get a sense of where she was and what was happening, Luna could feel that Badger was watching her, watching her with an increasingly malevolent stare. This was, Luna realized, a precursor to an attack.

The two dogs were separated by the length of the living room, but Luna knew Badger could leap from the bed and cross it in an instant. Luna prepared herself because she knew an aggressive challenge was coming.

Some time passed before Badger rose from his dog bed, his head down, his eyes fierce, and began padding his way toward where Luna had taken up safe station between the two chairs in which Winnie and Nolly sat talking and drinking coffee.

Badger picked up speed. The humans seemed unaware, not until Badger was upon her. Then Luna gave voice to her fear, shock, and rage as Badger engaged her, their teeth slashed, biting and growling, and Luna felt a sharp pain in her ear and the taste of Badger's lip came to her tongue, and then Winnie reached down and snatched Badger up into the air. Badger was growling and spitting, twisting in her arms while Luna retreated under Nolly's chair.

"Oh no!" the woman moaned. "Badger, why?"

Luna remained under the chair, a defensible space.

"I think it was Luna's fault," the man speculated after a moment.

The woman frowned. "Why do you say that?"

"I've been watching. Luna has just been staring at him, daring him to do something. He was provoked."

"Well, okay," Winnie agreed dubiously. "Should I put him back down on the floor?"

The man got up from his chair, grunting, his joints clicking, and reached under it for Luna. He picked her up, and she allowed herself to relax in his arms.

"Try it," Nolly suggested.

When she set Badger down, Badger came immediately over to Nolly's feet. Luna had her lips pulled back in a silent snarl.

"No, this isn't going to work," the man decided sadly.

A short time later, they put Badger in a back room. Luna curled up on the floor, relieved.

"All right, then, what are we going to do?" the woman asked.

"What can we do? We have to take Luna back to the shelter."

Winnie didn't like this. "But you heard what that young woman said. If we take Luna back, they'll put her down."

"Yes, but that's not our fault, Winnie. We did our best. It's just not working out."

"This is so bad," Winnie lamented. "I'll call the shelter and see if they have any ideas."

"Today's Saturday, though."

"All right, we'll keep the dogs separated until Monday. Put Luna out in the garage for the night, and then in the morning, let them out in the yard one at a time. Feed them in different rooms." Nolly shrugged. "It's a temporary solution, but it'll prevent a fight, I imagine."

"Are you sure Badger won't eventually just get used to her?"

"No, but look what happened. They drew blood, Winnie. What if one of them lost an eye or something?"

Winnie was silent. Luna looked up at her, sensing her deep grief. "Poor Luna," the woman muttered.

When Riggs was returned to his yard by Alysson, he found his place in the shade and pondered what had just happened. He had smelled and then seen Archie, and it jolted him out of his complacency.

Riggs had been doing what dogs do, figuring out the routine, trying to understand what the humans wanted from him, and then trying to deliver on those expectations, but this was not Liam's yard, and these people that he lived with were not Liam. He had realized that he had begun thinking of ways to help Mommy with the wild children she was raising, picturing a life here with them. Ingratiating himself with Daddy, winning the man over.

But that was wrong. Now that Riggs knew where to find Archie, he needed to get the pack back together and back with Liam. What else made sense?

Riggs trotted over to the gate. This time, when he lifted himself up on his back legs, he pawed at the metal latch. He sniffed it. He butted it with his head, and he lifted his nose against it. It rattled, and that rattle reminded him of the sound the gate made when Luna attacked it. This gave him encouragement and hope. Riggs dug at the latch. He lifted his nose again. Then, just like that, the gate popped backward a tiny amount.

Riggs dropped to his four feet and then dug at the corner, pulling the gate wide open. He stepped out through the gate and trotted down the driveway to the sidewalk.

He was free. Unhesitatingly, he turned in the direction Alysson had taken him earlier. He felt both guilty and exhilarated. He had to resist the temptation to run up into the yards, smelling where other males had marked, because he didn't have time for play.

His mission, of course, was simple. Go get Archie, lead Archie to the house where Liam would surely be waiting, and then they would all find Luna and Sabrina. The pack would be back together, and everyone would be happy.

Rounding up the others felt true, right, and basic to Riggs.

Riggs knew, generally, in what direction home lay. The mountains in the distance carried a clean smell with them that was ever present, serving as a directional beacon for any dog guiding himself through the world with his nose. All Riggs had to do was keep that smell on one side as he made his way toward the water that Alysson often walked toward but never reached. On the other side of the water, Riggs knew, were the smells that indicated home, or at least a way home.

Riggs walked onward, focused and determined. The food and

people smells were still present where he'd smelled Archie, but his pack mate was gone now. Riggs hesitated, then kept going forward. He passed where Alysson usually turned back, but didn't stop, the smell of water now compelling him, and he paused to drink from the stream when he reached it.

There were easy bridges over the stream, which had flat cement banks, so Riggs had no trouble crossing it. He continued on past that stream, keeping it behind him now.

It wasn't long before the hot sun bouncing off the pavement caused him to pant again. Whenever his spirits flagged, he would think about Liam. Liam would feed him. Liam would give him water. Liam was his person.

The day was mostly drained out of the sky when Riggs finally arrived at his home. There was no smell of Liam on the air, but Riggs confidently went to the door anyway. He sat in front of it and scratched at it and waited. When nothing happened, he barked and then he barked again, and this time, a woman opened the door. It was not Sabrina. Riggs was surprised and made no move to enter the house. The smells coming out of it were cooled by some mechanism Riggs did not understand and carried with that coolness the scent of two people, but neither was Liam. They were both women's scents. The woman in front of him was friendly, but puzzled.

"Hello, dog," the woman greeted. "Who are you?"

Riggs stared back at her. When she reached a hand toward his collar, he backed away suspiciously. What was happening? Where was Liam?

The woman turned and called into the house. "Hey, Shirley, come here. There's a dog at the door."

"A dog?"

"Just come here."

Riggs heard approaching footsteps, but he could tell they didn't belong to Liam.

24

Now there were two women on the stoop looking at Riggs, who had backed down the steps and was standing on the walk, gazing up at them. The first woman was tall, and from her fingers drifted a pungent, spicy odor Riggs had never smelled before. The second woman was redolent with a floral sweetness.

"You're okay, doggy. Are you okay?" the tall woman asked.

Riggs recognized the lack of threat but was still unhappy that Liam's scent was missing. He didn't know what to do. The flowery woman extended a hand, but he certainly wasn't about to approach either of them, even though they seem friendly. They were strangers. In Liam's house.

"I'll get something, a treat maybe," the tall woman suggested, disappearing into the cool depths of the home.

The flowery woman sat on the cement steps and patted her knee, but Riggs still remained wary. When the tall woman reappeared, she tossed Riggs a treat, and he snatched it out of the air and it was good, some sort of meat. He'd never had it before, but he recognized it as people food, tinged with the spice from the woman's fingers. Not a dog treat. There was no smell of dog in this house, or cats either, he realized to his relief. He would not want to live with cats.

"Should we call somebody? Animal control?" the tall woman asked.

"Yes," the other woman agreed. "That's who we should call."

Riggs saw some deliberation in their movements now. Some sort of decision had been made. His reaction when the woman with the treats came all the way down the steps and approached him was to turn and dart away.

Everything was all wrong. He did not want to be here now. He wanted to be with Liam, but Liam was gone. This was too much for him to understand. He just knew that he had to retreat, but where could he go? He had no particular goal in mind now.

Some distance away lay the other house, the noisy place with all the banging and sharp smells. Should he go there? Now?

Eventually, though, he began thinking about the generous bowl of food that Mommy would set out for him around this time every day. That bowl of food came to his mind and compelled him forward. Perhaps he should retreat back to the yard, eat the food, and then strike out again. Maybe, when he returned here, Liam would be home, and these two strange women would be gone. Or maybe Sabrina would arrive and tell the women to leave.

These were all things he just couldn't hold in his brain. He was so confused.

The shadows grew longer. The day would soon be ending. Riggs was tired. His nose took him now in the reverse direction of his travels. Soon the fragrance of water was in front of him once again, and he paused again for a drink, then kept pressing on. The clean smell from the hills brought a coolness that was welcome. His feet hurt a bit; he wanted to lie down. He was close now, and he began to salivate, thinking of the bowl of food.

When he heard a car slowing on the street next to him, he didn't think much of it until he heard Mommy's voice.

"Riggs. Riggs, come here."

Riggs froze. How had they found him, and what should he do now? His hard-won freedom seemed to him something he should not surrender, but the woman was calling him and he was hungry, and when people call dogs, the dogs have to obey. It was just what dogs do. In the end, he drooped his ears and made his way almost shamefully to the open car door. The older boy was in the car with him and gave him a treat. Riggs was beginning to like this older boy, and he certainly liked Mommy. The door shut, and the car drove off. It was not a fun car ride, because Riggs had the sense he was betraying Liam.

He felt like a bad dog.

Luna spent the weekend going from the garage to the backyard and back. Now she heard Badger's plaintive cries from down the hall as Nolly and Winnie opened the front door and led Luna out on a leash. Badger was upset because he understood that his people were leaving and taking Luna with them. Luna trotted expectantly to the car and was gratified when Winnie opened the door for her to leap in. As far as Luna was concerned, they were leaving this place, leaving Badger, and that was a good thing.

Car rides are entirely the province of humans, but Luna hoped this one was taking her to Liam and Sabrina.

Winnie wept quietly from the front seat, and Luna registered her sadness. Winnie was sad to be leaving Badger, Luna decided.

"Poor little girl," Winnie repeated more than once.

"We don't have a choice, Winnie," Nolly told her. "What are we going to do? Keep the dogs separated for the rest of their lives?"

"She just deserves better," Winnie lamented.

"I know that, but we can't save the world or even all the dogs in it," Nolly advised kindly. "Come on, Winnie. We tried."

Luna knew where she was before they even opened the door: back to the place with all the animals, the sad dogs. When they entered, Luna smelled Mrs. Kepler and Teme, but not Archie and not Riggs. Teme's shoulders slumped when she saw Luna, and Luna registered her disappointment. Mrs. Kepler seemed more stoic.

"Ah yes. Welcome back, Luna," Mrs. Kepler greeted softly.

"It just didn't work with Badger," Nolly apologized. "I don't know. It was so promising here at the shelter, but as soon as we got them home, they got into it."

"Isn't there anybody else?" Winnie asked plaintively. "I just hate to think of Luna being put down when none of this is her fault."

Mrs. Kepler pursed her lips. "Well, there's a brother to the man who died in the car accident, but he indicated he's living overseas and can't take her. The file doesn't have any other names."

"Is it . . . Will it happen today?" Nolly asked.

Teme and Mrs. Kepler glanced at each other. "We processed a few animals this morning, but now it won't happen again for several days. So, Luna, you're with us for a bit longer, sweetie."

Luna did not understand why everyone seemed so sad, but she did feel that it had something to do with her. She sat. She had nothing against these people. They were nice. She did not want them to be sad, especially if it was caused by something she had done, but she wanted to be home with Liam and Sabrina, and nothing could change that.

Eventually, Luna was led back to a different cage from the one she had occupied previously. The sounds were otherwise completely familiar, as were the smells. It was just a different part of the big room. She curled up on the thin pad at the back of her new kennel and lay down with a sigh. Something about this place depleted her energy and forced her into a nap.

Upon returning to the yard from which he'd escaped, Mommy produced a bowl of food, and Riggs plunged his face into it with gratitude, compelled by hunger to choke it down as if it were his first meal in days. He registered the tentative affection of the two older children in the family. They seemed more willing to approach him now, though when they reached out their hands, he had the sense they might snatch them back at any moment. He let them touch his fur and felt them relax. Most humans, when they petted a dog, were happy they had done so.

Daddy, however, remained hostile and stiff, insisting with gestures that Riggs go back into the yard.

"Put him on the line," he instructed the oldest child. "Oh, also, be sure you lock the gate."

Mommy arched her eyebrows. "Isn't that overkill?"

The man shook his head. "We're supposed to always lock the gate." He was speaking to the children, who listened somberly, but also glanced at his wife, making it clear he was actually lecturing her. "We don't want people just walking into the backyard. Not with the doors and windows open."

"Maybe if we ran the air conditioner . . ." Mommy started to suggest.

Daddy shook his head. "Our electric bill's high enough as it is."

Riggs was put on a rope that was attached to his collar at one end and was affixed somehow to the ground at the other. It felt like punishment, and he supposed it had something to do with the fact that he had managed to successfully extract himself from the backyard with the gate latch. Apparently, this was his new plight, to be on a line all day, albeit a long one.

He was still walked by Alysson in the midmorning and went with her hopefully and briskly toward the scent of water, expecting to find Archie's odors, but not locating his brother dog at all.

The next day, Alysson didn't come, and the house emptied of its human occupants. The place had a peculiar feel to it, hushed and vacant.

Feeling abandoned, Riggs became agitated. He wanted off the line. He paced, remembering his trek to Liam's house and the two women who greeted him there. Despite having no scent of Liam, Riggs still felt sure he needed to return there. That was home. Not here.

At one point, Riggs backed away from the line, pointing his nose at the stake driven into the ground. The collar slid up onto his head, brushing his ears before it fell to the ground with a clank.

Riggs shook himself. It was an odd sensation to go without a collar.

Riggs trotted optimistically to the gate, but despite a long assault on it, the latch didn't rattle and didn't move. Flummoxed, Riggs went around and into the house through the open sliding door. It was warm inside, warmer than it was out in the yard.

Riggs was padding from room to room, sniffing curiously, with no intent or goal, when he heard odd thuds coming from over his head. He trotted up the stairs and stuck his head out of the upstairs window.

The boys from next door had climbed back up on the roof and one at a time were sailing over the fence and into the pool. Riggs climbed out on the roof without really thinking, watching as the last of them took his dive. He thought about it. He thought about Luna opening the gate. He thought about what lay on the other side of the fence.

The boys in the swimming pool were splashing each other and not paying the dog any attention. Riggs tensed, crouching, ready to spring. It was a long way down, but the boys had done it. Did that mean that Riggs could do it?

25

"Hey, look!" one of the splashing boys shouted. He pointed at Riggs, and all four boys reacted.

"He's going to jump! Can he make it to the pool?"

"Hey!" one boy called. "Stop!"

Riggs tensed.

"He can make it. Hey, dog! Jump!" the first boy called. "Come!" He smacked the water with his hands, and that brought back a memory for Riggs. A long car ride to a lake. A dock jutted out into the water. Liam would run and leap off the dock, and Riggs and Luna would follow, but Luna always ran to the end of the wooden platform and halted momentarily, while Riggs ran and soared and made it to Liam first.

"Come!" the boy was yelling. He even sounded a little like Liam.

Riggs backed up and then sprinted and sprang, easily clearing the fence and landing with a solid splash into the pool. Briefly, he was in the unreal world underwater, and then he surfaced.

The swimming boys were yelling, "Oh, man!"

"Cool!"

"He just jumped off the roof! Hey, dog, that was awesome!"

They were grinning and swimming toward him, and their excitement and praise led Riggs to feel less like a bad dog for leaving the yard. He swam to the side of the pool and ran into a problem: he couldn't figure out how to get out. The edge was too high out of the water.

"Here, boy," one of the boys offered. He helpfully swam up behind Riggs, put a hand under the dog's bottom, and thrust him up onto the concrete padding around the pool.

Riggs shook himself and then gazed around in disappointment. He hadn't really improved his circumstances. This yard
was also completely fenced in.

The swimming boys were still splashing and tossing toys at
one another, so Riggs eased down on his stomach to watch. His
eyes flicked when one of them shouted, "Ball!" and tossed a toy
that bounced past his nose—Riggs wasn't here to play.

After a time, the boys heaved themselves out of the water
and wiped themselves down with towels. "Hey, come on!" one
of them called, and Riggs followed the boys as they filtered in
through the back door to their house. They fed him pieces of a
sandwich as they sat at the table. Riggs felt restless, wanting to
get back on his journey, but the sandwiches were roast beef.

When the boys stood up, Riggs knew it was time to go. There
was just one more barrier, the front door. He walked over to
it and sat, waiting for them to understand that he wanted out,
but nobody seemed to recognize what he needed. Instead, they
looked at their phones and murmured to each other and laughed.

Riggs thought about it. Not even Luna had ever opened a front
door. But Archie, in a way, had.

Riggs squatted.

"Oh, no, no, no!" one of the boys shouted.

He ran up and threw open the door, and with that, Riggs was
outside.

He immediately headed up the sidewalk, now collarless, off
leash, and on his way back to Liam.

Matteo's lunch invitation instantly made Sabrina nervous. Not
because of the man himself—short, gray-haired, spectacled, her
boss looked as harmless as someone's grandfather, and his manner was kind and warm—but Sabrina was still new to the tech
start-up world, still working to shed the cloisters of an academic

life, where "the principal would like to see you" was as ominous to teachers as it was to the students.

When Matteo smiled, his eyes crinkled, reinforcing the grandfather image, and maybe he even *was* a grandfather, though he was also CEO of a software company. Sabrina couldn't begin to guess how old he was.

"I just want to start off by saying how valuable you are to the company," Matteo told her after they'd ordered. "I didn't even know what a communications director was supposed to do."

"I didn't either," Sabrina confessed with a small laugh. She was already feeling better about this lunch. Matteo just had a way of putting people at ease.

"Do you like the work?"

"I do," Sabrina reflected. "I'm part grammarian, part editor, part technical writer."

"Plus press releases and my emails," Matteo added.

"That, too. I like the flexible hours and the fast pace of the work, so different from teaching."

"The hours are flexible. You can work as many as you want," Matteo agreed with a grin. Then his expression grew curious. "There's one thing I want to ask you, though."

Sabrina nodded, wary.

"On our website, your name is 'Ms. Sam.' Why Sam?"

"Oh." Sabrina nodded. "Sabrina A. Morgan. Sam."

"Ah. What's the *A* stand for? Anne?"

"Actually, my middle name is Lee."

Matteo frowned in noncomprehension, so Sabrina found herself explaining about her ex-boyfriend Merrick, back in Chicago. How he didn't know where she lived—Sabrina didn't want him to know. "It's why I had to change my cell phone number. That's kind of what he does, gets my number and then starts leaving me messages and texts. Not threatening to hurt me, more like what he thinks of as being . . . romantic."

"I understand," Matteo replied with a sympathetic nod. "It's

one of the hazards of the modern world. Can we help? We've got
a pretty good legal team I can put to your disposal."

"Honestly? Since I came to work, I haven't heard from him.
I'm thinking—and hoping—he just grew tired of it."

Out of the corner of her eye, Sabrina caught sight of a man
staring at her. When she turned, he glanced away, but she stiffened, aghast, because she recognized him.

It was Brad, Liam's brother, sitting across from an attractive
woman—it looked like a lunch date. Sabrina forced herself to
ignore him, but now had trouble concentrating on what Matteo was saying. Brad glanced over frequently, and she could feel
it each time he did. When he wasn't looking, she would glance
back.

This was certainly awkward, but it got worse when Matteo
regarded her curiously. "Everything okay?"

No *way* did she want to talk about Brad and Liam. She felt
certain she'd already introduced too much personal drama into
the conversation already. "I'm fine," she replied faintly.

Sabrina wanted to leave, but that wasn't going to happen. This
was her boss. Yet being in the same restaurant with Brad was
awful. What if he tried to talk to her? What would she say? What
would *he* say if she threw her salad in his face? Part of her wanted
to, wanted to do violence to this man in return for what he'd
done to her—except he'd lost his brother, his only remaining
family member, and Sabrina had pointed her thoughts in that direction whenever the anger boiled up within her. People in grief
do irrational things.

She just needed to get away without having any sort of interaction.

As if preplanned, Matteo stood up from the table to use the
restroom just moments after Brad's lunch date left for the same
reason.

Sabrina tried to ignore him, but Brad stared intently and un-
apologetically, trapping her. She took a deep, adult breath, stood,

and walked over to Brad, who watched her approach with cold eyes.

"Hello, Brad. How are you?" Sabrina asked in her most civilized tones. "I thought you moved to Germany."

"I had to come back for a few things. I'm not here long."

They stared at each other. Sabrina searched for something neutral to say. "You look well," she finally ventured.

"It's been rough," he replied stonily.

"I know, I'm sorry," Sabrina agreed. Though what had she to be sorry for? She regarded Brad a little more coolly, his self-pitying comment getting to her. "You never sent me any notice or anything, never invited me to the funeral. You banned me from the hospital—they wouldn't release any information at all. Nobody ghosts under situations like this, Brad. I deserved better. This didn't just happen to *you*."

Brad didn't respond to this. A wariness crossed his vision but then cleared. He stood up, signed a credit card slip, and put the credit card in his wallet. "I guess I should show you this," he stated coldly. He held out his phone.

Sabrina frowned. "What is it?"

"It's an email from the shelter advising me they're going to put Luna down tomorrow morning."

"Luna?" Sabrina gasped. "You told me you were going to find good homes for the dogs. She's still at the shelter?"

"They did find good homes for the dogs, they told me, but Luna apparently doesn't get along with anybody or any other dog. It's not a no-kill shelter, and I guess we're out of time."

"But you can't let this happen," Sabrina protested.

Brad raised his eyebrows. "*I* can't let this happen? That's pretty ironic coming from you, Sabrina. Who walked out on them? Who walked out on Liam?"

Sabrina shook her head. "I didn't . . . I told you, my sister . . . it wouldn't work."

Brad nodded. "Right. We each have our own lives. I'm going

back to Germany in two days, you live with your sister, Luna bites everybody. They told me Riggs and Archie are happy. And Liam . . ." Brad bitterly looked away, then back at Sabrina. "Dogs are just collateral damage when people are unreliable. The difference is I didn't have any responsibility—they weren't my dogs."

Brad's lunch companion came out of the restroom, and Brad signaled to her to meet him at the front of the restaurant. She nodded, and Brad turned contemptuously back to Sabrina. "Well, I gave you the information. You do with it what you want."

Sabrina watched him walk away, her mouth slightly open, unable to think of what to do next.

Riggs made his way back home with the unerring instinct of an animal who has traveled a path before. When he came to where he'd seen Archie, the food and people smells had left and taken the other dog's scent with them, so Riggs kept moving.

He arrived home while the sun was still high in the sky. The heat energized outdoor odors, and he sniffed eagerly for what he expected, which was the clear scents of Sabrina and Liam and the dog pack. Nothing in the yard or on the front porch greeted his nose except the smell of the two women who had been there the last time. Dismally, Riggs realized that Liam was still not home, which explained why the dogs weren't there either.

Riggs had gone from being a good dog with a destination to being a dog lost in the world. He stood in the shade and yawned anxiously, wondering where to go now.

26

Riggs lay in that yard for a long time, lifting his head hopefully each time a car approached. Waiting for his person here at home seemed the only reasonable action, though he was starting to feel sharp jabs of hunger.

When he dejectedly eased to his feet, it was without plan or strategy. He just knew, as all dogs know, that to eat, he needed someone to feed him. Liam wasn't here and might never come back—a dog's singular most dreaded fear, but one that occupies all canine minds when they're alone without their people.

The instinct to find people, and the faint but more concentrated smell of food in one particular direction, led him to follow his nose. He did not want to return to the house with the wild children and Mommy and Daddy despite the dinners that might be waiting there, because it seemed that family was determined to keep him from Liam.

There were dog smells coming to him from all directions as he padded along paved paths, which was slightly reassuring, but he steered away from people and canines when he encountered them. The odors were growing more dense—he didn't know it, but he was tracking toward downtown Denver. His stomach complained audibly, and his hunger fatigued him.

Night found him in an area lacking trees but packed with many buildings. He located a crust of bread and ate it noisily, but otherwise, despite food odors both fresh and sour, he was frustrated in his quest to find a meal.

This was an alien place to Riggs. It was as if the entire area were one big sidewalk, with scarcely any greenery or grass. Dogs had been here—many, many dogs—but Riggs was unsuccessful in finding them here now. His nose had misled him to a place that was hostile to life. It had been a mistake to come here.

Riggs curled up uncomfortably behind a tall metal box that sat on the street. Food smells leaked from the box—old, spoiled food smells that both intrigued and repelled him. It was a box, though, and to get into a box required human hands.

Riggs sighed, feeling miserable, thinking about Liam.

When Teme arrived at the shelter first thing Friday morning, there was a blond woman with long hair sitting on the front steps.

Teme was uneasy because she was opening the shelter by herself. Normally, Mr. Reed opened, but he had a doctor's appointment.

Teme's instincts told her there was something wrong with this woman. The way she held herself, the way she stared at Teme as Teme pulled into her employee parking slot, communicated an odd, almost frenzied energy. The woman jumped to her feet, and Teme bit her lip. She was aware that her car doors were locked, and she made no move to unlock them. Animal rescue attracted a lot of crazy people. Some wanted to do battle over the conditions and processes associated with shelters. Others felt that once an animal was a pet, it was a perversion, and the animals needed mercy killing.

When the woman remained on the steps, Teme felt a little more reassured. Had the woman come off those steps and charged the car, Teme wasn't sure what her plan was, but backing out and driving away didn't seem unreasonable.

Teme cautiously opened her car door and stepped out. The woman stayed on the steps. Another good sign.

"Can I help you?" Teme asked tentatively. Her car door was still open, and it would be a very quick and easy motion to sit back down and relock the doors.

The woman nodded. "I'm here about a dog."

Well, that might explain her agitation. Perhaps the woman's dog had gone missing. Certainly, Teme had seen it before. She shut her door and approached cautiously. "Hi," she greeted, only slightly less uneasily.

"I came yesterday, but you were closed!" the woman accused somewhat shrilly.

Teme nodded. "We're closed to the public Thursday afternoons. Sorry."

The woman swallowed. "My name is Sabrina Morgan. I'm here about a little dog named Luna. Do you know Luna?"

Teme brightened. "Oh!"

Sabrina seemed to read something in Teme's expression. "Please tell me you didn't put her down. Please."

"Oh, okay. I'm so sorry. I don't actually know. I wasn't here yesterday."

With that, Sabrina collapsed into tears, and Teme's mood changed completely.

"Oh, but let's go inside. Maybe everything is okay," Teme suggested compassionately.

Teme noted with concern that Sabrina could barely stay upright as they walked together through the doors.

"Do you want to sit down, maybe?" Teme asked Sabrina, who shook her head. "My name's Teme, by the way."

"Hi, Teme."

"You're Sabrina?"

Sabrina nodded.

"Can I ask how you know about Luna?"

"It's complicated, but the short version is that I used to live with her owner. Then a . . . person . . . showed me the email you sent about her being on death row."

Teme nodded as she put it together. "So you lived with the guy who . . ."

Sabrina swallowed. "Yes. He died in a car accident."

"I'm so sorry."

The cacophony of dogs barking had not ceased, it seemed, all night. They were certainly at it this morning, their voices faint through the heavy door, but that's just how things were here at the shelter. For Teme, the constant noise was so in the background she scarcely noticed it, but the sound seemed to make Sabrina apprehensive. Teme set down her purse and walked around the counter, clicking in to her computer.

"Our system's down," she announced disgustedly. She uttered that same phrase many times a week. When she glanced up, she saw that Sabrina was devastated by the news. "No, it's okay. Let's just go see," Teme suggested comfortingly. Nodding, frightened, Sabrina followed Teme as she opened the door to all the barking.

Riggs became aware of a gradual swelling of the noise that had battered at his ears all night long. At first, the cacophony and odors had been too much, overwhelming him and keeping him awake, even anxious, but gradually, feeling beaten down, Riggs drifted into a deep sleep and was able to ignore all distractions. Now, with light just filtering through the streets, Riggs stood, stretched, and yawned, shaking himself. He could smell that there had been a male dog nearby while he slept. There was no trace of him now.

His first thought was for food, but it was a dripping faucet that summoned Riggs, and he wound up lapping at a small pool of water until his thirst was satisfied. There were food smells everywhere, but there was no food. This was not a situation Riggs had ever encountered. When Liam or Sabrina were in the kitchen, there were similar smells, but there was always something offered by hand to accompany the odors. Now, though, different, competing, wonderful fragrances mingled with one another and danced away from him on the warm morning air without leading him in any particular direction.

This place he had found, with its noise, its cars, was absolutely reeking with deliciousness, and yet there was nothing for a good dog. Riggs noticed a real sense of active life as well, small animals who hid from Riggs and his nose when he sniffed along the edges of the alley. There were cats, too. Riggs could smell them, but like all cats, they were elusive and unfriendly to stray dogs. Riggs had no idea if they were watching him, nor was that really important right now. Once his hunger seized his imagination, there really was nothing else to do but try to find food.

Eventually, a wrapped piece of paper on the sidewalk revealed a crunchy roll inside with a tiny strip of meat and cheese clinging to it. Riggs devoured it ravenously. It was certainly not enough to put his hunger to sleep, but it dulled the sharp edge of discomfort and gave him some opportunity to ponder his circumstances.

People were out now, people walking the cement sidewalks, many of them with dogs. Riggs watched as these dogs reacted to his presence, staring, the males reflexively lifting their legs. Some of them ignored Riggs completely, and some raised the fur on the backs of their necks. The people with these dogs, though, that's what caught Riggs's attention. They would stare at him, but not with a smile.

Riggs was accustomed to people reaching out with open hands, to them kneeling and wanting kisses from him, and offering treats, and he could smell those treats now, in the pockets and pouches of the people who were walking their dogs, but there was nothing for Riggs. The people, when they saw him, gave him a hard glance, or they looked away and picked up their pace.

For the first time, Riggs understood that there was a difference between dogs who were alone and dogs who were with their people. Without his collar, and without a leash, and without Liam, that's who he was. He was a dog without a person.

Now what? His nose had led him to this vast area. People smells permeated everything. There was food and water to be found somehow, and with so many humans and dogs all around him, it seemed more likely that he would encounter Liam here than anywhere else he had been on his journey, but there was no Liam, and no smell of Luna, and no sign of Archie.

Riggs resolved to attend to his hunger first and then to find Liam and get the dog pack back together. That was his purpose. He trotted aimlessly along the sidewalk, his fur on one side brushing the buildings, sniffing hopefully.

When Riggs saw a dog like him, a male with no collar, dirty fur, and no people, Riggs instantly made to run up and greet him. The other dog fled, though, running as if Riggs were moving to attack him. It made no sense to Riggs, but he faltered and then slowed down, and then eventually stopped. Dogs without people were afraid of everything. That was the lesson he was learning.

Certainly, Riggs was afraid of the people, mostly men, who sat on the cement in a pile of their belongings and called to him when he trotted past. "Hey, dog!" they might yell. Riggs couldn't tell if these humans meant him harm, but they were very different from anyone Riggs had ever encountered.

Riggs was frustrated more by the dog scents than anything. He could tell some had made beds on pieces of cloth or behind boxes, but they weren't in their dens now. Where there were dogs, there would be food—his pack instincts told him that.

Riggs had never felt so alone.

Then an old and loud vehicle pulled to the curb, and everything changed.

27

Luna was asleep when the door opened, but her instincts yanked her into consciousness in an instant. Something, she realized, was happening. She climbed expectantly to her feet. She was even wagging. Not just something—something wonderful. Teme came around the corner, but it was the woman walking behind her that caught and held Luna's attention.

Sabrina.

"Luna!" Sabrina cried.

Luna whimpered and dashed to the gate, pawing at it furiously while Teme fumbled with the latch. The moment it swung open, Luna surged through it and launched herself into Sabrina's arms and was gathered like a child. "Oh, Luna," Sabrina choked, "I'm so sorry. I'm so sorry."

Luna cried and licked and loved her person. Sabrina had come, just as Luna had known she would.

"Well, it's obvious you two know each other," Teme observed with a chuckle.

Luna gazed adoringly at Sabrina, who was wiping away tears. Luna never wanted to be put down again. She wanted to be carried forever by Sabrina. "I thought Luna was adopted out, or I never would have left her here this long," Sabrina apologized.

"Oh, she was adopted," Teme replied, "but it didn't work out, I guess."

"What do I need to do? To take Luna home with me, I mean. I need to—" Sabrina gave a light laugh. "This is just sort of crazy."

"Why don't we go up front?" Teme suggested.

Sabrina followed her back through the heavy door. "Oh, Luna, you are so silly." Sabrina grinned at Teme. "No better makeup remover than a dog's tongue."

Teme sat behind the counter and laughed.

"Okay, I need to make some changes. I live with my sister. She has cats," Sabrina pondered.

"Oh," Teme replied dubiously. "Jack Russells are known to see cats as prey. It's probably not a good fit." Her face fell as she contemplated what this might mean.

"Right, of course! But I'm moving. I mean, I don't have a place yet to move into. I mean, I do, but not until September 3. The place belongs to my company, and it's sort of a perk that I get to move there. Instead of a big salary, I guess. They do allow dogs in the building. I was planning . . . I don't know what I was planning, actually. I just thought that by now—" She rolled her eyes at herself. "Am I giving too much information?"

"No, not at all," Teme assured her. "We need information. So to sort of parse it down, you're moving, and until then . . ." Teme trailed off. "We're sort of out of time for Luna," she finished apologetically.

"Oh! Then I'll check into a dog-friendly hotel. Today." Sabrina stopped talking and stared at Teme. "Are Archie and Riggs here, too?"

"Oh, no," Teme replied quickly. "I remember the dogs you're talking about. They all came in together, didn't they?"

"That's right. It was rather sudden."

"No, Archie and Riggs were each adopted out to separate families."

"Could I talk to those people?" Sabrina pressed hopefully.

Teme regretfully shook her head. "No, honestly, it's best if you don't. Let the dogs adjust to their new lives. It's been quite a while for Archie, and Riggs has been gone for more than a month."

Sabrina nodded and swallowed. "I don't think I could manage three dogs anyway."

"Do you work from home?" Teme asked casually. It was the

first of many questions on the checklist she would eventually need to complete, but to her, it was one of the most important. Since COVID, an increasing number of people had answered yes to that question, and to Teme, it made a huge difference.

"I work from home sometimes," Sabrina replied. "not every day, though. I was a schoolteacher. Now I'm—" She stopped and then smiled to herself. "Communications director," she said self-consciously, "for a small start-up company. I just was burned out on teaching, and this seemed like a good opportunity. I haven't been there all that long."

Teme nodded. "My mom was a schoolteacher. I think it's the hardest job in the world."

Sabrina smiled, and the two of them fully relaxed. Sabrina set Luna down, and the little dog immediately pressed against Sabrina's legs, determined not to be left behind.

"There are some questions I have to ask you," Teme began a bit awkwardly, "but I think I should tell you that we had pretty much given up hope for Luna. She hasn't been very friendly toward people. Not the way she is with you. And like I said, your instincts were right—she was on the schedule for, well, you know. So there's no chance we'll say no to you adopting her. You're her only hope, actually."

"Oh, Luna, you're the sweetest dog in the world. Why weren't you friendly?" Sabrina asked. Luna luxuriated in the sound of Sabrina saying her name. "So, right, I'll get a room at the hotel next to where I work," Sabrina reasoned out loud. She was putting it together. She had a dog now. She had Luna.

"I'm sure you'll figure it out," Teme agreed with an encouraging smile.

Riggs sensed that something was happening, a change to how things had been all morning, but wasn't sure what. All that had occurred to give him this feeling was that a man stepped out of his car. He was much shorter than Liam, smaller-boned, with light curly hair on his head the same color as Archie's fur. Unlike most people, though, this new man didn't look away, didn't increase his pace, but approached Riggs with an engaging smile, his eyes kind. He was here, Riggs felt, for him. Not to capture him—there was nothing threatening or devious in his motion—but just to see him.

Though the man wore an old, patterned shirt that carried its own earthy odor, his hands smelled like food.

"Dogs!" he called. "Hey, dogs! Come here."

Riggs watched in amazement as a small white dog emerged from an alley. Then a slightly larger black one came around the corner, and from down the street, seeming to emerge from a dumpster, a mottled brown-and-white dog trotted up energetically. "Here you go," the man proclaimed. He handed a piece of succulent-smelling turkey to the white dog—a big piece. "Good dog, Corona," he praised. He turned to the mottled dog. "Here you go, Budweiser. Oh, you need a bath." He tossed a piece of thigh meat through the air, and the small dog snagged it.

The smallest dog, long haired with a tiny face, approached timidly.

"Hi there, Modelo! You're so pretty. I don't know how your people managed to lose a full-blooded papillon, but there's no accounting for human behavior. And who are you?"

The man was looking directly at Riggs. Riggs hesitated uncertainly, but the smell of turkey drew him forward.

"You're new. Where do you come from? Are you friendly?"

Riggs wagged his nonexistent tail. He could not stop staring at the man's hands.

"Are you hungry, little one?" the man asked softly.

As he threw the hunk of poultry, the black dog tried to catch it, leaping into the air, but it went high, and Riggs pounced on it. Moist, delicious turkey.

"All right, Heineken," the man chuckled. "Here's yours."

The sound of dogs chewing stimulated Riggs into frantically choking down the meal as quickly as he could. When he looked up, the man had come over and was kneeling now, holding out another piece, which Riggs gratefully accepted.

"I'm going to call you Molson," he announced to Riggs. "You're Molson. That dog that looks like you is Budweiser, Corona's the white bully breed, the little Lab mix is Heineken, and the little princess is Modelo. Where's Michelob?" he asked.

The dogs looked at him, hearing the question but not knowing what he was saying.

After a time, other dogs came, and the kind man fed them as well. Riggs noted that the skittish, xenophobic behavior of the canines was mollified by the appearance of this one man, as if he were their Liam, their person. Some dogs even went so far as to sniff one another. Riggs stood still for a suspicious examination by the small white dog named Corona, contemplating this situation.

Though the dogs were free and off leash, this place Riggs had found was far different from any dog park. In a dog park, the friendly dogs formed and re-formed agile, moving packs, the youngest ones tearing around the enclosure with boundless energy while the older ones interacted with more dignity. Here, the dogs hid from people and one another and apparently only became normal dogs when this man appeared.

The canines were mostly still milling around, drawn by the scent of turkey in the man's pack, when a woman wearing a black outfit and a black hat, with large metal objects hanging from a shiny black belt, stepped around the corner. The dogs didn't react as if she were a threat, so Riggs didn't either.

"Hey there, Ron," the woman called, and that was how Riggs learned the man's name.

"Hey, Georgia." He gestured. "Got a new one. Name is Molson."

"Molson," Georgia whispered. She reached down to Riggs, and he sniffed her hand. It smelled like a rabbit. How would a woman have rabbit smells on her hands? Riggs had only smelled rabbits out in the grass, and they had always managed to elude him, though several times he was sure he had come close to catching one.

"He looks well fed. Must have been abandoned pretty recently," the woman—Georgia—commented as she ran a hand up and down Riggs's chest.

"Or ran away," Ron speculated.

Georgia nodded. "Maybe. But no collar, no tags. That's usually a sign that someone just dropped the poor guy off. Want me to take him to the municipal shelter?"

"If you feel like you have to," Ron replied carefully.

"No, what I feel like is I have to go home, to be honest. My shift's done. I'll take a photo, though, and ask the shelter to post it to their website."

"That's great. Tough night?" Ron asked.

Georgia shrugged. "I'm just tired in general. Just thought I'd take one more walk through the neighborhood. Take it easy, Ron."

"You too, Georgia."

The woman with the heavy objects on her belt departed, trailing a weariness behind her. Ron watched her go and then smiled and shook his head. "I'm not a night person," he informed the dogs. None of them knew what he was saying, but his turkey was real, and so was his affection. When Ron slid back into his car and announced, "See you tomorrow," the dogs immediately dispersed.

Riggs wasn't sure what was happening, but he absolutely did not want to be left by himself. The small dog named Budweiser trotted off, and Riggs followed him.

28

Budweiser gave Riggs a suspicious look when he realized Riggs was tracking him, but there wasn't much he could do, as Riggs had something of an innate capability when it came to following other creatures. Both dogs appreciated that the other was willing to halt progress for an intrigued sniff at some dropped or crushed object.

At the entrance to an alley, Budweiser hesitated, willing Riggs to move on, but Riggs remained by his side, and Budweiser gave up, resigned. As they entered the alley, Riggs appreciated a fresh pool of water in a place near the wall, where a hole in the broken concrete formed a natural bowl fed by a trickle from a metal pipe, and he stopped for a quick drink before hustling to catch up to the other dog. Riggs also noted that the alley was a dead end, making it more defensible. To one side was a low wall, and Budweiser maneuvered around this and climbed behind the wall to a soft and soiled mattress that had been tossed there by someone. With a sigh, the dog scratched at it, circled a few times, and lay down.

This was Budweiser's den. Would Budweiser allow Riggs to share it? Riggs tentatively put a foot on the mattress, and Budweiser treated him to a blank expression. Feeling encouraged, Riggs hopped up on the mattress. Riggs allowed himself to be sniffed and then returned the gesture. Budweiser sported the delectable fragrance of a canine who hadn't been subjected to a bath in a long, long time.

They were both males. Riggs was far younger, and something

had happened to Budweiser's rear quarters. Riggs could sense the pain there until Budweiser was able to adjust his position a certain way. The two dogs sprawled out on the mattress. Riggs took comfort from being part of a pack and, satisfied from having eaten from Ron's hand, fell asleep.

Riggs shadowed Budweiser from the moment the other dog woke up. Budweiser did not seem to have much reaction to being paired with another dog. Budweiser was without a pack, which seemed to Riggs how dogs lived on the streets. It made Riggs uneasy. Riggs preferred everything alive to be organized into cohesive units.

Trailing Budweiser, Riggs learned how to jump up into a dumpster and retrieve food. It was not easy. The dumpsters were very high, and the only ones worth assaulting needed to be redolent with the odor of edible food and be bulging with sacks of garbage so that their lids were propped open. The dumpsters with fully closed lids were impenetrable. Budweiser showed Riggs how to strategically leap and bite at the bags, and then fall to earth, dragging their bounty with them.

It always took many attempts, but eventually, a bag would drop to the ground and the two of them could tear it open. Most often, there was some sort of food to be had, though it wasn't always that tasty. Often, there was a sourness to whatever it was they were eating, and sometimes that sourness sat in Riggs's belly, but over the next several days, he received more or less enough to eat.

Ron came most mornings, bringing with him something wonderful to offer. The dogs loved Ron, Riggs realized, because he was a good man who fed dogs.

One afternoon, a different man appeared, and the dogs knew this man, too, but they reacted completely differently.

The first thing Riggs noticed about this new man was that he had a bearing to him that was unlike Liam or any other human Riggs had ever met. There was a way that he jerked his head to look around, and he was constantly muttering. He smelled like smoke; it was in his tissues, it was leaking from his eyes, on his breath—to Riggs it seemed as if this smoke man had come alive in a fire. He held a metal pipe in his hand, gripping it like a club.

When Budweiser and Riggs spotted Smoke Man, Smoke Man stared at them with rheumy eyes, and Budweiser wheeled around and ran. Not understanding what they were doing, Riggs automatically fled with the other dog.

"Hey!" the man screeched.

Riggs halted because a person was yelling at them, and a good dog should stop when someone does that. Riggs turned and glanced timidly behind him and saw the man, his face twisted in a frightening grimace, bearing down on him, the club coming up.

The Smoke Man, Riggs realized, intended to hurt him.

Riggs ran.

After a few days in a small room with no kitchen but just a bed, a chair, and a bathroom, Sabrina moved Luna again. This time, their home was in a very large building with big double glass doors and an elevator.

The word meant nothing when Sabrina said, "Let's get in the elevator," but soon Luna knew that's what the little room was called. It would shake, and the smells would change, and then the doors would sigh open and they would walk down a hallway, and Sabrina would touch some buttons that emitted a very tiny noise, and then they would be in Luna's new home.

There were no other dogs, but there was a bedroom and another bedroom—Riggs and Archie would be happy here. Boxes commanded most of the floor space. Every day, Sabrina played with these boxes, opening them and removing the contents, and usually putting the objects in a cupboard or setting them somewhere in a closet. Then the box itself would be folded up and stacked in the corner.

Luna didn't understand any of this but watched the activity carefully, content to be with Sabrina.

"I've got good news, Luna," Sabrina advised. "They're fine with me taking you to work tomorrow, so from now on, it's Take Your Dog to Work Day. When I'm not working here, you can come with me." Luna absorbed the tone of Sabrina's voice and understood that something good was happening, and that made Luna happy.

The next morning, they left the big building early and walked through cool morning air to another big building some distance away. Luna was surprised at the number of people that she met at this new place, but they were all friendly, and two of the women handed her small treats as they strolled through a bewildering maze of small half rooms with desks and chairs.

It was wonderful to be in a place where all the humans knew her name!

This seemed to be her new life—going every morning with Sabrina to a building full of friendly people or remaining in the home and taking a much shorter walk a little later. Either way, Sabrina liked to sit and make clicking noises all day, and Luna would loyally curl up at her feet.

Luna loved her new life because she was finally back with Sabrina. Now, Luna reasoned, they needed to go find Liam and Archie and, of course, Riggs.

Luna waited patiently for this to happen, and in a way, it did.

One glorious morning, Sabrina slept much later than usual and then dressed in shorts and put Luna in her car, driving a short distance. They jumped out of the car ride and found themselves at a wonderful place with a flowing stream and cement walks lining that stream and a trail with many dog markings and many friendly people.

Luna pulled at the end of her leash, smelling all the smells and greeting small dogs. She tended to shy away from the great big dogs; it just seemed like a good strategy. She loved the exotic fragrances of the small stream that separated the flow of dogs and people into two paved sections, so that if there were no animals on her side, there might be some to see and smell on the other.

Luna was utterly unsurprised to see Archie. His distinctive odors came first, of course. Luna lifted her head up and looked around, immediately spotting the shaggy, goofy dog on the other side of the river, being led at the end of a leash by a man with dark hair. The wind was cooler at Luna's back, so Archie should have detected her first, but Archie, being Archie, was so distracted by everything that it took a moment.

Luna watched her pack mate with bright eyes, putting it all together. Of course Sabrina would bring her to this place—Archie was here! Liam and Riggs would no doubt appear in short order.

When the smell finally registered with the small Labradoodle, Archie snapped his head around, searching, and spied Luna. The man walking with Archie had stopped and was awkwardly holding his phone, looking at it, and Archie didn't hesitate. He darted to the end of his leash and yanked it right out of the man's hand, then galloped straight at Luna, which meant he splashed without hesitation into the water. The river was not deep— Archie wasn't even forced to swim, he just lunged across in big, galumphing leaps. When he emerged from the river, he wasted no time shaking the water from his curly fur, and he ran joyously to Luna and jumped on her.

"Oh, wow!" Sabrina exclaimed.

The two dogs wrestled with the intimacy of littermates. Luna found herself a little irritated at how large Archie seemed. She had forgotten the dog was so much bigger, but Archie knew his place, and when Luna went for his throat in mock attack, Archie collapsed on the ground, stuck his legs up in the air, and allowed himself to be dominated.

"Archie, Archie," the man called from his side of the river. "What's gotten into you?" He held up a hand. "Hi. Sorry. Could you watch my dog? I'll come get him."

Sabrina nodded, but she was staring at the Labradoodle, reacting to the man calling his name. "Archie," she whispered in
wonder, "is that really you?"

Archie greeted Sabrina as enthusiastically as he greeted everybody in the world. She knelt and put out her hands, and he
sniffed her and jumped on her and licked her, deliriously happy.

The man who had been walking him came across a bridge.
It took him some time to find his way down to the crossing and
double back, and during that interval, the two dogs played, and
Sabrina laughed with delight. "I have no idea how this happened,"
she confessed. "But it's amazing!"

The man walked up, grinning. "That was all my bad," he confessed. "I was distracted and not really holding the leash very
tightly, and my dog took off. I honestly don't know what got into
him."

"I think I do," Sabrina replied. "This is Archie."

The man peered at her in puzzlement.

29

After evading Smoke Man that first day, Riggs shadowed Budweiser, unwilling to live solo when he could be in a pack of two. The wind was strong behind them, so they didn't smell anything until they turned a corner and Smoke Man was right there, already raising his pipe.

Everything was confusing and terrifying. Riggs froze and shrank down when the man charged at him, reacting like any bad dog would, hoping the human would forgive. Riggs was terrified when Smoke Man, harsh fury rising off his skin, raised his pipe over his head, but as it came down, Riggs couldn't help himself and dodged out of the way. The weapon narrowly missed Riggs's haunches, and as it struck the pavement, it clanged loudly, and the man shrieked—a raw, frightening sound.

Riggs wasn't sure what was happening. Nothing like this had ever occurred in his life. Budweiser, though, seemed to have a real sense of the danger they were in. The other dog wasn't looking back, wasn't wasting time observing this strange man with his vicious expression and odd odors. Budweiser was streaking away in full flight and vanishing around a corner. Riggs immediately elected to follow suit and scampered to catch up. Within a few footfalls, Smoke Man fell out of range with that pipe. His odors, however, continued to pursue him until Riggs had turned the corner and dashed up the sidewalk, gaining swiftly on Budweiser, whose painful hips slowed him down.

Riggs caught up with the other dog and reflected on the fact that it always made sense to follow Budweiser's lead. Budweiser, after all, had shown him how to hunt in the dumpsters, and now

Budweiser was leading him away from a man who was clearly angry about something the dogs had done. The business end of that pipe had landed very heavily, and Riggs could imagine what it might feel like to have that strike him in the ribs. He always tried not to make people angry, but it seemed now that the message from Budweiser was that strangers in general were to be avoided. The malevolence of the smoky-smelling man clung to Riggs like a bad odor in his fur, staying with him.

The idea that some people would seek to harm dogs was new information for Riggs, who had always believed that people were basically good and that humans would always take care of animals. Now that he lived away from Liam, life was not like that at all.

Away from Liam.

Riggs's thoughts turned back to his person. Living with Budweiser meant survival. Budweiser could find water and food, and there was that nice man, Ron, who would come around and offer dog treats almost every day, but in the end, Budweiser was just focused on surviving and nothing more. There didn't seem to be a sense of purpose in the other dog. No focus on trying to find a family or a pack. Budweiser had given up on humanity.

Riggs understood something now. It had been several days that he had been living on the streets, living successfully, thanks to Budweiser, though he was always much more hungry than he was accustomed to. But he wanted more than to just go on living; he wanted to find his person, to return to Liam and Sabrina and Archie and Luna, and to do that, Riggs would have to leave Budweiser behind.

Sabrina and the man with black hair stood with Archie and Luna on the cement path next to the river. The wet from Archie's fur dribbled onto his shadow. He was still focused on Luna, but the

Jack Russell could sense something happening between the two humans and was trying to pay attention to them.

"I adopted Archie a month ago," the man advised Sabrina. "How do you know him?"

"He used to belong to my boyfriend."

"Oh! No wonder he recognized your dog." The man beamed.

Sabrina smiled down at Luna. "Yes, that's sort of it. What happened was my boyfriend was in a fatal car accident, and his brother couldn't take the dogs. I couldn't either at that particular moment, so we wound up having to put them in the shelter."

"Ah," the man mused agreeably. "I get it. That must have been hard."

Sabrina swallowed and nodded. She glanced away, not wanting to share a vulnerable moment, and changed the subject. "It's just wonderful that they've reunited like this."

"Yes." The man grinned at her, and then his look clouded. "So, I'm sorry—you say it was a fatal accident?"

Sabrina nodded. "Yes." She caught her breath, then nodded again. "I mean, let's just say the brother and I don't get along. Long story, and in the end I was cut off from him. Liam, I mean. My boyfriend. He was in an irrecoverable coma, and then he passed away, but I never heard anything from Brad. That's the brother."

"Oh, that's terrible. I'm so sorry," the man commiserated.

"It gives me some insight as to how the dogs must feel. They don't know either—one day Liam was there, and then he was gone. I may not have all the details, but I have enough to give me some closure. Luna and Archie will never know. Do you think dogs wonder about stuff like that?"

"I feel like they must. But maybe they have a perspective we don't because they're here for such a short time. Maybe that makes them more accepting of change."

Sabrina absorbed this, nodding.

"So you had to do something, and you took them to the shelter," the man summarized.

Sabrina shrugged, not wanting to nitpick the narrative. "Like I said, at that moment, there weren't any other options. Shelters won't take a dog if you tell them you're hoping to come back and pick them up in a month or so. I had just quit my job, didn't have a place of my own, and Liam's brother was going to be living in Europe. Anyway, I guess the family that adopted Luna didn't want her and turned her back in, and I just happened to find out about it."

"Wow. All right, then. We should get the dogs together! Play-dates," the man suggested enthusiastically.

"Sure." Sabrina blinked and frowned. It seemed as if the man were suggesting something else.

"My name is Darren," he offered, holding out a hand.

"Sabrina. Sabrina Morgan." They shook hands.

Luna watched this, wondering precisely what was happening and how it was this man had been walking Archie. Where was Liam?

"Let me get your number," Darren suggested. "I'll call you. We can set up dog park days. Would that work?"

"Okay," Sabrina agreed slowly.

"Oh!" Darren exclaimed, picking up something in her tone. "Are you thinking you want Archie back?"

When hunger prodded Riggs to leave Budweiser's den, the other dog was hesitant to follow, and Riggs could understand why: the air was bringing them toxic whiffs of Smoke Man's presence. The menace was back out on the streets, and the wind informed Riggs's nose that the man was prowling, perhaps searching for dogs to attack.

But Riggs's living on the streets meant that he spent most of every day seeking his next meal, and he couldn't wait around for Budweiser to accompany him. His search eventually led him to a pregnant dumpster, white bags bulging at the top. In at least one of those bags were dog dinner food, Riggs realized. Further, Riggs saw the lid of the dumpster was flung open and mounds of full trash bags were piled up against it, preventing the lid from shutting. White bags were also stacked on the street, leaning up against the dumpster, but nothing in them smelled edible. The bags gave off, instead, a metallic and dusty odor. To tear into the plastic would be a waste of effort.

Riggs remembered Luna climbing up on the cold box to get food. Leaping and snagging random items from the dumpster took a lot of energy, but the way these bags were piled would enable Riggs to scale to the top. Tentatively, he began ascending. The bags shifted under his feet and were slippery, but still, he was able to easily mount the hill of plastic until the open dumpster was just a short leap away. Riggs gathered himself and propelled himself upward. He soared over the lip and into the trash-laden dumpster, and instantly, one of the bags, the one that had been bulging from the top, came down on him. Riggs dodged the threat, ripped into it, and found what had been attracting him—a big, flat box full of shreds of cheese and meat. He peeled the succulent food away from the cardboard and choked it down greedily. Further investigation found a greasy sack with bits of chicken and another one containing potatoes that had been fried in a delicious fat.

Riggs splayed his feet on the unstable bags, scarfed down the food, and sniffed for more delicacies. While doing so, he registered the sound of a rumbling truck, close by and getting closer.

When he could feel the thunder of the truck in his chest, he stopped hunting for food and froze. His newfound distrust of people led him to remain in the bottom of the dumpster, balanced carefully on a couple of bags, not daring to raise his head for fear of being spotted.

Suddenly and unexpectedly, the dumpster jolted. Riggs was flung to the side with the impact. What was happening?

He looked up. If he just scrambled, he could get out now. He started to climb the mountain of bags and then was astonished when everything changed as the dumpster itself hurtled straight up into the air. The dumpster tipped sideways and then, even more sickeningly, was upside down.

Riggs tumbled and fell and landed with a crash in a big pile of bags and cardboard and wood. He was overpowered with noise, a huge roar and a banging, and Riggs tried to make sense of it, digging to find air at the top of this pile. As he did so, a loud whine pierced the air, and the trash beneath him began to shift and crunch. The walls of this strange enclosure started to move in on Riggs; he was trapped and terrified. The bags crowded him, trash buried him, and Riggs struggled to reach air and light, digging upward and finding himself pinned under an increasingly deep pile.

Just as it seemed that all was lost, when the darkness closed over him and escape was impossible, there was a sudden lurch, and the whine desisted. The walls were no longer bearing down on him; they began to back away, and some of the trash loosened. He continued to struggle because his back legs were trapped. He clawed himself forward with his front legs, digging with his nose, breathing in the fetid air, scrambling.

The truck rumbled. It was going somewhere.

30

Sabrina had been forced to say no, she didn't want to take Archie back. She really couldn't—Luna was content to lie at her feet all day in the office, but from what Sabrina remembered of Archie, the young dog needed to be constantly entertained. And of the three dogs, Archie was the newest, so her relationship with him wasn't as solid as with Luna and Riggs. Plus, Archie obviously loved Darren. And Sabrina's apartment would feel pretty crowded with Archie there because that's what Archie brought to a situation—the sense of a lot of dog.

"Sorry, Archie," Sabrina told the Labradoodle wistfully. "I'm just starting to get my life under control."

"He does bring the chaos!" Darren agreed with a laugh. "I totally understand."

Sabrina said goodbye to a rather oblivious Archie dog and took Luna back to the car.

Several days passed with the mind-numbing routine of hanging out in the yard and waiting for Darren, but then things changed, and Archie was overjoyed because Darren came to get him in the early evening and took him for a car ride. It didn't matter where they were going; the fact of the car ride itself was enough to make Archie ecstatic. He bounced around in the back seat and barked out the window at a passing dog. When the window mysteriously raised itself in its frame, closing Archie off from the fresh air and the scents of dogs, Archie barked anyway.

Things became even better when the door was opened and Archie plunged out into some grass. He instantly smelled a very familiar dog. It was Luna! Sabrina opened the glass doors of a big building and Luna came racing out, and the two dogs greeted each other and wrestled in the grass.

Sabrina was dressed in shorts and a T-shirt and smiled at Darren as the two people snipped leashes into the collars of their respective dogs.

"Where do you want to go?" Darren asked.

Sabrina nodded toward the street. "There's a park up ahead. I like to take Luna there."

"Sounds good," Darren agreed. He fell into step next to Sabrina.

Archie could hardly believe how wonderful this day was turning out to be. He was back with Sabrina and Luna. There was no Liam, but Darren's heart seemed as big, and as far as Archie was concerned, if Darren and Sabrina decided to live in the large building with glass doors or the house with Mom and Theo and Darren, that would be fabulous. Archie would be with Luna, and certainly Riggs would be joining them all soon.

Archie briefly thought about the yard where he sat listlessly in the shade all day, waiting for something to happen. Of late, it wasn't always true that the man, Darren, would come for him. Many nights, Archie would wait in vain for someone to open the slider and come out and let him into the house. He had even spent the entire night out there in the grass several times.

It was not unpleasant. The night smells were different from those during the day. There were other animals to be detected in the night, and the cool air felt good. But it was lonely. Archie was just tired of being alone.

Luna almost seemed to understand this and tolerated Archie's initial burst of affection and energy.

"Well," Darren responded to a question from Sabrina, "I'm not divorced yet. I'm in that phase where it's all processing paperwork and disagreements and problems." Darren sighed. "This is the second time I've gone through this. In my life, I mean."

"I'm sorry to hear that," Sabrina observed politely.

"I'm living in a temporary place right now, completely furnished down to the napkins and full of men like me." He grinned wryly. "They should just put up a sign saying Divorced Hotel. Your place seems wonderful. I'm looking for something like that—not too far from downtown but in a residential area."

"It belongs to my company," Sabrina explained. "As part of my compensation, I get to live there at a big discount. The place I work for is a start-up." She laughed nervously. "I went from being in the teachers' union and having the most secure job in the world to working for a place where we never know on Monday if the company will still be in existence on Friday. I'm really enjoying the energy and the work, though. The people are all nice. The location's amazing."

"Your home is sort of what I'm looking for with Archie. The house I'm in now is typical suburbia, and it's going to my ex in the divorce. The yard's great for a Labradoodle, but I'm afraid my ex and her son are not big dog fans."

"Oh, who could not love Archie?" Sabrina wanted to know. "I'd take him myself if I could manage a puppy."

"Exactly," Darren agreed. He sighed again. "I feel like such a failure now. I never wanted to get divorced once, not to mention twice. I think my problem is I just rush into things too quickly. I commit to something without thinking it through."

Sabrina eyed him. "I've never met a man who commits too easily." They were silent for a moment. "Darren," Sabrina finally ventured, "if you're telling me you're not yet ready for a relationship, I want you to know I'm fine with that. I'm the same way. I'm still grieving Liam. I don't want a boyfriend. I don't want to date. You're nice, but I'm not going to want to take it any further. Not for a while, anyway."

Darren nodded, sensing that there was more. Luna glanced up at Sabrina, concerned about a sudden shift in the woman's mood. "The worst part of it is," Sabrina continued quietly, "Liam's brother, Brad, completely cut me out of the loop. All of a sudden, I wasn't allowed to visit. Did you know that the hospitals don't give out any information about patients anymore? They call it HIPAA. They said they needed to protect the patient's privacy, because his brother didn't list me anywhere in the paperwork. And when I called and asked how they protect the privacy of someone who's dead, they just told me they couldn't help me. Like I was nobody.

"Losing Liam was like a punch in the gut. I tried searching online, but I didn't come across any funeral notices or anything. That's so like Brad. He keeps everything to himself, he controls information. He won't respond to my texts or talk to me—his phone would go to voicemail after one ring, so I know he blocked me. Now I have a new number and he doesn't know it, but I'm not going to try to reach him. I only knew about Luna being in the shelter because I ran into Brad when I was out to lunch with my boss the other day. I was surprised to see him because I had heard that he had moved to Germany, and I guess he has, but he comes back every once in a while. Anyway, we talked briefly, and he was pretty hostile. He showed me this email that he had received about Luna that the shelter had put her on deathwatch and was about to euthanize her."

Luna kept glancing up at the mentions of her name. Archie was too busy sniffing around the base of a lamppost to notice and then was yanked as the couple kept walking, the leashes pulling the dogs along.

"I think Brad told me about Luna more to see if he could hurt me than anything," Sabrina finished quietly.

"Did you do something to make him so angry, or is he just a world-class jerk?"

Sabrina gave a wry smile to this. "I'm trying to be a good person and see things from his point of view, but it's hard. I know he loved Liam. And the night of the accident, as far as Brad knew, Liam and I had broken up. I needed to take some time, get some perspective, but I knew in my heart that Liam and I were going to work things out. But I'm sure in Brad's mind, I dumped his brother, and a few days later, Liam's dead. You don't have to be a psychiatrist to see how I could become the target of Brad's rage. And Brad was protective of Liam, kind of weirdly jealous—he didn't think I was good enough for Liam, but I don't think Brad believed anybody was good enough.

"Anyway, I went to the shelter and, thankfully, Luna was not yet, well, you know, put down, and now she lives with me." She looked up at Darren. "So where does Archie live now, if you've moved out?"

"It's far from ideal," Darren admitted. "My ex-wife doesn't at all care about Archie, and her son, Theo, was supposed to be Archie's person. Theo is like a lot of people today—his attention span's very short. For two days, Archie was the center of his universe, and then it became a chore to feed and water the dog. I try to get over there as often as I can, but I'm very busy with work, and then I have to call ahead now and make arrangements, or there's trouble. My wife, sorry, ex-wife—I guess I should say soon-to-be ex-wife—won't let me come over unannounced even if I stay in the backyard. And when she does allow it, she always wants to extract some sort of concession from me. Theo triangulated us, I think, and that's my fault as well. You shouldn't agree to marry a woman who has a child without really understanding what it's like to be a stepparent. It's not exactly an easy job." Darren barked out a short laugh. Then he rubbed his head. "Tell you the truth, I'm looking for a new job, hope to hear something anytime now."

It was a wonderful day. The dogs frolicked in the dog park together off leash but came instantly when Sabrina called, and then they walked back. Another walk! Archie stared at Luna in jubilant disbelief at their good fortune, but Luna seemed unimpressed.

Stepping along next to Luna, Archie felt at peace with the fact that they were all going to be together now. Archie would sleep on a dog bed next to Luna or on a human bed with Sabrina and Liam and Darren.

Except that wasn't the case. They stopped at Darren's car, and Archie was let in. The vehicle had its windows down so that he could stick his head out and look in astonishment at Luna, who gazed back, also confused. They were together. Why was Luna not being taken for the same car ride?

Luna watched as Darren and Sabrina spoke to each other, standing very close but not touching. It was clear there was some affection there, and that made Luna happy, but it was also obvious from their stiff postures that neither one of them was going to take a step forward into an embrace.

Luna understood something then. Archie and the man lived in one place, and Luna and Sabrina lived here. The man would probably bring Archie over all the time, and that was wonderful. Perhaps next time he would bring Riggs as well, but these two people were not planning to live together in the same house.

Clearly, what they all needed was Liam.

31

Riggs was still buried inside the huge metal bin. He struggled, pinned, pulling painfully with his limbs, physically dragging his rear quarters from under the entrapping garbage. He was aware of nothing else but the panicked need to get *out*. He finally clawed his way to the surface of the trash and shook himself. He had no idea where he was. It was dark here, shadows stark and the sky visible only through a space at the very top of the pile of garbage. Now that he was no longer fighting to free himself, he was aware of the stresses and pulls on his body that indicated he was moving. It was like a car-ride dumpster, but one that tumbled him and threatened to crush him if he slipped back under the shifting piles.

There were succulent food smells all around, but he was too terrified to pursue them. The noise of the engine beat at his ears, and his claws dug into the plastic bags, tearing them. He was aware of the sensation of a shuddering stop, throwing him forward, followed by a tremendously loud, grinding roar. Then, unbelievably, the sky was blotted out overhead, and a dumpster full of trash rained down on him. He dodged, scrambling, trying to get away, and was hit solidly with a heavy bag. It hurt. Riggs yelped, then found himself back under the pile, back in darkness. He fought against it, trying to climb, feeling the horribly oppressive sensation of the trash compressing all around him, the garbage making creaking noises and becoming more and more dense, suffocating him, squeezing, harder and harder to dig through, a nightmare of advancing walls. Riggs desperately dug his way back to the air, gasping when he found it, feeling as the walls relaxed their assault just in time.

Then the dumpster was driving again, and this time, Riggs felt the car ride accelerating, gaining speed.

He could not escape through the hatch in the ceiling; the walls were too high. Riggs tried to make sense of what was happening. The air whistling past overhead indicated they were moving some distance, the smells changing with the terrain. But this wasn't a normal car ride—there was nothing joyous about it. In fact, this felt like mortal danger to Riggs. He panted, whimpering, wanting Liam to come pick him up. Riggs remembered Liam's arms encircling him and lifting him out of the bathtub, and that's what Riggs wanted now. He would even accept a bath if only Liam would hug him to his chest, hold him, and keep him safe from a world gone mad.

Everything swayed each time the dumpster slowed and turned. Then, finally, with a long squeal and vibration, Riggs felt the ride coming to an end.

Now what?

Riggs felt himself being lifted—no, not lifted, *tilted*—as one end of the dumpster rose up while the other end seemed to descend. With a huge rattle and bang, everything started to shift beneath his paws, and Riggs found himself helplessly pulled down with an avalanche of trash bags, tumbling and falling as everything disgorged from the back of the moving dumpster. Once again, Riggs was buried, but by now, he had developed a certain skill and was able, with a little struggle, to pull himself to a place where he could find sunshine. Panting, he stopped for a moment, then squeezed his body entirely out from under the pile.

This was a truck bed like Liam's, but the thing was huge. Riggs was in the middle of an enormous mountain of trash stacked up in an open bin. Toward the back, the bin was open, and two humans stood there, wearing hats and masks, poking at the trash with long poles.

"Hey!" somebody yelled. "There's a dog!"

Riggs scampered away, dodging between piles of trash, running for his life.

Several days had passed without Darren visiting Archie, and Archie was nearly berserk with it. He'd dug holes, he'd chewed sprinkler heads, he'd barked at birds, but mostly he paced, restless energy like a fever in his muscles. As the weather had turned cooler in the afternoons, the back slider was firmly shut, and that meant Archie couldn't really smell Theo and Mom inside.

All dogs ponder their purpose, their relationships to the people in their lives. For Archie, purpose came down to this: he was near people, but not really with them. He was off the chain, but still alone. That's what everyone, from Face to Theo, wanted for him.

Darren carried himself with an odd melancholy when he opened the back gate. Archie greeted him joyously, spinning at his feet, crying and pawing at him. Archie accepted the treat, of course, but the real source of his joy was this man in front of him. He could sense that Darren loved him, loved him the way Liam had loved him. Archie knew that in Darren he had found a new person. In a way, it made him feel a touch of guilt, because he knew Riggs would not approve, but he had not seen Riggs for a long time, and wasn't it Darren, after all, who had reunited him with Sabrina and Luna? Riggs would want Archie to be with Luna—Archie sensed that. Though it seemed as if some time had passed since Archie had seen Luna. That was something else Archie had deduced about humans—they decided that sometimes they would wait long periods before seeing dogs. Darren did this, and so did Sabrina.

"Let's walk, buddy," Darren suggested.

It was off pattern to turn the direction they now headed.

Normally, a day walk meant Farmers Market. Archie joyously marked the unfamiliar territory, glancing up when Darren spoke.

"Been so long since I've had a Friday off, I feel like I'm truant from school," Darren remarked with a chuckle. "You're a good dog, Archie."

Archie glanced at Darren, picking up a wistful tone in the man's voice. "So, life's going to change for you again, I'm afraid. Since I only lived here in Denver because of my soon-to-be-ex and Theo, I decided to put my résumé out there." He shrugged. "Turns out, I'm more valuable on the market than I'd thought. I took a new gig and I'm moving to California. I know most people go from there to here instead of the other way around, but I think it's going to be a great opportunity for me. But . . . Archie, I'm so sorry." Darren bent down and looked into Archie's eyes. "I can't take you with me, buddy."

Archie tried to lick some of the sadness away from Darren by touching his nose and then his tongue to the man's outstretched palm. Darren responded by petting the curly fur on Archie's head.

"I'm afraid I'm going to have to take you back to the shelter. Theo will fight it, but we both know he can't handle the responsibility of dog ownership. Or anything else, honestly, which is a big reason why his mom and I are splitting—she's made it clear he can do no wrong, and I can voice no opinions." Darren sighed. "You know, I think I've learned a lesson here, Archie. People's lives are complicated. There are often so many moving parts, and as much as we love dogs, maybe it's not meant for all of us to have one. Maybe you need to think twice before taking on the responsibility." Darren grinned. "I certainly applied that philosophy when it came to having kids. I've had two wives now who wanted to have babies with me, and both times, something told me I should wait and see, and sure enough, those were good decisions. Anyway, I'm going to take you back to the shelter this week. I called them and let them know, and they promised me they would find you a really good home, Archie. Everybody loves you. All right? You'll find a family with a boy who wants to be with you, who wants to feed you, who doesn't just sit and stare at his phone all day." Darren bit off the bitterness that had crept into his voice. "Well, I guess I had higher expectations of my relationship with Theo, but there you have it." His smile at Archie was sad. "I've really let you down, but I promise you, life's going to get better."

Riggs could not make sense of his new life in the place of mounds of trash. All day, loud rumbles shook the air, which was redolent with odors that spanned the range from delicious to repulsive. Riggs had managed to find a hidden place under some abandoned machinery and cowered from the humans there—something told him he should evade being seen. At night, small creatures joined Riggs in foraging for food—but no dogs. There was water. Riggs could survive here a long time.

But did he want to?

One day, he heard people yelling, "There's that dog!" and Riggs knew he was in trouble. The alarmed shouts from the people told him as much. He scrambled away, evading the grasping gloves of the masked and helmeted man nearest him. He remembered Smoke Man and the club. This felt like the same situation—humans who wanted to hurt him.

He spotted two men and a woman, wearing similar outfits and hats, running clumsily toward him in their heavy rubber boots. They were clapping their hands and yelling at him.

Riggs turned and dashed in the opposite direction. He did not get far. There was a long, tall fence here, and as Riggs desperately ran along it, the barrier seemed to go on and on without end. He could sense that the oddly garbed people were long behind him now, but where was he going? He came to a corner in the fence and faltered, panting with exertion and fear.

He turned back the way he came and saw a truck with a blinking light headed his way. The truck reminded him of Liam's vehicle—it was shaped the same—but when it slid to a halt, the man who stepped out wasn't Liam.

He had a pipe.

No, not a pipe. It was a pole with a loop at the end of it. Riggs backed up.

"Get him in the corner!" the man with the pole shouted.

Two more people came out of the truck and moved sideways, menacingly, their arms out as if to snag Riggs if he tried to get away. He backed up, uncertain, afraid.

"Hey, dog. Hey, dog," the woman called kindly. Her voice sounded nice, but after Smoke Man, Riggs didn't trust anyone he didn't already know. Riggs retreated, but he was in the corner of the fence. The fence was high—there was no escape. He lowered his head, looking for the spot where he would run between the people. There was no room; they were right there.

"That's it," the man with the pole called.

The people were edging forward warily, cutting him off, and Riggs knew with absolute dread that he was about to be caught.

32

Riggs desperately darted to one side and was blocked, and then darted to the other side and was blocked again, the people relentlessly closing in. He was a herder being herded, and that led to a sense of defeat. He feinted forward and froze as the woman made to cut him off. Surrounded, he cowered, cringing, and then saw the pole right there in front of his face and felt the noose slipping over his neck like a collar. He turned to run and then couldn't—the loop around his neck held him fast. He dodged and twisted, struggling, trying to escape that loop. Even when he turned and faced the pole and backed up, a method that had always worked in the past, there was no shaking this particular collar. It was tight and controlling. Despondently, Riggs realized he was captured.

The three people who approached him did so extremely cautiously, watching him.

"He seems friendly," one of the men observed. "Or at least not too unfriendly."

"Good dog. Good dog," the woman soothed.

Riggs wagged his tail stub tentatively. She seemed nice, and when she extended her hand, he was shocked to see a dog treat there on her open palm.

"Be careful," one of the men warned.

The woman kept her eyes on Riggs. They were kind eyes, they reminded him of Sabrina's, and when that treat came within reach, Riggs, distrusting but hungry, put his head slightly forward and delicately picked it up out of her flat hand.

"Good dog," the woman praised again.

"Well, all right," the man chuckled, sounding relieved. "That went easier than it usually does."

"Well, usually, they wander up here and aren't chauffeured," another man suggested.

The people laughed softly. It was not an unfriendly sound, and Riggs peered at them hopefully. Life had taught him that not everyone was like Liam and Sabrina. Ron was kind and gentle, but he didn't want to hold the dogs and didn't try to take them home. Smoke Man wanted to hurt them. Teme was loving but jammed Riggs into a cage. These people seemed a bit like Ron, and when another treat, then another, was offered by the woman, Riggs felt himself relaxing.

For a while, nothing happened. Then the woman produced a leash and led Riggs over to a post by the fence. The leash went under his four legs and around his chest in such a fashion that escape proved impossible—struggling just drew the straps tighter.

The air was cool and dry, and now that he was no longer trying to hide, Riggs could enjoy the heady, pungent fragrances flowing from the garbage being trucked in. He waited patiently. People who put dogs on ropes are in charge of dogs, he had learned, and though the terrain was unfamiliar, this situation was really no different from any other where he'd been leashed. If Liam had been there, he would have said, "Stay."

Riggs closed his eyes, thinking of Luna loyally frozen next to him, both doing Stay for Liam while Archie climbed on them and barked.

Eventually, the woman came over and picked Riggs up off the ground, unwrapping his leash as she did so. "Such a pretty dog. I wish I could take you home. I love Australian shepherds," the woman whispered softly.

"I always thought Aussies were larger," the man with her objected.

The woman shrugged. "I guess it's a small one. Miniature or something. Come on, little dog." The woman carried Riggs over to the back of a pickup truck and put Riggs there. They slammed the tailgate. The man went around to the front.

"All right. See you tomorrow. Do you know where the municipal shelter is?" the woman asked.

The man nodded. "Yeah, my daughter volunteers there sometimes. I'll let you know what they say. Maybe he's been microchipped."

"That'd be great," the woman responded.

The man climbed into the front, and the truck sagged a little. Riggs took stock of his surroundings. He'd never been for a car ride in the bed of Liam's truck but had always thought it would be fun.

Some old dirt and rags were all he could find to sniff on the floor, but succulent odors came to his nose as the truck began to move. Soon, it was bumping along, and Riggs had to extend his claws to keep from sliding around on the metal bed.

Where were they going? Riggs lifted his nose and tried to find a familiar scent line. There wasn't one really except the area where he and Budweiser lived, now at a considerable distance, still giving off a very distinctive, dense odor of people, foods, and machines.

The truck moved very quickly for some time. Then it slowed and stopped, and then it turned, and then it stopped. Riggs raised himself on his back legs. He didn't know where he was, but he knew something, which was that this person had put him into this truck for a car ride to an unknown destination, and that destination was unlikely to have any of the pack or Liam or Sabrina waiting for him. The next time the vehicle stopped, Riggs gathered himself and launched into the air, landing gracefully on the cement.

The man immediately opened the door to his truck and jumped out. "Hey, come!" he shouted. That was a word that Riggs not only knew but that stabbed him directly in his instinct to obey humans, and normally, he would have responded, except he had learned something from the smoky-smelling man and decided that, in this case, it would be acceptably good dog behavior if he ignored the command. Riggs turned and resolutely headed toward where his nose told him he would eventually find Budweiser, little Modelo, Ron, and everyone else.

Sabrina walked with Marcy down the sidewalk, Luna skipping gaily ahead of them on her leash.

"It's just that everything is different now, you know?" Marcy was saying. Apparently, they were still talking about the pregnancy, an event taking on epic proportions in their lives.

"The weather's gotten colder," Sabrina agreed. "Like, ten degrees in the past five minutes."

Marcy laughed. "No, I mean I have a human being growing inside of me, Sabrina."

"That's probably due to the pregnancy."

Marcy was quiet for a moment. "So, what's with you and the dog guy? Warren? You think he's going to ask you out?"

"Darren. Apparently, the prospect frightened him so much he's moving to California," Sabrina replied dryly. "He's a little old for me anyway."

"But you said there was an attraction."

"A little," Sabrina admitted. "We decided, though, that it wasn't really going anywhere. It can't—he's not even divorced, and he says it takes a long time when it's contested. This is before his new job and move to California was even a topic. And anyway, it's too soon after Liam."

Marcy sighed and stroked the nearly nonexistent bump that was her belly. "I just want for you what I have."

"I did think that's where you were headed." Sabrina looked at the sky. "I think it's going to rain."

"What do you want, sis?" Marcy probed, unwilling to let it go.

Sabrina was quiet for a moment. "I thought I knew. I thought I wanted to be like you, have your life. Get married, get pregnant. Be a mom to my own kids, instead of being a teacher to others'. Then I lost Liam, and I realized that's what I really want. He's what I want. I'd give anything to have it back the way it was."

Fat raindrops began smacking them, the impacts almost painful. Luna stared at Sabrina for an explanation. Marcy wrapped both hands around her belly as if the precipitation were threatening her pregnancy.

"It's hailing!" Sabrina announced as they turned and dashed back to Marcy's house. Luna ran out the leash, leading them in their flight when Sabrina dropped the nylon line. Luna didn't understand what they were doing, but she loved doing it.

Riggs registered the change in weather as something that seemed to happen frequently this time of year, when the summer matured and there were bugs in the air and the grasses underfoot were brittle and brown. It began with a rumbling and a shift in the wind that brought cooler temperatures and the smell of rain. Today, though, as Riggs plodded along, following his senses, trying to make his way back to the place where there were so many people and so many machines and so many food smells, the rain that came seemed harsh and abusive, almost judgmental, matching Riggs's mood. He felt like a bad dog.

When the sky darkened even further and the lashing rain became hard, penetrating balls of ice that bounced and hurt when they struck his fur, Riggs fled the punishment, eventually finding a sagging front porch to an old home with tires and metal parts in the yard. He hid under there, listening to the racket that these strange ice balls made as they stormed out of the sky and lashed the earth. He was tired and hungry again and took no comfort in the thought that when the weather finally let up, there would be puddles of fresh water to drink. He was alone and miserable. He missed Budweiser, he missed his dog pack, and of course, most of all, he missed Liam.

He settled down, momentarily shutting his eyes, and then he snapped them open, realizing that at some point during the assault from the sky, he had drifted off to sleep. It was now later in the day. The winds had died down, and the clouds had miraculously scudded away, leaving the air cleansed and rejuvenated, but Riggs still felt like a lost dog.

Walking along a busy road with the cars flying past, sounding angry as their tires hit wet spots that threw water high in the air, Riggs came across an animal. It was very large and lay with its glistening hooves perfectly still, black eyes open, antlers thrust into the dirt, mouth closed. Riggs stood over the huge creature, examining it for some time. He did not understand precisely, but this animal was not asleep. It was deep into a state of being different from sleep and would never wake up. It would never do anything again.

In a way, Riggs felt as if there was a message in this animal, a message of failure. The animal was lying here because something had happened to it and it had no more will to go on, and that was how Riggs felt himself.

Would he ever find Liam? Riggs was not so sure now. He was losing his sense of purpose.

But there was still sun in the sky and breath in his body. He was hungry but could still move, still press on. After one last, long look at the carcass at the side of the road, Riggs resumed his journey.

33

This time, when they encountered each other, it seemed as if Budweiser was looking as much for Riggs as Riggs was looking for him. There was something comforting to both of them that their size and coloring was so similar—they felt a link—not as strong as being littermates but, together, they were gradually forming a pack.

The two of them reunited on a street they had traveled before, one with a peculiar odor filtering out from the back of a place where people liked to eat and clink glasses and yell at one another. The distinctive smells remained in Riggs's nose even after he and Budweiser headed back to the area where they felt the safest, the mattress in the alcove behind the half-height wall.

Once in the safe place, Riggs withstood Budweiser's careful examination. Clearly, Riggs had acquired some new odors in the place with all the garbage. The smells were not unpleasant, though, and Budweiser was appreciative. They curled up together close enough to touch on the dead mattress behind the wall, letting the evening's darkness overtake the sky, content, at least for the moment.

The next morning, barely dawn, Ron's aging vehicle with its distinctive rattle called the dogs from all their hiding places. Budweiser and Riggs joined Modelo and Corona and a few other canines that Riggs recognized, confidently approaching Ron, who carried a sack filled with succulent odors.

"Hey there, dogs!" he greeted cheerfully. "Hi, Molson. Hey,

Budweiser. Hey, Modelo. How are you guys doing? Where's
Michelob gone?"

Ron handed out his treats. The dogs modeled their behavior
off one another and awaited their turns. They were all as hungry as Riggs—it was on their breaths as they crowded eagerly
forward—but they knew it would be wrong to lunge for a bigger
share. People don't like that; they want dogs to be orderly and po-
lite, so, to Riggs's approval, that's how they all behaved, waiting
patiently for their own share.

When a sharp yelp of pain split the air, all of the dogs turned
in unison and stared in the direction of that sudden, frightening
noise.

A dog had just been hurt.

Ron heard it, too, and turned and walked rapidly in the direction of that agonized squeal. The dogs followed Ron. They would
always follow Ron, not just because of the treats but because of
his kind hands, his gentle voice. They turned the corner and saw
a dog limping and whimpering but moving as quickly as it could,
running away. It was Michelob, a larger dog, Heineken-size but
not a Labrador mix, with Riggs's bobbed tail, black-and-white
coloring, and long, shaggy fur.

Michelob was hurt.

Down the street on the same sidewalk was Smoke Man, striding malevolently after the fleeing canine. The club was in his
hand.

"Hey, what'd you do to Michelob?" Ron yelled. "Are you
crazy?"

The man halted but was still scowling, his mouth moving silently and his eyes inflamed with anger. Ron marched toward
him, the dogs cowering, reluctantly following from the rear.

"Who are you? What are you doing here? You don't belong
here!" Ron shouted. The fury in his voice was raw and frightening to the dogs.

The stress of this human interaction was too much for the little dog named Modelo, who slunk off, belly low, desperate to get away.

Ron fearlessly walked right up to the man. "I asked you a question!" he shouted.

Ron was a small man, Riggs now realized, small in comparison to the smoky-smelling man, and much smaller in comparison to Liam.

Smoke Man took a step back, lifting his pipe menacingly, his meaning clear. Ron pulled up, out of range of the club, his hands on his hips. "Did you just hit the dog? Why would you do that?"

Riggs had never seen a face contort with such malice as Smoke Man's, who bared his teeth and shouted a hoarse, unintelligible cry before lunging forward and swinging the pipe sideways into Ron's ribs. Ron staggered, folded over, and sat on the ground, whooping in air.

Smoke Man raised his pipe for another blow.

Riggs reacted as one with the pack. He and Budweiser and the others leaped forward and went after the assailant, snarling and snapping, up on back legs as they ruthlessly closed their jaws on the man's flesh.

Riggs went after Smoke Man's legs and sank his teeth into the moldy-tasting cloth, finding muscle with his fangs. The man shrieked with pain and dropped the pipe, falling to his knees, bringing his face within range. Riggs and Budweiser lunged.

"No!" Ron yelled desperately. "Dogs! No!"

The word arrested them. Ron was displeased. They faltered and looked questioningly back at Ron.

"Hey, stop! What's happening?" a familiar voice called authoritatively. "Back off, dogs!"

The command was sharp even if the words weren't clear. The dogs turned and saw Officer Georgia running up. She and another man both had their hands on their belts. Riggs and Budweiser broke away, shaking themselves, frightened. The larger, black dog, Heineken, shrank, his belly to the ground.

"What's happening here?" Georgia demanded.

"Dogs bit me," Smoke Man hissed through clenched teeth. "They attacked me for no reason."

"Go, dogs," the man with Officer Georgia urged, waving his arms. Budweiser and Riggs took a few steps back, and Heineken rose to his feet and scrambled away.

Ron was shaking his head. "This guy was trying to kill the dogs with a lead pipe, and when I confronted him, he went after me. He got me in the side with that thing. The dogs saved me. He was going to hit my head with a pipe! I think he broke my ribs."

"Okay," Officer Georgia commanded firmly to Smoke Man. One hand was extended, and the other was still on her belt. "You, sir, don't touch that pipe. Understand me?" Officer Georgia strode up and kicked the pipe away with a sweep of her foot.

Her friend, the other man, bent over Ron. "Do you have any weapons on you, sir?" he asked.

Ron shook his head. "Of course not," he wheezed.

Officer Georgia stood over Smoke Man. In a loud voice, Georgia demanded, "Do you have any weapons except the pipe?"

Smoke Man shook his head. "I think I'm bleeding. My leg is bleeding," he muttered.

"I can feel where my rib's been shattered," Ron added through clenched teeth.

"Georgia, we need to call the sergeant, animal control, and an ambulance," her friend urged.

Georgia cocked her head. "Maybe not ACO," she countered. "I know these dogs. They're feral, but peaceful. Ron feeds them. If that's what he was doing and this asshole came up and started hitting the dogs, the dogs had every right to defend themselves and especially to defend Ron."

Georgia's friend was shaking his head. "Man, did you see what

I saw? The dogs were swarming this poor bastard. We got to call it in."

Georgia sighed.

"It's like it's a whole pack of man-eaters," her friend insisted.

"All right, I'll call ACO, but I don't think you're understanding the whole situation here. These are a bunch of smaller-than-average dogs, Brian, not a pack of wolves."

When loud cars came rolling up with people to help Ron and give him a ride, they also turned to take away Smoke Man, who now had his wrists behind him and seemed really angry. The remaining dogs took advantage of the activity to disperse.

Riggs stuck with Budweiser. Michelob's scent had vanished around the corner, and with it, the sense of pain in that leg that he held curled up off the ground.

Riggs felt like a bad dog. He had never bitten a person before and certainly had never tasted human blood. The anger and the yelling and the loud cars all shook him, and he paced and paced their short alleyway in front of the enclosure with the mattress. Riggs could not shake the sure sense that something really bad was about to happen.

That afternoon, it did. They were roused from a nap by the sound of yelling and cars and people talking animatedly. Budweiser and Riggs snuck out from behind the short wall and trotted out to see what was going on. They were somewhat shocked to see several people in padded clothing chasing down little Modelo. Michelob, his wounded leg held off the ground, was already in a cage in the back of one of the many trucks that were pulled up to the curb.

A woman was standing and talking at another man, who held a video camera on his shoulder—none of the dogs had the slightest idea what it was or what the people were doing. "A crackdown on the stray-dog problem in downtown Denver," she intoned.

A tall woman Riggs had never seen before noticed him standing with Budweiser, who was frozen in shock. She carried a stick with the loop at the end of it, and Riggs knew exactly what was happening.

It was a Farmers Market day. Archie knew this without really understanding how he knew. There was just something about the nature of the noises within the house, the cars on the street, the smells in the air.

When Darren appeared and put the leash into his collar, Archie could scarcely contain his excitement, even though Darren seemed oddly subdued. Archie twisted at the end of the leash, bounding up and in all directions, turning back to paw at Darren before lunging forward again. "You silly dog," Darren observed, the same odd sadness in his voice.

Farmers Market meant all the food smells and the happy people, a place where Archie would be tied to a pole and greeted by so many loving hands. The dog wagged at the thought of it.

Why did Darren seem so withdrawn? How could you not be happy on such a wonderful day?

At the Farmers Market, Archie drank in the food odors, the smell of the moving water a short distance away where he'd encountered Luna and had reunited with Sabrina, the bushes where he could curl up and stay cool. He took in the heat bouncing off the buildings nearby and the feel of the rough cement under his feet.

He was with Darren, his new person, at his favorite place. It was the best part of Archie's life.

"This is our last trip here, buddy," Darren told him wistfully. "I'm so sorry. I called the shelter, and I'm taking you back there the day after tomorrow."

Archie gazed up at Darren adoringly.

"You're a good dog, Archie. A wonderful dog. I mean it." Darren swallowed, his eyes moist. "Sometimes things don't always turn out as planned. But they'll find you a good home, Archie. I promise you. You'll have a better life than you do now, that's for sure."

Darren sighed. He was looking around, taking in the sights. Then he lowered his gaze to meet Archie's eyes. "Guess I'll go say goodbye to everyone here. I won't be long."

Archie watched Darren vanish into the crowd.

34

Riggs knew these people were not there to take them to be with Liam. Their movements were tense and deliberate, and those poles with their loops gave Riggs an instant memory of being snagged and led forcefully away. They were taking the dogs the way they had taken Ron.

Riggs thought of the cage with the thin bed and the room of barking dogs and Teme and the sadness in every dog's voice and intuited that might be where the captured dogs were headed now.

A couple of the people held succulent food in their gloved hands, waving it around and luring a few of the smaller dogs forward. These dogs were younger; they didn't know you can't always trust people.

But Riggs knew. He turned and ran and faltered only when he realized that Budweiser was not keeping pace. Budweiser seemed fascinated by those waving hands with the meaty treats. Riggs hesitated. He pictured going back for his friend, but the people were too close, those loops down low at dog level.

Riggs fled, running in a straight line down the sidewalk. He headed toward the water smells because they were there, powerful and present, but he had no sense of a destination beyond the river, just the sure conviction he needed to be away from where the people were rounding up dogs.

Riggs kept his head down. A woman called to him as he ran, and he ignored her. He would stay away from humans, even the friendly ones. Even the people with dogs. He didn't trust anyone but Sabrina and Liam.

Soon the water was right there in front of him, and he climbed down to the cement path along the moving stream. After a quick drink of water, he headed along that path, feeling the cool breeze on what would have normally been a wonderful day to be alive. But people were turning against dogs today, and Riggs was afraid. He needed to find Liam. Liam would make everything right.

At a turn in the stream, Riggs was lured up the banks toward some big buildings, where an astonishingly varied assortment of food smells drifted on the air—food and people and even some dogs.

He would keep his distance, but he wanted to see what all these food odors were about.

And then he detected another smell, one that he recognized. Archie.

Archie loved the children coming up to him at Farmers Market. They petted him and gave him little tastes of cookies and ice cream. He loved the friendly people and the dogs, many of whom stopped to wag and sniff.

With most dogs, large or small, Archie often wound up with his back in the dirt, waving his paws in the air, completely submissive. As he played, though, he kept an eye out for Darren, catching the scent of his person occasionally as Darren moved between stalls, purchasing small items, most of them completely uninteresting, inedible things like vegetables.

Archie sensed another dog approaching and turned, and astonishingly, there was Riggs, right in front of him. Riggs advanced cautiously, but Archie was ebullient, leaping in the air and twisting, getting tangled in his own leash, flopping on the ground, and then dancing up, trying to climb on top of Riggs, who seemed unusually grim, even for Riggs. The two dogs sniffed each other, Archie's tail thrashing the air with excitement.

For Riggs, this reunion was incomprehensible, but here was

Archie at the end of a leash, the collar loose around his neck, playing and dancing, the smell of a strange man in his fur. Had his pack mate been here the entire time since being led away by Teme, so long ago?

Riggs didn't understand much, but the sense of urgency from earlier still drove him, made him skittish and wary. He had just found the youngest member of the pack, but there was no time to play—they needed to *go*. There were people pursuing dogs and grabbing them and shoving them into cages on trucks, but Riggs had no way of communicating this to Archie.

He did know, though, that Archie looked to him to lead. He would follow Riggs, and they would run from people and be safe, except that Archie was tied to a pole. If only Luna were here, perhaps she would figure out how to help Archie off his leash.

"Hello, dogs!" a young girl called cheerfully. Archie turned to her and rolled in the dirt, and Riggs pulled back warily, keeping his distance, until she left. It smelled suspiciously as if she'd given Archie some beef jerky.

This was why they needed to escape. Archie would grant indiscriminate love to anyone who came along, and a treat just made him that much more seducible. All dogs were susceptible, Riggs knew. Budweiser was a dog of the streets, but even he had been enthralled when he smelled the delectable offerings of the people with the loops of rope on their poles.

Thinking of escape led Riggs to remembering being tied up in the backyard and how he was able to slip out of an entrapping leash by backing away from it. Riggs pondered how to communicate this to Archie, who was spinning and yiping joyously because a woman was strolling past with a tired dachshund. Archie knew how to celebrate, but right now, Riggs needed him to focus.

When Riggs moved forward, Archie was instantly cowed, understanding that Riggs had something on his mind other than play. Archie tried to dance out of the way, but Riggs kept pressing, cutting off Archie's movements laterally, forcing him to back up as the only option. Soon, Archie was at the end of his leash and could retreat no farther. Yet Riggs pressed on, his chest a barrier, darting his head back and forth as Archie made to lunge to the side to escape the other dog's relentless advance.

Now, Archie was almost being strangled by his collar. He was panicking, the rope taut to the pole, Riggs still pressing forward inexorably. The collar rode up against the back of Archie's skull, digging in, and Archie did what any dog would do and ducked, his face lowered so that it was pointing straight down the line, and that's when the collar slid over his head and into the dirt with a dull clank.

Archie shook himself vigorously, and if he was impressed or astounded by what had just happened, he gave no indication at all.

When Riggs turned and headed back toward the cement paths bracketing the moving water, Archie followed willingly. Archie remembered that it was in this area where Sabrina and Luna had been waiting for them and concluded that perhaps that was what was happening now. He'd always assumed that eventually Riggs would appear and guide him back to the pack.

The only hesitation Archie felt was when they began to descend the banks to the path along the river. That's when Archie turned, looking for Darren but not finding him or his scent easily. Darren was in among all those people and food smells somewhere, and Archie felt like a bad dog to be abandoning him, but Riggs was his leader, and Riggs wanted him to go forward, so that's what Archie did.

Soon the two of them were trotting briskly along the cement path. Riggs had no real destination in mind. He was looking for food because he was always looking for food. Budweiser had taught him that. They had plenty of water in this river. Downstream was layered with a higher density of people and food, but that was where dogs were being rounded up and put in cages, so Riggs led Archie in the other direction. His nose told him that soon he'd be encountering houses like the one Liam lived in, spaced farther apart and with few people tossing food on the sidewalk, but it would be safer.

When the cement path and the river passed under a busy, noisy road, the dogs climbed up a set of stairs cut into the banks. There were short, busy buildings here—the noises and odors were not nearly as packed together as they were where Budweiser lived, but people were cooking and eating in the small cluster of structures. Archie followed willingly.

They trotted up a driveway because Riggs sensed that in this narrow passageway between two buildings there were trash cans that might be successfully hunted. The first bin was much smaller than the one in which he had been trapped, but it smelled very promising. Archie panted, not really understanding but willing to go along.

Archie had never in his life scavenged for his own food. For him, this lark was fun and a great adventure, but he didn't know that Riggs was hunting. Archie was hoping that soon they would find the right people to take them in and give them proper dog dinners.

Riggs circled the bin, his nose up. This was easier in that it was shorter, but harder in that the bin was topped with a lid keeping the odors inside. There was some chicken in there, Riggs was sure. He paced back and forth while Archie watched in noncomprehension. Riggs wasn't sure how he was going to get in there, but the fragrant chicken had him fixated.

When a car pulled up and across the driveway at the far end, Riggs registered its arrival but didn't really react. When another vehicle turned slowly into the driveway at the near end and eased its way toward them, he was not alarmed, but he did alert. The chicken suddenly seemed less important.

When he saw that the car kept coming, Riggs suddenly froze, drawing his companion's curious look.

He and Archie, Riggs realized, were being hunted.

Two men slid out of the car at the end of the alley, and they were holding sticks with loops of rope at the end of them. That meant the only escape was away from them, directly at the approaching automobile. Riggs cautiously advanced toward the slow-moving car.

Archie held back, all his instincts screaming that it was wrong to walk directly toward a moving vehicle, but that's where Riggs was headed. Archie wrestled with conflicting impulses and finally followed Riggs, but tentatively, his ears back.

The car halted its advance. The doors popped open and people stepped out of either side, and they, too, had sticks with loops of rope at the ends of them. Riggs did not know who they were, but he knew he and Archie were trapped.

35

It was with a sense of dismal acceptance that Riggs watched Archie scamper happily up to the menacing people and accept the loop of rope around his neck as if it were the most unremarkable process in the world. But what other choice was there? Riggs sat and waited solemnly. There was no escape from this. When the noose tightened around his throat, he didn't wag his little stub, but he didn't resist. He followed the people and jumped into a cage in the back of their vehicle.

The dogs were caught.

The people were soft-talking, and Archie licked their fingers. Riggs curled up in a sullen ball and ignored them.

"You're both such good dogs!" the man not driving chirped at them.

Riggs understood what he was being told, but he did not feel like a good dog.

As the vehicle moved, the smells outside became more and more familiar, and once they were led out into a parking lot on short, heavy-roped leashes, Archie and Riggs both knew exactly where they were. The faint sound of the ever-present barking of the dogs in the big room came to their ears, as did the smells from the yard. This was where they had been taken by Brad after Liam failed to come home one day.

Riggs had lived with Mommy and Daddy and the wild boys, and he had lived on the streets with Budweiser and had been hungry all the time, but this place was worse, more lonely, more desperate.

Archie shook himself with optimism, perhaps believing Liam was waiting inside for them.

Riggs thought briefly of trying to escape but knew it would ultimately be futile to resist. The rope around his neck would tighten, and he would be dragged to a cage. That was just how these things were.

When they were led in, Mrs. Kepler and Teme seemed to be waiting for them.

"Oh my God!" Teme shrieked. She came around her counter and dropped to her knees and extended her hands. "Archie!"

Archie greeted Teme as if the two of them had been separated for an eternity. When Teme turned and extended her hand to Riggs, he reluctantly licked it. This was not home, but Riggs could tell that Teme did actually care about them both.

"Okay, this is so weird," Teme told Mrs. Kepler as she accepted papers from the people who had driven the dogs here. "Archie was supposed to be here as an owner's surrender Monday. I swear, I just talked to the man last week. He's moving. He's getting divorced."

Riggs watched the two men who had brought him to this place leave without a backward glance, then turned his attention to Teme, letting her pet him.

"I told him, 'Sure, bring Archie in.' Everybody loves Archie. We had a waiting list for him last time. But, Riggs, what are you doing here? Were you with Archie? Nobody told us you were coming!"

Mrs. Kepler was shaking her head. "I don't remember these dogs."

"Well, no. No reason you should," Teme agreed. "It was in July. There were three dogs. The owner was killed in a car crash, I think it was, and there was no family except a brother who lives somewhere overseas. You remember Luna, of course. The Jack Russell?"

She straightened, and Archie put a paw on her knee, and she smiled down at the dog and gave him a treat and then tossed one to Riggs. No fool, Riggs snatched it out of the air, though his eye was on the front door. Perhaps someone would soon be opening it, providing him an opportunity to dash outside. Once there, he knew he could elude the people who wanted to put in him a cage.

Mrs. Kepler frowned. "Well, all right, regardless of their history, we've got the dogs back, plus all the others animal control brought in today."

Archie wagged exuberantly when Mr. Reed came and spoke to them, though the man didn't seem to recognize them. He did put them in cages next to each other, though, so that Riggs could have the familiar scent of Archie on one side of him in his cage while Riggs curled up on the pad in the back of his own.

There were plenty of new dog smells in the room, plus two Riggs recognized: Budweiser and Modelo were both in cages, though Riggs hadn't spotted them when Mr. Reed led him to his enclosure. From the sense of what time it was in the day and the sounds of the dogs, Riggs knew that the people would be bringing dinner around soon. He would be fed, and he had water. Sometimes that was all a dog could hope for.

But fed or not, watered or not, it wasn't Liam's house, and their person wasn't here.

Riggs had found Archie. The pack was partially back together. But the most important aspect of what Riggs was supposed to accomplish, reuniting the dogs with Liam, had yet to take place. He thought of that failed animal lying in the dust by the side of the road, blank eyes open, and that's how Riggs felt lying on his pad, his eyes opened, his ears under assault from the barking dogs. He was like that motionless animal, a failure.

Teme and Mrs. Kepler huddled over Teme's computer. "See, I had him in the schedule," Teme told Mrs. Kepler. "Archie was supposed to be here Monday at ten o'clock."

"But he was brought in by animal control."

"I guess he got loose somehow," Teme speculated. "What a weird coincidence."

"All right. Well, we should call the man, I suppose," Mrs. Kepler observed.

"Really? I mean, do we think he'll come down now, pay the fine, pick up Archie, then surrender him all over again in two days?"

Mrs. Kepler slowly shook her head. "You make a good point. All right. Let's just send him an email."

"You know who I think we should call, though?" Teme continued.

"Who?"

"We were just talking about Luna. She was one of three dogs from the same place. When we adopted her out, we updated her file." Teme tapped the computer screen with a fingernail. "See? Sabrina Morgan."

Brad had fallen so soundly asleep he wasn't even aware that he was sprawled in a rather uncomfortable chair, his mouth open and his head back as if he were visiting the dentist, so it was a shock when a voice in the room pierced his unconsciousness and jolted him awake.

"What are you doing here?" the voice challenged.

Brad blinked and looked around to get his bearings. *Oh yes*. It all came back to him. The hospital sounds—murmurs and beeps. He snapped his eyes to Liam's.

Liam was staring at him. It had been *his* question that had awakened Brad. Brad leaped out of his chair. "Did you just say something?" he demanded.

Liam nodded slowly, his confusion strong on his face. "What's going on?"

"Oh." For a moment, Brad was so overwhelmed, it was all he

could do to stand there in front of his brother without breaking down. He hastily wiped his eyes and took the few steps to his brother's bedside. "You've been pretty incoherent since you started waking up, brother. Do you remember anything?"

Liam shook his head. The effort seemed to be painful. "No, I . . ." He frowned, staring off into the distance. "Not really," he finally admitted. "How long have I been asleep?"

"Asleep," Brad repeated disbelievingly. He sighed wearily. He backed up and went over to the chair and dragged it up so that he could sit next to his brother. "I have so much to tell you, Liam. It's going to be a little difficult to explain. Let me know if I'm going too fast. Okay, buddy?" Brad reached out and touched Liam's arm. Then he withdrew his hand, marveling that for so long that arm had felt slack and even dead, and now it responded to the fingertips on it by tensing slightly. Liam was alive. "So, do you remember that you were in a car accident?"

"A car accident?" Liam repeated, pondering. "No. A car?"

"Well, your truck."

"Oh. Is it okay?"

Brad had to laugh at that. "Your truck? Man, your truck has been sent to the crusher or whatever they do with something so mangled. You were knocked into a coma."

Liam clearly didn't believe this part.

"No, seriously, you've been out." Brad shook his head. "I don't even know how to say this, brother, but your accident was June 20. It's August 24. More than sixty days, bro."

Liam's face went slack with shock. "How can that be?" he responded in a small, quiet voice.

"Well, I got to say, that's the big question." Brad pointed emphatically at Liam. "They told me you weren't going to make it. They wanted to *remove your feeding tube.* I said no, that wasn't going to happen as long as I was in charge. You've just kind of been in the twilight zone all summer." Brad's lips twisted bitterly at the memory. "Your first doctor actually told me you were 'taking up a bed.' Here, in a facility dedicated to comatose patients. Then this new doc came on board, and she was wonderful. She was the first person to tell me you might recover. It turned out everyone had written you off, and no one thought to check your calcium levels. Once they fixed that, you started waking up, and they called me to come home. Anyway. Okay."

Brad waited patiently for Liam to process this before continuing, "It was about a week ago you started babbling, looking around, flexing your arms. I was over in Frankfurt. I got on the first plane back. Man, when I walked in, there didn't seem to be any change, but then I saw what they were talking about. Every once in a long while, you'd suddenly be twitching and muttering, and sometimes your eyes would look right at me, but they didn't see anything. It was like watching you come back from the dead, man."

"I—"

"I know you probably have a lot of questions," Brad interrupted. "Okay, so you didn't die, and that's the most important news of all. I don't know if you even remember, but we signed power of attorneys for each other, and so I've been handling all your medical decisions. I moved your stuff into storage and closed on your house with those people from California. They were sort of strange, but the check cleared. Oh, and I've kind of been running your crew. Well, not really. You always tell me I don't even know which end of the hammer to hold, but that house you bought, I went ahead and closed on it and everything. I've been paying your guys to keep working."

"Okay," Liam mused slowly. "Wow." He was silent for a full minute, shaking his head a little in disbelief. Then he looked up and met Brad's eyes. "How are my dogs?"

36

Whew, that question. Brad's discomfort was obvious, and he knew it, so he tried to feign a different reason for his facial expression. "Would you just let me tell everything in order? I don't want to get it confused. Anyway, like I was saying, the house is basically done. I mean, I had to make the call on some stuff that you didn't specify, some underlay for the floor, but you'd pretty much mapped the whole thing out, so we just followed your blueprint, literally. I drove by there on the way in this morning, and the driveway's even paved. You've got a new house, brother."

Liam looked bemused, as if Brad had lapsed into a foreign language.

"So, yes, your truck was totaled." Brad nodded. "I filed the claim, deposited the money in your account. I've been just pretty much overseas working, but, you know, with email and electronic banking, I've been able to stay on top of everything. When I came back to the States, I stopped in to see you, and every time, I had a conversation with the doctors about the so-called futility of keeping you going. I don't know, maybe they wanted to rent the room out for a higher rate or something." Brad smiled at his lame joke, but Liam was still wearing that bewildered expression. It made Brad sick to see it. Not for the first time, he tried to imagine all this from Liam's perspective—you wake up in a hospital, months have passed, everything's different.

"I guess . . ." Liam whispered, then stopped himself.

Brad nodded encouragingly for Liam to go on.

"I guess I'm scared what you're going to tell me about my three dogs."

Brad looked away, then nodded and looked back, steeling himself. All right, then. "Okay, this is going to be hard to hear, but you were supposed to die. Remember that. I couldn't take the dogs. I was going to Germany, remember? I have a job over there now." Brad nodded emphatically. "You told me I should take it. You practically demanded I take it. Do you remember that?"

"So they're . . . gone?"

"I took them to a shelter that promised to find them new families," Brad equivocated, thinking about the email concerning Luna. "Happy families, Liam."

Liam put a hand to his face and, to Brad's dismay, wept. For a long time, that was the loudest sound in the room. Brad didn't say anything, couldn't say anything, for several minutes. He was forced to just sit there and watch his brother's grief. "I didn't have a choice, Liam," Brad finally pleaded. "If I didn't get on that plane, I would have lost the job. You told me you'd kill me if I didn't go to Germany, but that meant there was no time to try to figure out a long-term plan."

Liam processed this. "Couldn't Sabrina—" he began to venture.

"Sabrina?" Brad interrupted with a snort, seeming glad to have a target for his anger. "No. She was living in a house full of cats. Said there was no way she could help. She turned her back on your dogs, man. She flaked. That's just what she does."

Liam stared inward and then met Brad's eyes. "So what are you telling me about Sabrina?"

Brad sucked in a breath. Again, the perspective: for Liam, this was happening immediately after leaving Marcy's house. He didn't have any idea what had been going on since June. "This is going to be really hard to hear, brother. Sabrina's with somebody else now. I saw her out with him. Look, everyone probably told her to move on. You guys had broken up, after all. And then with the accident, no one thought you were going to come out of the coma."

"I was going to propose," Liam protested, his voice a croak. He covered his eyes again, racked with silent sobs.

Brad stood there, his teeth clenched in pain, watching his brother go through it, second-guessing his every decision.

Sabrina walked in the shelter door with Luna on the leash. She looked around the reception area with disbelief on her face—this whole thing seemed unreal.

Teme sprang up. "I knew you'd come!" She moved around the counter and surprised Sabrina by embracing her.

Sabrina fumbled a hug back.

"Oh, thank you, thank you for coming," Teme gushed.

"I've been so worried. It's really Archie and Riggs?"

Teme nodded. "We verified it with the chip. We called the number, of course, but it's been disconnected. I guess that was your boyfriend's phone. I mean . . ." Teme trailed off, looking for a hint.

"Yes, he was killed in a car accident," Sabrina confirmed. The words shocked her to say them out loud, as they always did, but she had to get used to it.

"We called the people in the file, the new owners. As I said, Archie's adoptive family is going through a . . . crisis. The parents are getting a divorce, and the husband is moving to California."

"Darren," Sabrina agreed with a nod. "I know him, a little."

"Oh! Did he tell you he was surrendering Archie back to us?"

Sabrina shook her head. "We aren't really that close. We walked the dogs together a few times, that's all. I did know about the divorce, and from what I understand, the boy wasn't that into taking care of the dog."

"Right, that's what he told us," Teme agreed.

"And what about the family that adopted Riggs?"

Teme's gaze became troubled. "I spoke to the husband there,

and it was a different story. Turns out, he never really wanted Riggs, just did it, he said, so that his wife would be happy. He said Riggs ran away constantly and was always biting his kids."

"Riggs?" Sabrina objected sharply. "That doesn't sound like him at all."

Teme shrugged. "I didn't get a good vibe off the guy."

Sabrina was silent for a moment. "So, I guess, what should we do?"

"It depends on what you want to do."

Sabrina gave her a helpless look. "Can I be honest? I mean, I have a condo with a dog park area, and I take Luna to work with me when I'm not working from home, but there's no way I could take all three dogs, so I don't know what I can do."

"Well, I know a dog walker who's really good, and he could come over and walk your dogs for you while you're at work," Teme replied enthusiastically. "Would that help?"

Sabrina smiled, amused. "You're like everyone I've ever met in rescue," she noted. "Always trying to find homes for the animals."

"Good homes, of course," Teme agreed simply. "That's not just my job, it's my passion. Rescue is like a giant machine that needs to keep moving at top speed. You heard about the roundup of the stray dogs from downtown? One of them—she'd been hit with something, and her leg was broken—had a chip, and her owners were here in like five hours. And another one, she and Riggs were like buddies when they were both out in the yard together, was a full-blooded papillon. We put her photo up and got maybe thirty queries in one hour. But Riggs and Archie? They're a pack. I hate to break up packs. They found their way back to each other on the streets! And I know you'll be a good home for your dogs, and they are kind of your dogs, aren't they? You couldn't take them before, but your situation's changed. It's no longer impossible. Maybe just try it? See how it goes?"

Sabrina looked dazed. "I suppose," she finally murmured. She looked down at Luna, who was cowering away from the noise behind the door that she knew led back to the cages. "It's okay, Luna," Sabrina soothed. She knelt and picked up the little dog, cuddling her to her chest. "It's okay. We're not going back there."

"Okay?" Teme pressed.

Sabrina's expression was mournful. "When Liam had his accident, we'd been broken up, but neither of us really liked life without the other. I was living with my sister and my job situation was impossible, and then a drunk driver crossed into his lane and took away the man I loved. I had to make the hardest decisions right then, right when I wasn't in a position to do so. But I can't tell you how many nights I fell asleep crying over the fact that I couldn't manage to hold on to the dogs. I was just overwhelmed at the time. So having Luna back is a miracle. I'll . . . Yes. I'll take them home with me." Sabrina laughed softly. "I have no idea how it's going to work, but I'll take Riggs and Archie. And also the phone number of that dog walker."

Teme smiled. "I'll be right back."

Luna watched in relief as Teme went by herself through that door, reacting visibly to the smells and sounds as it opened.

Liam, with the help of Brad on one side and an exceptionally strongnurse on the other, was now sitting up in the bed. His stare was full of disbelief as he processed the physical sensations of having been asleep for a summer.

"How do you feel?" Brad asked solicitously.

Liam shook his head. "I feel like I've never been so exhausted in my life. I can barely lift my own arms."

"Right. They said that's what would happen, but you're going to be fine. I'm going to stay with you and help you get better. I've already arranged for physical therapy to come out to the house daily once you're released. You're going to get back into shape in no time, I promise." Brad grinned. "I can't wait for you to see the house. It turned out great."

"Do you have my phone?" Liam asked.

Brad pursed his lips and then shook his head. "No. You were supposed to die, remember? I think your phone is somewhere in a junkyard in what's left of your truck. I shut off the account because I didn't see any sense in keeping it active. We'll get a new one. Don't worry."

"Sabrina's number's in there. My phone, I mean. It's not like I've got it memorized. I just punch Sabrina's name and connect."

"Yeah, okay," Brad muttered. He looked away and then back. "Let's just get you in shape enough to check out and get home."

"Do you know how to reach her?"

"Sabrina? No, I told you, I saw her on a date with her boyfriend. It's not like we communicate."

Liam's eyes flickered a bit at the word *boyfriend.*

"The doctors are going to be here soon and check you out for themselves—they probably don't believe you're conscious. When they give you a clean bill of health, you're going to inpatient rehab, and as soon as you can take care of yourself, we're out of here." Brad's grin trembled. "I know to you this is like a bad nap, but I really thought I'd lost you, brother."

Liam stared down at his hands, pondering this, and then lifted his eyes. "How am I going to reach Sabrina, Brad?"

37

Riggs sprang to his feet when Teme approached. Somehow, he knew that her entry into the large enclosure had something to do with him. Archie, watching Riggs, did the same thing, gazing at his pack mate expectantly.

Archie dashed to the gate when Teme reached down to let him out first. The loop slipped over his head, and he wagged and tried to jump up on Teme to play. Riggs watched disapprovingly. Dogs were not supposed to jump up on people. When Teme opened his own cage door, Riggs slid out silently and waited patiently, as a lesson to Archie, for that loop to slide over his own head.

Now what?

As Teme's hands touched Riggs's head, he jolted in surprise and sniffed wildly at her kind fingers. Unmistakably, among all the dog odors fresh and stale, a new one was painted on her skin, and Riggs knew whose it was.

Luna's.

Archie picked up on Riggs's excitement and was galvanized, yawning and panting and twirling. Riggs was disgusted that almost immediately their two leashes were a tangle.

Teme laughed. "Oh, Archie, you are such a goof dog."

Riggs waited impatiently for Teme to untwist the leashes. Archie licked her hand. Riggs held his nose up, trying to find Luna in this place of loud dogs. Budweiser and Heineken and Modelo were gone now, and Michelob had barely arrived before he was taken away by a man whom Riggs instantly intuited was Michelob's person. Luna was definitely not here either—he couldn't lift her scent from the riot of odors, save for the strong and insistent fragrances on Teme's hands.

Riggs strained on the leash when they were finally on the move, and Archie strained because Riggs was straining. They passed cages with dogs, and Archie wanted to stop and socialize, but Riggs was determined to keep moving and Archie didn't want to challenge him.

The big door opened, and Luna and Sabrina were waiting on the other side.

Archie, of course, was all over Sabrina, crying and licking and whirling, but Riggs focused on Luna. The two dogs were nose-to-nose, wagging, and then Riggs climbed up on top of the Jack Russell, needing to press against her. She nibbled gently at his neck, and there was so much love in the gesture, Riggs whimpered.

Sabrina was crying. Clutching Archie with one arm, she groped for Riggs, and all three dogs came into her embrace.

Teme smiled, tears flowing unashamedly. "Oh," she breathed. "This is why I do this."

Luna pressed up against her person, her dog pack surrounding her, finally at peace.

"What do I need to do? I mean, is there paperwork?"

Teme glanced around as if looking for Mrs. Kepler. "Just go," she urged. "I'll take care of everything."

Sabrina wiped her eyes and stood, smiling down at the dogs, who sat attentively at her feet as if awaiting orders. "You dogs want to go home?" she asked softly.

Liam struggled to get out of Brad's car, waving off the proffered arm. "I can do this," he chided irritably.

Brad raised innocent hands. "Whatever you say, boss."

Finally standing upright, Liam launched himself up the side-walk, noting the inlaid flagstone with approval. His cane had three prongs at the bottom for stability, and he seemed impatient with himself that he needed it. He glanced around. "Where is everybody?"

"Like I said, they're pretty much done. I don't think they're working much on anything new, though—construction's sort of dried up right now. When I told them you were coming out of it, I think part of their relief was the idea you'd have jobs for them."

"That's going to take some time," Liam observed dourly.

"Sure." Brad was cheerful, eager for Liam to see inside.

Liam panted and stopped halfway up the front steps, getting a grip on himself and pushing Brad's helpful hand away when it was automatically extended. "I can do this," Liam repeated.

Inside the house, they toured from room to room. Liam saw that the engineered wood flooring was flawlessly placed, and the appliances, knobs, and faucets were all the ones he'd selected. Normally, as a house was being remodeled, he was on hand for every stage, but this was evolution from naked studs to finished home in what felt like one giant step.

In one of the bedrooms, a flat glass panel was affixed to the wall. "What's that thing?" Liam asked.

"It's an electromagnetically charged weight lifting station," Brad responded. "It's called a Tonal, and you can set the weight as high or low as you want. It's where you're going to do all your strength exercises when you're ready. Meanwhile, the physical therapist comes six days a week, and you'll be doing pretty much nothing but sit-ups and push-ups all day long. It'll be like the marines."

"Okay. Neither one of us have ever been in the marines," Liam responded dryly. "I don't think you know what you're talking about."

"Yes, I mean we could've been marines," Brad speculated.

"They probably were intimidated. Didn't want us showing them up with our physical prowess."

"I'm sure that's it."

The house seemed empty to Liam, and he realized it was because as it was being built, he pictured his dogs following him around, lying at his feet, playing in the backyard. Of course, Sabrina would come home from school, and he would have dinner with her, and they'd talk about their days and their plans.

Sabrina's touch was everywhere. The kitchen was lifted from one featured in a magazine that she had declared "perfect." He'd grabbed that magazine when she wasn't looking, and it was the model for what he'd had built. The flooring was precisely what Sabrina had picked out as her favorite, and the bathtub was a model she'd envied at her sister's house. In most ways, this was Sabrina's house more than Liam's.

Except that Sabrina was gone, and so were the dogs. Maybe moving in here wasn't such a good idea now. Did he really want to rattle around this empty place by himself?

Brad observed Liam staring blankly at a wall and guessed what was happening. "This is going to be really rough, isn't it?" Brad murmured softly. "There's no easy way to do this."

Liam gave him a sad smile. "No," he agreed. "There's no easy way to do this."

Chason was a tall, thin man with an easy grin. He was in his early twenties and had settled on a career in dog walking as the best use of his college degree. He liked to be paid in cash. His grin was so relaxed and easy it made Sabrina envious—when you were a dog walker, you probably never sat up until two in the morning trying to finish a report for finance people.

Chason was often escorted by more than one dog when he knocked on Sabrina's door. Her three dogs went with him the first day as if being led to prison but came back so happy Sabrina decided to give it time, and by the end of the first week, they would assemble at the door, impatient for Chason's arrival.

The next week, Sabrina trusted him enough to give him the access code to her front door. She had cameras positioned in the entryway and both in and out of the condo, so she would know if he was a burglar, but all he was interested in when he came inside was loving the dogs, giving them treats, and walking them down the sidewalk to his big vehicle. It was a three-bench van, and every dog sat in the same seat every day as if it were a school bus and they had all been assigned where to sit.

Luna liked to position herself with her face near the window, while Archie preferred the very back, where he was usually by himself and could run back and forth, patrolling for squirrels and dogs out each window. Riggs would've wanted the front seat, but often there was a large bulldog sitting there who Riggs decided was not going to be dislodged. It made Sabrina smile to see what good dogs they were being and how happy they were to be with their school bus pals. Then they would drive away, vanishing from Sabrina's view through the cameras, headed to the dog park and other walks.

From the looks of him, Chason spent pretty much his whole day walking. He would probably live to be two hundred years old.

For a time, all was well. Riggs enjoyed walking with the dogs and the ride with Chason to the dog park. He loved Sabrina and was happy to climb up on her bed, find room between the two other dogs, and lie down with a sigh every night, but after several days, he began to feel restless. Before, he'd had a mission, a purpose, and that was to find the pack and find Liam and Sabrina, and he had accomplished most of those things, albeit much of it seemingly by accident. Yet the job was incomplete. They were all together except Liam. Where was he?

Compelled to find an answer to that question, Riggs began going and waiting expectantly by the front door. Surely, any day now, he would hear the sound of Liam's work boots striding up the steps and feel the change in the room when Liam entered.

"Oh, Riggs," Sabrina murmured softly. She went over and knelt by the dog, who glanced at her but then returned his stare to the front door. Sabrina put her arms around him and buried her face in his soft fur. "I'm so, so sorry, Riggs. I know this must make no sense to you."

Luna wasn't precisely jealous of this interaction, but she didn't like the fact that Riggs was getting all the attention, so she clicked her way across the tile floor of the entryway and shoved her nose up so that she, too, could enjoy Sabrina's love. Irritatingly, this drew Archie's attention, and he came galumphing across the floor and crashed into all of them, knocking Sabrina sprawling.

Riggs had to restrain himself from snapping at the younger dog. There had been something happening between him and Sabrina that Riggs was trying to process, and Archie, by barreling into the middle of it, had spoiled the mood.

Riggs stared up at Sabrina, and her return look was full of sympathy, but, as with all humans, her mind was unreadable.

38

Brad grilled hamburgers for dinner and served beer with them. Liam realized that it had been a long time since he had brought a beer bottle to his lips—not just because of how long he'd been doing physical rehab in the hospital but in real terms—he hadn't been going to the bar much in his coma. It tasted good.

Brad went about the meal preparations with a tense air about him, though, and Liam watched him warily. Brad would get like this—quiet, moody, and pensive—usually before announcing something Liam wasn't going to like, so Liam waited patiently for his brother to get to it.

The burgers were good, a little overdone, but that's how Brad cooked. Liam always went the other way, and Brad often wound up popping whatever it was into the microwave for twenty seconds or so to bring things up to the temperature he preferred. They were mostly silent while Liam waited for Brad to say whatever it was he was going to say. The longer he took, Liam figured, the worse it was.

"I've reached the decision," Brad announced. His expression was grim. Liam nodded for him to go on. "I'm going to move back—I mean, to the United States. Quit the gig in Germany."

"No, you're not," Liam responded calmly. "You said you've used up all your special leave and it's time to go back. So go back."

"Look, I knew you'd object, but it's obvious I need to be here to take care of you," Brad explained.

"No, you don't, Brad. Honestly, I've got this. I'm getting

stronger every day. It feels like I've already been in boot camp for a year." Liam laughed.

"I don't want to leave you alone," Brad insisted. "The way you mope around the place, it's like you're depressed."

"I'm not depressed, I'm in pain. Physical therapy *hurts*. Every muscle I've got is sore, even the ones I didn't know I had."

"I know you, Liam. You need to be around people. This"— Brad gestured to the walls—"is going to feel like prison to you once I'm gone."

"Prison with two-hour visits from a physical therapy sadist," Liam suggested lightly. Then his expression turned serious. "I won't be alone, Brad. I've been looking online for houses to flip, and I'm going to put out my feelers for home remodeling jobs. Something will come up, and then I'll be with my crew."

Brad looked away unhappily, not persuaded.

"Look, I so appreciate everything you've done for me. Not just since the accident but my whole life. When our parents left, you were my rock. You know how much that meant to me? I so looked up to you, and when you said you'd handle everything, I figured it was handled. You were a kid, but you took on adult responsibilities. I wouldn't be who I am if it weren't for you, brother. I owe you everything."

Liam's voice had hoarsened. "And I get how it must have been when I had my accident. They said I was going to die and they wanted to pull out the feeding tube, and you told them to go to hell. You stayed on top of everything. I mean, I don't know how you did it without being here to supervise, but the house is great, exactly as I envisioned it. You did that, Brad. You continue to be the best big brother in the world."

Brad shrugged. "You've got a good crew. They'd call me with a question, and I'd say, 'Well, whatever you think is best,' and that's it."

"All right," Liam agreed with a chuckle. They were quiet for a while. "I would be really angry at you if you left this job, Brad. You've worked so hard to get this contract, and it's your dream. Are you sure you're not just running from some fräulein who's got her hooks into you?"

Brad shook his head. "No. I mean, well, no."

That made Liam laugh. They were quiet for a moment. "Part of being the momma bear is shoving the baby bears out of the cave and telling them to go take care of themselves."

"Where'd you hear that?" Brad snorted. "Bears? Come on."

"Okay, birds, then. Snakes. I don't care. The point is, you took over as my parent and you did a good job. And when I needed you, you were there for me. And I'll always need you, but I don't need you *here*. Okay? You're a phone call and a plane away if something happens. Go."

Brad sighed. "I picture you walking around in this place by yourself, and it makes me sort of sick to my stomach."

"Then stop picturing it. I won't be alone for long, I promise."

"Yeah." Brad grinned. "You always were the handsome one. I'd bring home a date, and the next thing I knew, she'd be asking me for your phone number."

"That never happened."

"It happened once," Brad countered.

They were both grinning, but then Liam's smile faded.

"Well, speaking of that, I called Sabrina's school today."

Brad instantly reacted, scowling. "Why would you do that? I told you she's with somebody else now."

"Because, Brad, I need to talk to her. Dude, I was going to propose to that woman. Anyway"—Liam looked sad and shook his head—"she's not there anymore. She quit, like, right after my accident, and the only email I had for her is the one at the school. That's why I called. It bounced. She's pretty good at keeping herself unsearchable on the Web. I don't have her phone number, because you shut off my phone, and my cloud account, when I signed back on, didn't retain any information. Guess that's what happens when your brother notifies the phone company you're deceased."

Brad just gave him a weary look. "Okay, I made a mistake. I'm sorry. But I don't think calling her is a good idea. You need to move on with your life, man. Look, you were supposed to die in that hospital room, but you didn't. You were not supposed to come out of the coma, but you did. And now you're here, and now you're getting your strength back, and the two of us—"

"Not the two of us, Brad," Liam interrupted impatiently. "You said it yourself—you don't know anything about construction. You just told people to do what they thought best."

"Isn't that kind of what you do?" Brad challenged. They grinned at each other.

"Fair enough," Liam agreed, "but still, I expect you to get back on that plane, get back to Germany, and conquer Europe. Meanwhile, I need to get my business going, and I've got the physical therapist coming every single day, it seems."

"Except Sundays," Brad interjected.

"Except Sundays. I really do appreciate everything you've done for me, but it's time to let me fully recover, and that means being on my own again."

Brad didn't say anything, but Liam knew his brother and knew he'd soon be on a plane back to Germany.

The dog park was a wonderful place. Riggs tolerated the chaotic scramble of dogs chasing one another because the people would sit on picnic tables and talk and be unbothered by it. If they had wanted the dogs to be corralled into a corner of the dog park, Riggs would've been up to the task, but clearly, it didn't bother anybody.

As it was, he liked to patrol the perimeter, keeping an eye on things. Luna stuck pretty close to Chason but then, occasionally, would race around, jumping on a rubber ring that she had found somewhere that she seemed to enjoy torturing. Archie was the most social. He was always wrestling with some dog or another or was the member of a melee running together with no obvious destination in mind, swerving and stopping and tumbling endlessly.

Every so often, the double gates would clang as someone came into or exited the enclosure. Riggs had been to that gate. He had observed the mechanism. A person would open the outer gate with a dog, come in, close the outer gate, walk across a small fenced-in area, and open the inner gate, usually stooping at that point to unleash the incoming dog. There was no way to work the latch, Luna-style, to escape.

Even if it were possible, Riggs couldn't imagine what would happen even if he managed to pop the latch on the inner gate. It wasn't like the outer gate would open as well. It felt hopeless, but more and more, that's what Riggs fixated on. Not so much those gates but somehow, at some point, getting out of the dog park and finding his way back to Liam. That was the final step in what Riggs had set out to accomplish at the beginning of the summer.

The nights were cooler now, reminding Riggs that there would be snow soon. Occasionally, Riggs thought of Budweiser and Modelo and the other dogs, wondering what had happened to them. Were they out of the shelter and back on the streets? How would they survive in the winter when everything would be coated with snow?

Riggs, at one point on his patrol, watched a large, blocky-headed black Labrador trying desperately to get at a tennis ball that lay on just the other side of the fence. Here, they were situated behind an enormous tree, so the dog's owner couldn't see that the Labrador was digging frantically at the soil under the fencing. The dog's name was Henry. His owner was a smiling older man who liked to sit at the picnic table and talk to a thin woman named Audrey, who belonged to a dog named Chance. Audrey would sit and listen and nod while Henry's owner talked.

Henry was a big dog. His head was huge. For him to squirm under the fence would take quite some excavating. Riggs watched as the dog clawed at the dirt, sending it flying behind him. It was amazing how much earth Henry was able to dislodge, but it was futile. Despite all his efforts, he was not able to get all the way to the ball. Riggs watched quietly as Henry stuck his head under, but that was not enough. He clawed, he dug, he even cried a little. Dogs like these, Riggs knew from experience, would become so fixated on a ball that they could think of nothing else. Riggs felt that balls were useful and fun when a person threw them, but when one was just lying around, it was of little value.

Henry was simply too big for his hole.

But Riggs was much smaller.

39

By unstated mutual agreement, Liam had retaken the kitchen. Brad set the table and accepted his eggs with a grateful smile.

"Time's your flight tomorrow night?" Liam asked his brother.

"Nine thirty."

"Don't know how you sleep on airplanes."

Brad shrugged, chewing.

Liam reached for his coffee and gazed at his brother over the top of it. "Thought of something," he remarked to Brad. "I'll wait till you're gone, though."

Brad eyed him warily. "What?"

"Marcy."

Brad blinked.

"Sabrina's sister. I don't have her number, but I can find her house. I can ask *her* how to get in touch."

Brad sighed and sat back in his chair, folding his arms. "You can't drive yet."

"I can Uber. Stop. I know how you feel about Sabrina, but I have to do this."

Brad looked away, his expression grave.

"What is it?" Liam demanded. "Spill."

Brad nodded, steeling himself, looking resigned as he met Liam's eyes. "I haven't been completely honest about Sabrina. About what she thinks. She said some things, and I didn't try to correct her."

Liam stared at his brother.

Riggs had to admire Henry's tenacity. The big Lab kept up his frenzied digging despite the futility of the project. Riggs helpfully lifted his leg on the big tree behind him, offering this encouragement to the black dog.

"Henry," the Labrador's person finally called.

Henry backed out with a grunt and gave Riggs a disgusted look, as if sharing the notion that something was terribly wrong here, because the ball was on one side of the fence and all the dogs were on the other. When Henry padded away, Riggs eased over to the depression under the fence and peered at it.

Henry had done an impressive job of almost successfully scooping out a tunnel to the ball. Riggs eyed the result, thinking that Luna could slide through easily. Archie might take some effort. Could Riggs climb under?

When Chason called, Riggs returned to him to go home to Sabrina.

The next day, Chason brought them all back to the dog park. Riggs trotted over behind the big tree to see if Henry was still digging, but Henry wasn't in the dog park that day, so Riggs took another look at the hole under the fence. He dug at the dirt, and it was soft there, and he was able to continue Henry's work.

He sensed a dog behind him and turned, and it was Luna, watching him with intelligent eyes. Did Luna understand what Riggs was thinking? Riggs did not know, but Luna was not leaving his side. She didn't help dig, but she watched carefully.

Riggs was able to wriggle almost all the way under the fence when Archie came bounding up to see what was going on. The Labradoodle immediately concluded it was all about the ball and shouldered Riggs aside. His digging brought all the energy of a puppy. Dirt flew, and Riggs blinked as some of it sprayed him in the face. Eventually, Archie, straining, grunting, and groaning, was actually able to shove the ball with his snout. It rolled away from him. Frustrated, Archie backed out and gave Luna a look as if asking, "Well, you're the smallest. Won't you go get the toy?"

When Riggs tried to pass through, he was stuck for a moment, and it felt as if he would be pinned there beneath that fence, but then with just a little bit more straining and digging, he squirmed out. Luna watched him, now on the other side of the fence, tilting her head, trying to figure it out. Archie wanted to be on the side with Riggs, or maybe he just wanted the ball, but he went at that hole with everything he had. He dug and squirmed and twisted, and Riggs watched, impressed as Archie emerged on his side of the fence. Immediately, Archie pounced on the ball and gave Riggs a triumphant expression.

Luna and Riggs stared at each other. Luna probably understood what Riggs was intending. The question was, would she join the pack, or would she stay in the dog park so that she could be taken home to Sabrina?

"Archie!" That was Chason, calling for the Labradoodle. Archie jerked his head up in amazement as if it were only now that he realized he was completely out of the dog park.

Riggs didn't have any more time. A human was calling them. He gazed at Luna, who stared implacably back. He understood that she might not want to join them, though it would be easier for her to escape under that fence than it had been for the other two. But he was disappointed. The pack belonged together.

Riggs turned, and Archie followed. They trotted through the trees to the sidewalk, hesitated, and then picked a direction.

Chason had easily rounded up the rest of his charges—a boxer named Cappy and an old beagle named Mr. Tibbs—but Sabrina's dogs were still missing in action. He'd gone from being mildly irritated to being slightly concerned, though there was no way they could have left the dog park without him seeing, was there?

He put his hands to his mouth and yelled out each dog's name in turn, but no one came running. And running from where? The dog park had a few trees, but it was ludicrous to think that all three dogs might be hiding behind one. Chason stood, frowning, and slowly walked the perimeter of the dog park, not sure what he was looking for. Cappy the boxer trotted willingly alongside Chason, but Mr. Tibbs decided the shade under the picnic table was just too alluring.

Eventually, Chason found a hole under the fence along the back, hidden from view by the trunk of a large tree. He bent and examined the dirt and clearly saw claw marks.

He pulled out his phone to call Sabrina.

Before Riggs smelled Luna, he somehow felt her, knew she was coming up behind them. Archie turned in surprise and greeted the Jack Russell as if she'd been missing for days, but Riggs and Luna just touched noses briefly before moving on.

Archie and Luna fell into a natural pattern of following Riggs as he steadily led them away from the dog park. Riggs wondered if they felt as much as a bad dog as he did, but it was just simply impossible for Riggs to do anything now but go in search of Liam. It had been his primary focus since the mysterious day of their person's disappearance.

But where was he leading them?

His initial thought had been to return to their home, where the Liam smell had receded and where two women now answered the door. His instincts, though, told him that was far away, a long day's trot.

They could return to Sabrina—Riggs could easily lead them there. But Sabrina hadn't been able to find Liam either, if she were even looking.

Where they were now, though, was much closer to the loud, noisy house, the one with all the banging sounds and clean, sharp smells.

Because of its proximity and because Riggs just didn't know what else to do, he led the dogs in the direction of the noisy house. Archie kept going off mission, stopping to lift his leg, to pursue interesting odors, and, at one point, to chase after a loose cat, but Luna sensed Riggs's purpose and tracked steadily behind him. Archie would figure out he'd fallen behind and then race to catch up, leaping on the other dogs joyously.

Riggs couldn't help himself—he picked up his pace a bit as his nose told him they were getting close. The increased speed enforced a bit more discipline, and Archie focused on keeping up, following willingly, right up to the point where they turned the final corner, and then the young dog halted as if arrested by the end of a leash.

Luna and Riggs both stopped and sniffed at him curiously, picking up on his distress.

Archie knew where they were. He did not want to go back on that chain. He did not want that man, Face, to take care of him. Archie wanted to stay with the dog pack, but not at the expense of returning to live with Face.

Riggs put up with Archie's reticence for a very short period of time before physically moving against Archie, as he had done a few times in the past, pushing Archie forward. Archie was confused. Why would Riggs be doing this? Where were they going?

Archie surprised both Riggs and himself by refusing to be pressured. His feet were planted as if dug in, and he wasn't moving. Riggs and Luna sniffed each other, deciding.

They left Archie and continued on.

Archie bowed and barked. Neither of the other dogs looked back. Archie whimpered. They were leaving him! Distressed, Archie broke from his resolve and scampered after the other two dogs. The pull of the pack was just too powerful.

Luna and Riggs both smelled it at exactly the same moment. They were close, passing a place where a large machine was digging its neck into a hole, snorting and bellowing in a way that reminded Riggs of his trip in the trash dumpster, when the scent of a very specific person came to them. A fresh scent, one that they would recognize anywhere.

Liam.

Riggs could feel Luna's excitement as he broke into a flat-out run, racing to the door. Nothing registered—not that this house was different, not that there was a full yard, not that there was a fence around the back. All he knew was that Liam was here, here now.

Archie hung back, ready to flee if Face came out that door. Riggs scratched emphatically at the door, barking, his stub of a tail wriggling. Luna joined him, and she also barked.

The man who opened the door wasn't Liam. It was Brad, whom Riggs no longer trusted but who was in this house, and the smell of Liam came flooding out through the gap made by the open door. "Oh my God," Brad gasped. He turned and yelled into the house, "Liam, you're not going to believe this!"

Brad was blocking the entrance with his legs. Luna, smaller, dove into the tight space between them, and the man staggered back. "Oh!" he exclaimed.

Luna was in. Riggs impatiently squirmed around Brad's legs, fighting to get beyond the obstruction. Liam was here. Riggs gave voice in a high, loud cry, pushing and shoving until he was past Brad, following Luna, following his nose, scampering through the unfamiliar entryway. His nails scrabbled on the wood floor, fighting for purchase.

Behind him, he could sense that Archie had abandoned his reluctance and was coming up the walkway at high speed. Brad turned to follow Riggs, not quite shutting the door, and Archie hit it joyously, pushing it open.

Luna vanished around the corner, and Riggs pursued. He found himself in a big room with couches and chairs, and Luna was flying across the floor, and there, lying on a rug, was Liam.

40

Luna sailed through the air and landed squarely on Liam's chest. "Oomf!" he grunted, and then a moment later, Riggs was there, too, both dogs lying on Liam's chest, licking his face, crying, pushing into him as he gathered them in his arms. "Oh my God. Riggs. Luna. How in the world?" His eyes widened in shock as Archie darted into the room, running up to join the mayhem, adding his own flavor to it.

"I can't believe this. I cannot believe this," Liam repeated over and over. He looked to Brad, and both men were weeping. "Did you do this?"

Brad shook his head helplessly. "No, they just came in the door."

"My God," Liam breathed. He kissed each dog's face. He held them and let his tears flow. His dogs were back. "This is wonderful. This is so wonderful."

It took the dogs a long time before they would allow Liam to stand up, and even then, they pushed against him, reaching their muzzles to his hands, wanting him to keep stroking them.

"Where have you been? How did you do this?" Liam asked the dog pack.

They spent the rest of the afternoon cuddled with Liam on the couch. Archie eventually jumped down, but he remained close to the other two, who wanted to sit together in Liam's lap.

Brad left, and when he returned, there were cans to be opened, cans with glorious dog food.

"What do we do, do you think?" Liam asked his brother.

Brad spread his hands. "What can we do? These are your dogs. They somehow came back to you."

"But don't you think . . . I mean, it's been months. They've been living together somewhere. Somebody adopted them, and that person's going to be looking for them," Liam objected.

"I'd say the dogs have been looking for *you*," Brad pointed out mildly. "And what are we supposed to do, ask them where they've been?"

"We could contact the shelter," Liam mused.

Brad looked troubled. "I don't know. That just seems like we'd be calling attention to ourselves. Right now, these are lost dogs, lost and then found by their original owner. What if they send the dog patrol to pick them up?"

"Dog patrol?"

"Whatever they're called. Maybe there's some sort of law, chain of title, or something. Liam, look at them."

Liam dutifully gazed at the dogs, who were all staring rapturously back at him.

"They're your dogs. Whoever adopted them didn't do a very good job of taking care of them, because they're here now. They escaped. You really want them to go back to jail?"

Liam shook his head and put his hand out for all the dogs to sniff and lick. "No. They've been through enough. You're right, they're my dogs, all three of them. Oh, wait."

"What is it?"

"This tag on Luna, it's got a phone number."

Initially overlooked, a brass tag, lying flat, was affixed to the leather collar.

"The other two also have them," Liam added. "Same number."

"No name, though," Brad pointed out.

"Well, this complicates things," Liam observed.

The dogs slept on Liam's bed that night, but Luna was a bit restless. Riggs thought he understood why. Yes, the pack was together, and, yes, they were back with Liam, but why wasn't Sabrina here?

Several times, Luna awoke, expecting to hear Sabrina entering the room.

The next morning, the dogs tracked a lot of activity, and it made them anxious. Brad was walking back and forth, carrying items in a manner that Riggs and Luna had come to associate with long car rides. There was just something about this uniquely human activity they recognized. Archie, of course, was able to interpret nothing except the uneasiness in the other dogs.

While Brad packed, Liam lay on the floor and lifted his arms and legs, and Archie jumped on his face. "Archie!" Liam sputtered. Then the dogs barked ferociously because a man came to the door, and they wanted him to know how dangerous things were for intruders in the new house. The man walked in, and the dogs, subdued, sniffed him and Archie hopefully brought him a rope toy. His name was Darwin, and he was lean and smelled of the out-of-doors. He and Liam played a game with stretchy bands and a ball too large to chase, and then Darwin stood and watched Liam lift his legs and arms.

"I think I'm done with physical therapy!" Liam declared happily to this Darwin man.

"Maybe another month. How's Tonal going?"

"It hurts. This hurts. You hurt," Liam replied.

The men laughed, and Riggs and Luna curled up together in a dog bed, a little uneasy because there was this new stranger, but when Darwin departed, he did not attempt to take the pack with him.

Brad and Liam shared a meal at the table, and the dogs sat attentively and were rewarded for their alertness. Then Brad went into the back and carried out some boxes with handles, setting them by the door. This, too, was behavior consistent with long car rides, and Riggs and Luna both registered it with rising alarm.

Archie examined the boxes, sniffing in a way that Riggs knew meant he was considering lifting his leg on them, but in the end, Archie glanced at Riggs and thought better of it.

"Still no answer on the collar phone number?" Brad inquired as he cleared his plate.

Liam shook his head. "Straight to voicemail, and it's the phone company's greeting with just the number, no name."

"It's the right choice, though, not to leave a message," Brad remarked supportively.

"Yeah, and I did like you suggested and I'm blocking the number from this end, because I don't want anyone tracing the dogs back to me until we have a conversation. But maybe that's making it a stalemate—they don't answer, because I block my number, and I don't leave a message, because I don't want them hiring a lawyer to take my dogs away."

Later, Liam sat by himself at the table. The dogs gathered at his feet, not just because the table was a good place from which to be handed treats but because they wanted to be as close to Liam as possible. He opened a thin box and had made a clicking noise with his fingers on it.

The dogs all felt it when alarm jolted through Liam. He stiffened and gasped. "Oh no," he moaned softly.

Sabrina had told Chason not to feel bad about the dogs escaping. Of course she said that. What else could she say? But she didn't really mean it, and he was out driving around anyway, trying to find them. And now her home, which seemed so overly stuffed with canines when the full pack was in residence, felt vacant and lonely. She paced, looking hopefully out the big window that gave her a view of the street.

She called Teme and explained what had happened.

Teme was shocked. "All three of them? Even Luna?"

"I know. It makes no sense."

"You and Luna have a special relationship," Teme observed.

"I know," Sabrina repeated. "But she's been with Riggs longer. I just don't understand why they would run away."

"Riggs was living on the street," Teme reminded her. "He was caught up in that sweep animal control executed after that man was attacked, though it turned out the guy was a felon with outstanding warrants for, are you ready? Assault on a police officer."

"Fine," Sabrina replied faintly. "So are you thinking they might be downtown? Living on the streets?"

"I can ask ACO to keep a lookout," Teme volunteered.

Sabrina briefed Teme on everything she'd done to try to locate the dogs, but it wasn't much—what could she do? "I didn't even update their chips," Sabrina lamented. "I was going to, but I've been so busy with the new job . . ." She trailed off.

"We'll find them," Teme vowed.

When they hung up, Sabrina resumed her pacing. Where were her dogs?

"What time's your flight?" Liam asked.

Brad looked at his wristwatch. "I got another half an hour or so before I need to call a car." He cocked his head at his brother, picking up on something. "Everything okay?"

"Come here," Liam replied curtly.

"What is it? What's wrong?"

"I want to show you something," Liam explained, gesturing toward the screen on his laptop. His voice was cold, and Brad frowned curiously before coming over to look over Liam's shoulder.

"Recognize these dogs?" Liam challenged. Brad gave him a blank look. They were looking at photographs of Riggs and Luna, and then there was another of Archie by himself.

"What's this?"

"It's a web version of putting missing dog posters on phone poles. Those are my dogs. Someone's looking for them."

"Oh. Huh," Brad replied, processing.

Liam pointed at the screen. "Not 'huh,' Brad. Look at this

photo, where Archie's all shaved. See how the woman's cropped out, all you can see is her arm? Recognize the arm? Because I sure as hell do. I took this photograph. She says to email Ms. Sam, but that's Sabrina. Sabrina is the person looking for these dogs."

Brad's mouth dropped open. He gazed at Liam, not understanding.

Liam's return expression was hard and unforgiving. "You lied to me, Brad, the same way you lied to her about me being dead. You told me she couldn't take the dogs. But this says they're *her* dogs. So she did take them! She took them and they got away, and now they're here and she's looking for them."

Brad shook his head. "No! I didn't lie to you, Liam. I swear she said she couldn't take the dogs. Sabrina was my first impulse. When you had your accident, I told her she needed to take care of the dogs, and she told me she couldn't. She said she quit her waitressing job and couldn't afford to move and that her sister had like fourteen cats or something, and it was impossible. You know Luna's attitude about cats. It never would have worked."

"Then how do you explain this, Brad?"

"I don't know! When I saw her on her date, I told her that Luna was on death row at the shelter." Liam gasped, and Brad held up a hand. "I didn't see any point in telling you that part because Luna's alive, right here, okay? But Sabrina didn't say anything about adopting Luna or having the other two dogs. She just acted all embarrassed because she was out with some guy."

"You got a bad habit of hiding the truth from people, Brad," Liam grated harshly, "and it's come back to bite you in the ass. You lied about what really happened with Mom and Dad. You told me they were coming back."

"I know, brother. I just wanted to protect you from hurt."

"Okay, but it's time to stop doing that!" Liam nearly shouted. The dogs stirred uneasily.

"You're right," Brad agreed mournfully. "I know I screwed up everything. I'm sorry, Liam. I can see how it just made things worse."

After a long silence, Liam turned back to his laptop. "When did you see her?"

"I don't know, late summer."

Liam pursed his lips.

"Liam, I swear to you, I did not lie. She absolutely told me she couldn't keep the dogs."

Liam gazed into his brother's eyes. "I believe you, Brad."

The long silence between them felt healing to them both. Then Brad sighed. "So I guess the question is, what are you going to do now?"

41

Liam glared at Brad. "I'm going to figure out how to fix this mess you've made, is what I'm going to do."

Brad's shoulders slumped. "I know it's a mess. They told me to say goodbye to you, Liam, that you wouldn't be alive when I got back. It was the hardest thing I've ever had to do, and I didn't feel like I had a choice. They told me at the shelter they would give the dogs to a good home, but they didn't say it would be with Sabrina. I mean, I was doing my best at the time."

Liam considered this. He stood and embraced his brother. "I didn't think about how hard it was. I'm sorry. Whatever happened with the dogs, it's not your fault. I believe you."

Brad hastily wiped his eyes as Liam released him and tapped the screen with a fingernail. "There's an email address."

"What are you going to do?" Brad asked softly.

"Well, what *you're* going to do," Liam responded, "is to get in an Uber, go to the airport, and fly back to Germany, and what *I'm* going to do is send Sabrina an email."

Brad stared at him, and a sardonic grin spread across his face. "Send her an email. It's going to be like, 'Hi, I have the dogs and, P.S., I'm not dead.'"

Liam's expression was blank for a moment. "Okay, you're right," he agreed slowly. "I guess I don't want to do that via email. I wouldn't do it with a phone message, either."

"Needs to be in person," Brad agreed.

"Well," Liam speculated, "I think Sabrina's too suspicious. If a stranger, out of the blue, sends an email and says he's got the dogs, she's not going to say, 'Well, bring 'em on over.' She'll see right away that that's not a good idea. She doesn't want anyone to know where she lives."

"Plus she would recognize your email," Brad added.

"True. Well, I've got a couple of old ones I've never used with her before. I'll send her an email from there, and I'll tell her the dogs are in the backyard and she should come over and get them while I'm not home. That way, she'll feel like she doesn't even have to talk to a stranger. She just opens the gate and the dogs will come out. That's what I'll tell her."

"There's really no good way to do this, is there, Liam?" Brad asked.

Liam shook his head. "No." He looked at Brad. "Well, it's my problem. I'll figure it out. I think that's what I'm going to do, though. It feels the safest. Once she's got the gate open, I'll walk out and say hi."

"I wish I could be here for that," Brad observed with a grin.

"Do you think she married this guy, the one she was seeing?" Liam asked anxiously.

"I don't know, Liam. How would I know something like that? That would be awfully quick, though. Don't women want to be engaged for at least a year, draw out the agony?"

The day after Brad left, the house was still filled with his presence, but there was an emptiness to the place, and the dogs could tell he was gone and, potentially, not coming back. That's what people did. They left, and they either came back or they didn't. It wasn't up to the dogs to determine what they were going to do.

After a breakfast and some time spent rolling on the floor with Liam, the dogs were put out into the backyard. Archie was relaxed now. He understood Face wasn't here. Liam was here. The pack was here. This was home. Luna was still tense, but Archie had settled comfortably into this new life. People were wondrous beings who kept changing everything, and Archie had decided the best thing a dog could do was go along with all of it.

Liam showered and cleaned himself up as best he could, and

then he paced in the living room. The sweep hand on his watch crept around and around so slowly, it almost made him sick to look at. "Hey. I'm Liam, nice to meet you," he said at one point, sticking out his hand as if talking to a ghost. He imagined this person, this man, the new man, coming with Sabrina. That's what had kept him up last night. Of course she wouldn't come by herself. She would bring her boyfriend, or her fiancé, or husband, or whoever the hell he was, and Liam would have to just grin and take it.

When he heard the wheels on his newly paved driveway, he ran to the window and sucked in his breath. As she stepped out of the car, Sabrina swept her hair back with one hand, and it was the same gesture that had captivated him the very first time he ever caught sight of her.

She was alone.

For a moment, all he could do was watch as she shut the car door and glanced speculatively up at the house. She turned her head and looked at the side gate, hesitating. When she walked to that gate, the dogs caught her scent and began barking frantically. Luna was leaping so high she nearly cleared the fence. She was so excited that when the gate opened, she barreled right into Sabrina.

"Oh, dogs," Sabrina murmured. Luna was trying to climb up, and so Sabrina lifted the Jack Russell and held the little dog like an infant. Luna, whimpering, licked Sabrina's face. Archie ran to some bushes and raised his leg in celebration. Riggs wagged his stub and pressed up against Sabrina's legs and closed his eyes when she reached down with her free hand to stroke his fur.

The pack was together, and now the people were together. Riggs had done what he was meant to do.

"Okay. All right, guys. Are you ready for a car ride?" Sabrina sang. The dogs were frenzied at these words. Luna would not stop kissing her face. "All right, Luna. That's enough. That's enough," Sabrina laughed. "Oh, I'm so relieved." Sabrina heard the front door open of the house and glanced up with raised eyebrows, ready to greet whoever it was, and then her face fell in shock.

Liam came down the steps, holding his hands up as if surrendering to the authorities. "Sabrina, I don't know what you heard, but I've been in a coma. I mean, I couldn't . . . I'm so sorry."

Liam stopped several feet away, searching her face with his eyes. All he saw there was an expression approaching horror. He didn't know what to say or what she could be feeling. Was she even glad to see him? He swallowed, hesitating. He wanted nothing more than to close the distance between the two of them, but he had a sense that perhaps that was the wrong thing to do. Sabrina's mouth finally closed. She gently put Luna on the ground.

"Oh my God, Liam," she whispered. When she ran to him, Liam spread his arms and folded her against his chest, his eyes shut. Sabrina sobbed into his shoulder, and the dogs circled at their feet, feeling the strong emotions, glancing at each other nervously, unable to process what was happening. "Liam. Liam. I thought you were—" Sabrina couldn't even say it.

Liam nodded. "I know. They told you I was dead."

Sabrina pulled back to gaze into his eyes. "Well, no, what they said was you were going to die. And then I . . . saw something. I thought you *were* dead. And your brother . . ."

Liam nodded. "Brad just left. For what it's worth, he knows how badly he screwed up. I think he feels really awful about what happened. But, well, you know Brad, he's really protective of me. I think if he had his way, he would keep me locked up like Rapunzel or something."

"Rapunzel," Sabrina repeated, dazed.

Liam correctly read her expression. "I guess this is a shock."

Sabrina wiped her eyes and hastily nodded.

"Okay, why don't we slow it down, give you a chance to get used to everything. Come on, I want to show you the house."

The dogs led the people through the front door.

Sabrina looked around. "What is this place?"

"It's the home I told you about. When I bought it, it was just being framed in, but it's finished now. While I was in the hospital, Brad had the crew do it all just the way I asked. Come see the kitchen."

Sabrina numbly followed him into the kitchen and glanced around. Her eyes were glassy. He wasn't sure she was seeing what he was trying to show her.

"These are the cabinets you said you wanted," he boasted. "Remember? You picked them out."

She turned her astounded eyes on him. "I feel as if I'm dreaming, Liam. None of this feels real."

"It's real, I promise." He held her for a long moment and felt her respond, squeezing him back, and hope flooded through him. "Okay. I'll show you the rest of the house. I think you're going to like it."

In one of the bedrooms upstairs, the walls were painted with a rainbow. It was, however, bereft of any furniture. Sabrina took it all in, still looking dazed.

"I've been calling this one the nursery," Liam advised.

She turned her gaze on him and blinked, not getting it.

Liam took a breath. He was rushing it, but he couldn't wait any longer. "I don't remember anything about my coma, but I do remember waking up in the hospital and being told I was supposed to die. Kind of puts things in perspective. What's really important."

The dogs all sat as if on command, their eyes on Liam.

"Sabrina, the night of my accident, I had a question on my mind. Something I wanted to ask you. Well, less a question, I suppose, than maybe a proposal. It had to do with this."

He reached into his pocket, dug around, and pulled out the small box. She stared at it numbly. He opened it and the sparkle leaped to her eyes. "Say yes to me now, Sabrina, and I promise we'll be together forever."

Liam sucked in a breath. If the other guy was a factor, she

would tell him now, and his life might be jolted off course yet again.

Sabrina was crying again, but as she embraced Liam, Riggs could feel no sadness in her. "Of course. God, I've missed you, Liam. Of course I'll marry you."

Luna and Riggs exchanged glances, and Riggs wondered if the Jack Russell understood what was happening. Archie didn't, that was clear from the way he yawned and then dropped to his belly, tense with all the emotions, but bored with the lack of activity.

Riggs was content. They were all together, his humans and his dog pack. This was how it should be.

Epilogue

MICHELOB

Michelob's actual name was Ozzy. His bloodlines suggested terrier with spaniel with something else, and his brown eyes were serene when they held a human's. He couldn't exactly remember how he wound up living without his people—he didn't really realize he was being left behind when his family departed in their multiple cars, leaving him at the Chatfield Reservoir, and then when he tried to cross C-470, a nice woman pulled over and invited him for a car ride, and he went willingly. The woman took him to a neighborhood with houses fairly close together and hit the brakes sharply when he barked at a dog chasing a ball. "Is this where you live?" the woman asked, opening the door.

What Michelob remembered much more clearly than that first day was living on the streets of Denver, drawn by food and people smells, though his family of David and Janice and their many wonderful children weren't among those his nose could find.

The bad man with the pipe broke Michelob's tibia. At animal induction, Mrs. Kepler was almost immeasurably sad. "We won't be able to help this one," she mourned.

There were other organizations in Denver that could take and heal wounded pets, all of them unfortunately full, but Teme set about sending a broadcast email anyway, while Mr. Reed gave the dog something for pain.

"Got a read on the chip," Mr. Reed announced triumphantly a little while later.

Within a few hours, a Chevy Suburban wheeled into the

parking lot with a screech, and the doors popped open like it was an FBI raid. David and Janice and several of their grown children burst in the door and they were crying, and Teme and Mrs. Kepler and even Mr. Reed teared up when the limping dog was led out and everyone screamed, "Ozzy!" and Michelob sobbed, licking his people, relieved to at last be rescued.

Later, after his surgery, after he was fully recovered, Michelob, now fully back to being Ozzy, might take a moment to remember his other dog friends and life on the street, but for the most part, the whole sad incident was forgotten.

CORONA

So many bully breeds found their way into the system that Teme was pessimistic that they'd ever find Corona a home, but Corona's eyes had an odd, almost sad expression in them that was compelling. Corona's life started in a small car with no wheels and no doors, surrounded by a large litter of white puppies, all of whom found their own way to their own fates. A street dog, the only things Corona craved were the kindness of a human hand, a sense of home, and a person to protect her and love her.

Her view of the dog fair was that it was nice to be outside, even restrained to a small cage, and when a family trooped by the smallest member, a female child, halted, fixated by Corona's deep, mournful eyes.

"Come on, Tracy," the father of the family eventually called. They seemed on a mission to visit and reject every dog in every cage with scant inspection, a task distracting them from tracking their youngest daughter as she returned to Corona's cage more than once.

"We call her Snowball," Teme advised cheerfully when the family returned for the third time to drag Tracy away. "Want me to let her out? She's very friendly."

Corona trotted straight out of that cage and into Tracy's arms and then her home. Being the baby of the family earns some indulgences and when Tracy demanded that, irrespective of what the rest of the family did, she deserved her own pet, no one argued. Corona responded to the name Snowball and the love of her person, Tracy, and now that her life made sense, Snowball never bothered to think of her life on the streets.

MODELO

Some people don't deserve the blessings that come with dog ownership, and the couple who paid $1,200 for the papillon puppy they named Princess Leia fell into that category. Given the couple's penchant for loud, frightening screaming matches in front of the little dog, it was probably inevitable that their household pet would become collateral damage in the ongoing battle that was their human relationship. When, during an outdoor lunch off the Sixteenth Street promenade, the woman—Monika— stormed angrily away from the table, the man—Steve—reached down and unsnapped the papillon's collar and allowed the beautiful canine to wander away.

Once in the shelter, Mrs. Kepler gazed into Modelo's dirty, snarled fur and said, "Oh my." Mr. Reed gave Modelo a bath before the picture went up on the website.

The woman who adopted Modelo arrived in a Mercedes CLS and filled out her application as if applying for sainthood. She was desperate to prove she could provide a good life for the little dog, and, reviewing the form, Teme idly asked Mrs. Kepler if she thought the woman would be interested in adopting a person.

Modelo's new name was, interestingly, Princess. It seemed to the little dog to be only fitting. She wore her jeweled collar and even the tiny tiara without any sense that it was anything but deserved. Princess lived a life of pampered luxury, carefully groomed, always on soft pillows, never giving a moment's thought to her brief life on the street.

HEINEKEN

Heineken lived at the shelter for two months before being adopted. He hadn't meant to live on the streets, but as an unaltered male, he was overcome with an irresistible impulse when a female dog's compelling odors lured him to join a pack of restless, frustrated males circling outside a fenced-in enclosure. Three days of prowling gave him no access, no satisfaction, and a physical hunger that drew him to the city's dense food odors.

Whatever other DNA was in Heineken besides Labrador was overwhelmed, and eventually, Teme arranged for the dog, rechristened Scoop and now neutered, to be transferred to a Labrador rescue. Dedicated breed rescue operations belie the common wisdom that the only place to get a specific dog type is through a breeder, and it wasn't more than two weeks after arriving at the new shelter that Scoop was adopted by a man who liked to Jeep up into the mountains and go camping. Heineken had lived on cement surfaces, but Scoop spent his days dashing into mountain streams, gazing suspiciously at moose, chasing squirrels, and barking at ducks. He liked to sleep with his head on his person's chest, pinning the man down as if worried his human might abscond during the night. Life was so wonderful now, Heineken almost couldn't remember his other existence as a dog of the streets.

BUDWEISER

Budweiser was initially adopted as a puppy and lived for a time with a couple of young men who were more neglectful than caring. It was a crowded house with four main human residents and many people filtering in and out and a lot of music and a lot of sticky liquids spilled for Budweiser's tongue to lick up. At one point, loud people came and dragged the four men away with their hands shackled behind their backs, and the doors and gates were all left open. Budweiser ate some dropped food and then departed, wandering away, winding up living for nearly two years on the streets—a long time for a dog to fend for itself.

In the shelter, Budweiser could smell Riggs, and Riggs could smell Budweiser. They both shared Aussie bloodlines, though Budweiser's family tree was more complicated. Perhaps the common ancestry explained why Budweiser let Riggs share his den.

Budweiser was smart and alert, an instant favorite with the shelter staff, who were very happy one particular day to lead the dog out into the fenced-off private greeting yard. Budweiser knew the people waiting for him there: Ron and Officer Georgia. He greeted them warmly, even crying a little at their familiar odors.

"See?" Ron said to Georgia. "Told you."

When Georgia left that day, Budweiser—shortened to Bud— sat in the back seat, scarcely able to believe his fortunes. Georgia was a police officer and a single woman, and she and Budweiser formed an instant family unit.

Georgia often brought home the distinctive odor of the streets, and Bud always sniffed her clothing carefully. The memories the fragrances evoked weren't particularly pleasant, but he always remembered Riggs fondly and hoped his friend found a person of his own to love him.

LUNA

Luna still sometimes went to the building with many rooms and many nice people when Sabrina left in the morning, and sometimes, she remained home with Riggs and Archie. For Luna, the days with Sabrina were the best, but there was never any worry that Sabrina would vanish again. Something had relaxed in the home, a dissipation of a previous tension.

"I think it was the grind of the school year that was getting to me. I work twice as many hours now, but I'm only half as tired," she confided to Liam. Luna lazily listened to Sabrina's voice and was satisfied to hear only contentment. That's how Luna would have described her life if she'd known the word: contented.

RIGGS

Riggs was forever vigilant, keeping track of Luna and Archie, allowing both of them only so much opportunity to inflict mayhem on their toys before he eased out of his bed and restored order.

He never really liked it when Liam left the house but was satisfied that his human's scent was always close by. The dogs had learned that Liam had come across yet another noisy house, this one just a few lots down from their home, and that's where he spent all his time. He came home for lunch with Sabrina and the canines many days, and never neglected to hand over small morsels to his three dogs.

"I have news," Liam announced to Sabrina at one such meal. "That couple from Boston that bought the vacant lot three houses down made up their mind, and I'm going to start finalizing their plans when their check clears. My commute is even shorter than yours used to be."

Riggs often recalled his time lost on the streets with a restless anxiety, a feeling only made better when Luna, or Sabrina, or of course Liam or even Archie sought Riggs out to cuddle. He knew this, though: everyone in the pack was happy now, and that's all that mattered.

ARCHIE

Archie understood now why he'd spent so many hours on the chain. It was so that Liam could find him in this very place and then move in with the dog pack. Life had been very unstable, with different people and locations, but, looking back, it seemed to Archie that he'd ultimately been very happy no matter what was going on. Now, of course, he was overjoyed because he had people and a pack.

When it occurred to him to think about it, Archie considered himself to have the most wonderful life a dog could possibly have. But normally, he was enjoying himself too much to think about it.

Acknowledgments

I'm one of those people who actually reads author acknowledgments, and, it would seem, so are you. Can we agree, then, that some writers are better at this than others, with me being one of the others? I'm always shocked when someone will take two paragraphs to thank four people and that's it. I spend that much time thanking my socks!

When I turn in my acknowledgments, my agent always reminds me I'm not getting paid per word. But to thank everyone who has ever helped me get to this point, where *My Three Dogs* is my thirty-sixth published novel (or thirty-seventh, thirty-eighth, or thirty-ninth—I've turned in several but the publication order hasn't yet been set) I need a lot of words!

Perhaps I should begin with my great-great grandfather, who fled the blizzards and cold of Canada to move to Michigan because his map didn't show Florida. My ancestors shoveled a lot of snow so that I could grow up to be an author. I must, at the very least, thank them for reproducing.

My parents are no longer with us, but when they were alive they encouraged me to get a real job. But then, when it appeared I was serious about this author thing, they did everything possible to help me realize my dream, including buying me those socks I'm so grateful for. I didn't thank them enough when I could, and there's a lesson in there for the few people reading this: thank people. It doesn't cost anything and gives so much. Thanks, Mom, thanks, Dad.

I have two older sisters that I treat as if they are the same person, though I suspect a DNA test would show otherwise.

I dedicated one of my mystery novels—*Repo Madness*—to the both of them, and I'm correcting that inconsideration with this novel, which is dedicated to my big sister, Amy Cameron. She's a career educator and has been teaching my novels to her students, even in math class, for as long as I've been a published author. The other sister, Julie Cameron, is a doctor who prescribes her patients my novel *The Midnight Plan of the Repo Man* and refuses to treat them for any illness, including accidental amputation, until they can recite at least two passages from the Repo series. Thank you, Amy and Julie, for your support, kindness, and tolerance.

Okay, since you insist on bringing them up, yes, I'm very proud of the Repo novels, which tell the story of a repo man in northern Michigan who solves murders and has a persistent voice in his head that he argues with. Pick up the first one, *Midnight Plan*, and you'll be hooked, I promise. And thank you, Forge Publishing, for supporting those novels even though they aren't dog books. See? I turned shameless self-promotion into a thank-you. Cost me nothing. Thank you, socks.

I can't move on from family without acknowledging that everyone related to me by blood or marriage has graciously supported my career. They go to my movies, come to my signings, buy my books, invite me to speak at their schools, feed me cookies. They all have the sort of real jobs my father had in mind for me, and they let me strip-mine their experiences for plot points and character ideas. So I'm going to thank, in an order that I can attest is utterly random: Brad Barlow, Ray Varuolo, Georgia Lee Cameron, Chelsea Hatch, Chase Cameron, and then Eloise, Ewan, Garrett, Gordon Bruce, Sadie, Arlo, Dawson, and the soon-to-be-born William. Thank you, James Hatch and Kristen Cameron. I'm blessed to have so many direct relatives, especially if my publisher changes its mind and decides to pay me by the word.

I'm not going to thank my cousins or old girlfriends directly, because there are far too many of the former and only a couple of the latter—all of whom have unfriended me on Facebook.

When it comes to *My Three Dogs*: thank you to my editor, Kristin Sevick, who really cares about this novel and who helped me unsnarl the timeline so that Liam wasn't in a coma for a decade. A good editor makes all the difference—I so appreciate you, Kristin. Thank you Linda Quinton for being involved in every stage of this novel, and thank you to the team at Forge: Devi, Lucille, Sarah, Eileen, Anthony, Troix—all I do is write the books; you do the rest. Without you, there wouldn't be a "Bruce Brand," and people would just be wondering around in their thankless socks, sobbing at the lack of dog books.

If the running socks references aren't working for you, blame my editor.

Thank you, Jason Vogel, for telling me everything I needed to know about garbage collection in Denver, CO. If you hadn't talked to me, I'd have been forced to climb into a dumpster to see what happens next, and then people would be saying, "Look, someone finally threw out that dog author."

I think it's hilarious that when people ask what line of work I'm in I can say "showbiz." Thank you, Gavin Polone, for producing the three movies, so far, based on my books (*A Dog's Purpose*, *A Dog's Way Home*, and *A Dog's Journey*, if you're interested). Thank you, Sheri Kelton, for managing my showbiz career, and thanks, Steve Younger, for negotiating contracts that give me cookies as one of the deal points.

Thank you, Dan Angel and Jane Charles, for working to get two of my best novels, *Emory's Gift* and *A Dog's Perfect Christmas*, onto the screen. It's so hard to get a movie made even if everyone agrees the story is "perfect" and the script is "perfect" and the author is "overweight." You've been tirelessly promoting both works. I so appreciate you both.

As for my writing career: My agent for two decades, Scott Miller, is a decent human being who has always listened to what

I've wanted and then said he'll get it for me except the cookies. Scott, you've guided my writing career to where it is today and I'm eternally grateful.

I have so many author friends and I wish I could thank them all because they energize me whenever my enthusiasm is flagging. Katherine Applegate sometimes allows me to do book events with her so that people will actually come. You're a wonderful writer and person, Katherine. And Adriana Trigiani is my mentor, even though she's so much younger than I am—Adriana, you are an astounding talent and munificent friend.

Speaking of socks, Evie Michon gave me a pair that are never supposed to wear out! The same can be said for her daughter. Thanks for giving me her and also Teddy, Maria, Jakob, Maya, and Ethan.

Lee Child, Andrew Gross, Nelson DeMille—thank you for supporting my Repo series, it means the world to me that you love those books! (I know what you're thinking: *I wish these darn acknowledgments would end so I could run out and buy that* Midnight Plan of the Repo Man *novel!*)

You're probably going to have to order the Repo series online, because bookstores no longer routinely stock them, except I do have some diehard booksellers who tell everyone who enters their stores "you need to read this book!" Okay, that's an exaggeration, they probably don't tell infants in strollers. Those children are given *Lily to the Rescue*.

While you're online, please consider buying *Emory's Gift* so that you can brag that you read the book before it was a movie. This will make you very popular—I'm trying to make all my readers popular since I failed in that effort with myself.

I'm assuming you're so popular that several people have already given you *A Dog's Perfect Christmas*.

Thank you, Larissa Wohl, for picking my novel, *A Dog's Perfect Christmas*, as the very first novel in your worldwide book club. What an honor!

Thank you, Jamie Gornstein Tighe, for the marathon way you've promoted my novels and the ceaseless effort to set up that book signing. This year!

I began writing novels back when it took a chisel and a blow from a mallet. I pounded out a few really bad books on a manual typewriter in the back of a workshop run by the Wright brothers. Thomas Edison built me my first electric typewriter, and I wrote one novel on a Commodore 64 with cassette-tape drive. This last part is true and all of this is to say, a human's fingers have only so many books in them and anything I can do to avoid typing, I will do. The first draft of this novel was written via dictation, using an Apogee electronics microphone so sensitive it heard my *thoughts*. Thank you everyone at Apogee, especially Marlene Passaro and Betty Bennett, for donating the equipment that keeps my fingers from divorcing me.

If you've ever heard of me through social media, it's because of the crack team that . . . okay, why "crack" team? Are they cracked? Anyway, Mindy Wells Hoffbauer, Jill Enders, Julia Hart, Chase Cameron, Elliott Crowe, Breeze Vincinz, and Susan Andrews have all helped keep me current whenever electrons need to be whipped up for marketing purposes. Thanks, everyone. (I'm sure there's a joke with "current" and "electrons," please feel free to write it, plus also my next novel.)

There is a secret group of *A Dog's Purpose* fans on Facebook (friend Susan Andrews if you'd like to join) and in 2024 we will have *more*, meaning more secrets, more giveaways, more insider information. Come join us!

Thank you, Dr. Deb Mangelsdorf, for being my go-to for all questions about veterinary medicine. Without you I'd be as lost as I was in geometry.

Thank you, Frannie Lederman, for the real Lily to the Rescue and for saving me from the bloody elevator.

Thank you, Elizabeth Kennedy, for introducing me to Sammie Rose so that I have yet another child making fun of me. Thank you, Zoanne Clack, for introducing me to Theo, Sonata, and Matisse so that I can hang out at the cool kids' table. Thank you, Samantha Dunn, for your wonderful writing and for introducing me to Ben so I have someone to hang the star on the Christmas Tree.

And . . . scene. These are the longest acknowledgments I've ever written, and I'm missing so many important people, but, as we all know, my fingers start to ache. I didn't thank Hayes, the Rundstroms, Robert Schaumburg, etc., because I really need to get back to writing my next book. But if I've thanked you before, please know I'm still grateful, and if I haven't yet thanked you by name, it's because I'm a jerk.

Oh! And best for last: A few years ago I met this woman and we became writing partners, then life partners. Her name is Cathryn Michon, and she's famous for many things but not her cooking. She's a director (she'll be directing *A Dog's Perfect Christmas*) an actor, a singer, an author (her latest book, due September 2024, is *I'm Still Here* and it's perfect) a stand-up comedian, and I'd recommend her as a wife except I've got an exclusive on that. Thank you, Cathryn, for being on and by my side.

About the Author

W. BRUCE CAMERON is the #1 *New York Times* and *USA Today* bestselling author of *A Dog's Purpose*, *A Dog's Way Home*, and *A Dog's Journey* (all now major motion pictures), *The Dog Master*, *A Dog's Promise*, the Puppy Tales for young readers (starting with *Ellie's Story* and *Bailey's Story*), *The Dogs of Christmas*, *The Midnight Plan of the Repo Man*, and others. He lives in California.